She was there. She was sitting on a log by the shore. A raccoon — an early riser, as the sun was just setting — was eating breadcrumbs out of her hand. It spotted me first and scampered away.

'You!' said Erica. She stood up straight with her hands on her hips. 'Is it you?'

I walked to her, then hesitated. Was she angry? Wild? Frightened? Or loving . . .?

'You look like mud pie. Go jump in the lake.'

I think she meant it. 'Can't,' I said. 'These are my only clothes.'

'Take 'em off.' She waited. She tapped her foot. 'Go on.'

I just stood there. I wasn't going to take off my clothes.

'Where'd you get that Navy jacket?'

'Whore in Illinois. Said I reminded her of her husband.'

'You!'

'What?'

'You got to play every fiddle you can find.'

Famous Potatoes

Joe Cottonwood

CORGI BOOKS
A DIVISION OF TRANSWORLD PUBLISHERS LTD

FAMOUS POTATOES

A CORGI BOOK 0 552 11607 6

First publication in Great Britain

PRINTING HISTORY
Corgi edition published 1981

Copyright © 1978 by Joseph Cottonwood

The author wishes to thank Charles
Scribner's Sons for permission to
quote from Ernest Hemingway.

Conditions of sale
1: This book is sold subject to the condition that
it shall not, by way of trade *or otherwise*,
be lent, re-sold, hired out or otherwise
circulated without the publisher's prior consent in
any form of binding or cover other than that in
which it is published *and without a similar condition
including this condition being imposed on the
subsequent purchaser*.
2: This book is sold subject to the Standard Conditions
of Sale of Net Books and may not be re-sold in the U.K.
below the net price fixed by the publishers for the book.

This book is set in 10/11 Baskerville

Corgi Books are published by
Transworld Publishers Ltd.,
Century House, 61–63 Uxbridge Road,
Ealing, London, W5 5SA

Made and printed in United States of America
by Arcata Graphics
Buffalo, New York

Some other places were not so good
but maybe we were not so good when
we were in them.

Ernest Hemingway
The Short Stories

LEONARD AND CLYDE, just out of jail
Clyde picked his nose with a ten penny nail
Leonard read a Bible, said, 'Hear me, oh Lord,
Take me to Heaven in this Forty-nine Ford.'

Mother America
What have you done?
All of your children
Out on the run.

—Tony's Dance Band

SUBURBIA

I was a nice boy from the suburbs. In high school my best friend was named John. We were good students, near the top of our class.

At night we stole signs. It became a ritual for us. I borrowed my father's Chevy; John swiped his mother's whiskey. We cruised, grabbed a sign, cruised some more. We grabbed so many that we ran out of places to hide them. We gave them to our classmates: ONE WAY for the scholar, SPEED LIMIT for the slow learner, NO TRESPASSING for the shy one, YIELD for the nice girl, DO NOT ENTER for the virgin, FOR SALE for the bad girl, ALCOHOLIC BEVERAGES PROHIBITED for the football captain. We became connoisseurs. We aimed for the special prize: PLEASE DO NOT WALK ON GRAVES from the military cemetery, or TRY US! WE'RE NOT EXPENSIVE—WE JUST LOOK THAT WAY! from a motel, or SHRIVER from the driveway of Sargent Shriver, the director of the Peace Corps who lived a few miles from us in a wealthier part of the suburbs. The Shrivers had a horse that kept jumping the fence around their yard and trampling the neighbors' gardens. We figured we were striking a blow for the common man by stealing their sign.

John and I came from one car families (worse yet, one *old* car with chipped paint, big tailfins, many dents), and we had to mow lawns and shovel snow for pocket money, while it seemed that all the other kids had their own cars and a fat weekly allowance. It brought us closer, feeling poor.

Our sign stealing days ended the night we tried to chop down the Coppertone ad. We were hacking away at this

9

mammoth billboard with that picture of a dog pulling down the little girl's bathing suit and exposing her precious white fanny. I forget what we were planning to do with it. A police car pulled up, and we were too drunk to run. It was quite a scene at the station when our parents came down. My dad was confused. He had no idea what he was supposed to do. My mother was embarrassed — for herself, not for me. John's dad was outraged. He was shoving John around like a kid trying to start a fight. John's mother, a semi-alcoholic, thought the whole evening was simply hilarious. The police were annoyed. There were no charges. We promised never to do it again, and agreed to drop by for a few chats with the 'youth counselor.'

The youth counselor turned out to be EMIT GODWIN, PROBATION OFFICER according to the black lettering on the frosted glass of the office door (which, I confess, we briefly considered stealing). Mr. Godwin was a nice guy, an old man who was slowly losing his mind. He'd already lost his hair. He gave us a couple of half-assed lectures which among other things revealed to us that we were Double Arrow Buddies. You see, some friendships are mostly one way. Mr. Godwin diagrammed a one-way friendship on the blackboard:

$$A \; \text{\Large\Uparrow} \longrightarrow \text{\Large\Uparrow} \; B$$

In this case A needs the friendship of B. A makes all the moves. B likes A, but if A stopped making most of the moves, B would drift away. Now sometimes you get a friendship like C and D:

$$C \; \text{\Large\Uparrow} \rightleftarrows \text{\Large\Uparrow} \; D$$

Here C needs the friendship of D, just like A needed B. But D also needs the friendship of C, and so they are Double Arrow Buddies.

Smirk. It became a private joke: 'Well John, I wouldn't do

10

this for just anybody, but since you're my Double Arrow Buddy . . .'

Poor Mr. Godwin. When he retired (I think they pushed him out), we sent a card signed with a double arrow. But I think he was right about one thing: our sign stealing — our 'petty vandalism' as he called it, and of course that's what it really was — our petty vandalism was motivated not by want or need (who needs signs?) and not by resentment (well, there was a *little* resentment), but mainly we were motivated by friendship. It was something we could do together. 'And Friendship,' Mr. Godwin said, 'and I mean Friendship with a capital F, is a noble motivation indeed — and a rare one.'

Besides the night we were arrested and the day Kennedy was shot, the only other excitement in high school was Miss Putts. She was a sweet old lady with a kind face and striking white hair. She taught twelfth grade English. We called her Putt-Putt Putts because she drove a little Morris Minor that sounded like a toy.

John and I had both been burned in English. We'd always liked to read, but suddenly in eleventh grade we were supposed to *study* the books — not just read them and remember the plot and the names of the characters but also *analyze* them, recognize *symbols* and *themes*. Suddenly books became puzzles to solve, and plots became moral theses. We hated it. We hated it. We barely passed. Then in twelfth grade with Miss Putts I somehow couldn't take it seriously any more. I started making fun of the work. I found a cigarette to be a death symbol, and telephone poles were crosses for Christ to bear, and pencils were sex symbols and on and on. John picked it up, and soon we were finding symbols in toenails and punctuation marks. Putt-Putt *loved* it. English became our favorite class. We couldn't believe our success. 'I detect a note of irreverence,' Miss Putts would say if we laid it on a bit too heavy, but as long as we sounded vaguely reasonable she'd beam with approval. Once when I compared drinking a glass of water with a symbolic attempt to drown oneself, she said, 'Willy, are you making fun of me?' And I said no. I wasn't

11

making fun of her. I *liked* her. It was the subject that was ridiculous.

One day Miss Putts bought a gun and drove to her sister's house. Her sister was dying of cancer, hopelessly suffering. Putt-Putt shot her twice in the head, then drove to the parking lot of a shopping center where she wrote a grammatically perfect note in elegant script, and then right there in the front seat of the Morris Minor between the K mart and the A & P, she put the gun to her heart.

We were stunned. Teachers don't do that sort of thing, especially English teachers, especially sweet old ladies. We analyzed the suicide note:

. . . could not bear to see any more suffering . . .

'Bear,' John said. 'A pun on "bare." Baring the truth. Bare as her ass.' We were drinking bad whiskey in John's basement, trying desperately to be witty and smug, studying the note as it was quoted in the newspaper.

My sister faced a certain death. It was only a question of time . . .

'My sister,' I said. 'Like "my brother." Meaning we are all sisters and brothers in the Family of Man. Facing certain death. Only a question of time. If time is a question, what is the answer?'

John made a face. 'I'm sick of this bullshit.'

'Me too.'

We never played the English game again. We sent flowers to Miss Putts' funeral, signing the card with a double arrow.

After we went away to college we never saw each other. We didn't even phone or write letters. Whatever had held us together in high school—being smartasses, for example—didn't apply any more, and to be friends in college we'd have to start all over. I guess neither of us wanted to make the effort. Anyway, there were geographical problems. John went to Yale and then to medical school in St. Louis. I went to a small midwestern college where I was initiated into the pleasures of hemp, which grew wild near the campus. Unfortunately these were still the Dark Ages, and my Good Citizen roommate reported me to the dean. I was dismissed. Soon I was drafted. After boot camp I drove a bulldozer in Vietnam until one night a sergeant asked me if I wanted to turn two hundred bucks. I would be given a pass. I would drive a truck to Saigon and back. One night's work. Two hundred American dollars. I went. I got stopped by some MPs. The truck was full of black market cigarettes. I spent six months in a sweltering stockade. Sleeping in the bunk below me was Cro-Magnon, a man who'd killed ten American soldiers, two of them *after* he'd been put in the stockade. I was a bit nervous. Once I saw Cro-Magnon walk into a wall by mistake. He demanded an apology. The wall refused. Cro-Magnon swore at the wall, calling it every name in the Army vocabulary. The wall ignored him. Finally he hit the wall. He punched it again and again. The guards had to carry him away. I slept lightly, knowing he was down there. The only amusement in the stockade was racing cockroaches. We each had our pet roach which we kept in a jar and fed with our own bread. We pampered our bugs as long as they ran for us. If one balked, though—even if it was a star runner—if it balked just once, we had the law of the camp: if you don't run, you don't live. We'd stomp the son of a bitch right there on the starting line. I've thought about that law. I think it says a lot.

After six months they let me out with a dishonorable discharge. I'd entered the Army less than two years before, so I felt like I'd put one over on Uncle Sam—I'd gotten out four months early. My father said he couldn't pull any strings, but there must've been one thin piece of twine because he got me a job washing test tubes and cleaning rat cages. Home was unbearable. My parents tried—after all, they were liberals—but I guess I'd simply outgrown the whole scene. I saw an index card on a bulletin board asking for riders to help with the driving to San Francisco. I went. Being a skilled and experienced technician, I soon found a job in San Francisco —washing test tubes and cleaning rat cages. I had a room in the Fillmore District. At that time San Francisco was in the forefront of a chemical revolution, and I joined the peasants who were storming the Bastille. At the same time I was spending every spare moment at work watching how they operated their little computer, which was next door to the rat room. It was easy. Soon I talked my way into operating, and doubled my salary. After a few months they installed a bigger computer, and I was promoted to operate it. I'd moved in with a painter named Melinda who was pretty fond of amphetamines, and soon I was fond of them, too. I talked my way into operating a 360/65, which at that time was probably the biggest machine in the city. I had a flair for the work. I was also zooming on speed. One day Melinda went out for some wine and never came back. A few days later I dropped acid and walked through a plate glass window. I decided to cool it. When my wounds had healed I took a bus to Boston. I found a job operating a 360/50 for an insurance company. I didn't cool it. I was an out and out speed freak, skinny and shaking. I lived next to a nice couple named Jim and Mary—nice, but terrible judges of character. One day Mary said a friend of theirs wanted to buy some hash. I told them I didn't deal, but I could get some and sell it at cost. Their friend was no friend. It was a setup. My father flew up to Boston and told me he'd help if I agreed to go to this place in the mountains where I could be 'cured.' If not, I could rot in jail. Naturally I agreed. His lawyer beat the rap—illegal entrapment—and off I went to the mountains. It was a nice old resort in the Appalachians that used to treat tuberculosis before penicillin came along. Now it used the same treatment—clean air and cold nights— for drug addicts. The sign over the driveway said MUSHROOM MOUNTAIN SANITARIUM. I lived in a big white house on a hill surrounded by pine trees. At night I slept under an open window covered by heavy wool blankets. Ever since, I've always loved the smell of wool. I used to lie in bed and count the shooting stars and listen to the owls and the rustle of the night. One of the other patients was Erica. She was only fifteen. She wasn't an addict, but she'd had some weird kind of reaction to LSD—maybe she was allergic to it, or maybe it was bad acid, some animal tranquilizer or God knows what —and she'd lost the coordination in her fingers, and sometimes she'd have spasms run through her body from head to toe. The spasms were creepy. It looked like an orgasm, but there was fear in her eyes. Erica and I would climb the mountain to a lake where she taught me how to fish. We were usually the only people there. We'd fish and picnic and skip stones and make love, and if we caught anything we'd fry it on a fire. Erica could talk to the birds. If she heard a dove she'd sit on a rock and coo, and it would coo back from far away, and she'd coo again, and the dove would answer from a closer tree, and she'd coo again and the dove would come closer and closer until it was sitting on a branch right over her head. She went home before me. She gave me her address in Wheeling, West Virginia. When I got out a month later I took a bus to Wheeling and got a job operating a Univac for a bank. I had to lie about my background, but I knew that a good operator is hard to find. I hoped that as soon as the bank saw how good I was, they'd forget about checking references. Erica was living with her parents in an old gray rowhouse shaded by elm trees on a cliff above the Ohio River. The front porch had a chair hanging by a chain from the roof, and you could swing in the chair and watch the river go by. I was living in a flop-house down by the bus station. The only other tenants were winos and burned out prostitutes. They were all psychopaths. There was screaming and doors slamming all night long. When I wasn't at work I tried to spend every minute with Erica. Her parents came from Harlan County, Kentucky. Her dad played fiddle and her mother played a mean harmonica. Erica sang. I told them they should write to a record company and sign a contract. They didn't think they were any good. They just wanted to have a good time. Her dad was happy driving a delivery truck for Coca-Cola. He was a Teamster, and proud of it. When Erica got pregnant, her folks wanted me to move in. Instead I took her to a Justice of the Peace and then to an apartment I'd found in another part of town. She didn't like it. Too far from the river, she said, but she moved in with me. The baby came out strange. It was blue and didn't cry and looked like a moron. It died after two weeks. I was sorry it had turned out that way, but I was glad it had died. Erica was broken-hearted. She blamed it on the

LSD. She blamed it on me. She blamed it on the apartment that was too far from the river. One day she split. I called her folks—they hadn't seen her. Three days later she was picked up in Pittsburgh. They sent her home. She went to live with her parents. She was having spasms again. I tried to get her to go fishing with me, or to go up in the mountains to talk with the birds. She refused. Her coordination got worse. Her folks sent her back to the sanitarium in the mountains. She lost weight, and when I visited she wouldn't see me. I was going mad. I loved her but she was driving me crazy, and I obviously wasn't doing her any good, either. I had to go. If you don't run, you don't live.

I hitchhiked to Cincinnati, then decided to try hopping a freight. I'd never done it. I walked around the trainyard looking for a good long train. I figured the more cars, the more likely it would be a long distance run. I saw one pulling out that was so long I couldn't see the engine or the caboose. I ran alongside and climbed onto a flatcar that had a truck trailer lashed to it. That was a mistake. I was exposed to the wind and the sun, and somebody could spot me. As soon as the train stopped for the first time, I selected a boxcar. It was nice. For the rest of the day I sat by the open door of the boxcar while the land rumbled past my eyes. I pretended I was sitting still, and the land was moving. In the evening the train stopped in Vincennes, Indiana. I was hungry, so I got off and found a cafe. After supper I felt so good that I just wanted to walk down the tracks. Dry autumn grass was hanging over the gravel, and swallows were swooping and diving. I didn't know it at the time, but this was my last night as a legal citizen. The air smelled clean and crisp and full of life.

I slept in an abandoned railroad station. Occasionally through the night a long freight would clatter on by, shaking me awake from the pillow of dust. For the rest of the night there was only the sound of dry grass scraping in the wind, and a mysterious machine that I could hear somewhere beneath the floorboards. What the machine did I'll never know. The station was locked, waterless, abandoned—the town had died and disappeared—and yet every five minutes

16

or so this cursed electric motor would whistle to a start, hum along for several seconds, and drive a piston clank-clank-clank until it shook the floorboards. Then it shut itself off and lay dormant for another five minutes or so, while the grass scraped and the wind blew. To me that machine symbolizes the Midwest, and I often think of it even today—a persistent, mysterious industrial force coming to life and dying again and again amid the land of wind and dry grass.

ST. LOUIS

Sam the trucker had a box of big white pills. He called them White Lightnin'. I'd heard of the L.A. Turnaround — a pill truckers use to drive New York to Los Angeles and back — but White Lightnin' was something new.

'Help 'self,' Sam said grinning, wagging a toothpick, tapping a ring on the steering wheel.

Why not.

I knew good and well why not, but I popped one anyway. It left a chalky white dust on my fingers.

'Chew.'

I bit. It tasted like kerosene and guano and bats' whiskers, and when I swallowed, my stomach growled with rage. But my head sang. It was no benny. Soon my mind raced forward and ran circles around the conversation — Sam was recalling how he grew up on a chicken farm in East Texas — while my fingertips felt heavy and numb. Chicken farming was failing and Sam's parents were dying as we rolled over Illinois flatlands, so when he inherited half the farm he traded it for a truck. Land for wheels. He knew every cathouse from Boston to New Orleans, every back room casino from Miami to Seattle, every grimy truckstop from Chicago to San Diego.

He was full of it. I let him talk — words were music and I tapped my heavy toes — but with White Lightnin' I could think whole sentences between each word that he uttered, and the sentences were thoughts that I didn't want to hear: I am running away from love. I am a coward. I am a rat.

Sam delivered the soybeans and myself to a mill in East St. Louis.

'There's an easy-goin' cathouse behind a bar—Ernie's—on Thirty-eighth Street.'

'Yeah? Thanks.'

'See you there. Hoo-wee!'

But I had no intention. I wanted to be West of the Mississippi (magic words), and there she was—Big Muddy—shimmering in afternoon sunlight, and beyond her I could see brown balls of smog rolling under the Gateway Arch.

I knew somebody in St. Louis: John, my Double Arrow Buddy. For all these years he'd been chipping away at the mountain of knowledge, and soon he'd be king of the rockpile. A doctor, and what had I done with those years? What had I gained? What did I know? I wondered how John would react after all this time.

'Could I speak to John, please?'

'Speaking.'

'Hey, John, this is your old Double Arrow Buddy!'

'Huh?'

'Willy! Remember?'

'Oh.'

I almost hung up. I was talking into a tunnel seven years long, standing alone in a phone booth in a city I did not know.

'John?'

'Oh Willy! *Willy!* Hey! Where *are* you?'

John was fine. He was married, and he smoked a pipe. He lived on the third floor of an old apartment building on Pershing Avenue. I guess you can figure the age of the building by the name of the street. Lucy, his wife, said they didn't use architects in those days. The builders slapped up walls on a whim. In their apartment the back door was in the bathroom instead of the kitchen. To take out the garbage, you had to squeeze between the toilet and the bathtub.

John wanted to take me out for dinner. We walked up the block and around the corner to a place called Romey's. The sidewalks were full of students. Romey's was on a corner directly across from the university, but inside the pizza joint were only expressionless men and hard-looking women. I asked John why the students didn't eat here.

19

He shrugged. He'd never been here before.

The waitress threw the menus at us. She slopped the water glasses and didn't wipe up the puddles.

I ordered a beer with the pizza, and then another. I was coming down from White Lightnin', and I needed to hold my head together.

A man in dark glasses seemed to be in charge of the juke box. Every once in a while he'd cruise over and punch a few buttons—Sinatra, and Tom Jones.

I told John what I'd been doing with my life, and he told me about a summer in Europe and another working as a waiter in Yellowstone National Park. Other than that, he'd simply been going to school. And Lucy, who was in graduate school in anthropology, had spent her summers with her folks on Nantucket Island. Incredible! I thought of all the things I'd done in the last seven years, and here these two were still students, still going to school, still being told what to do.

I looked up from our conversation to see a shaggy-haired kid shuffle in and over to the juke box. As he leaned into the glow of the machine to read the selections, you could see that he'd patched the back of his old sheepskin jacket with an American flag.

Conversation stopped. The man in dark glasses started walking for the juke box. At the tables the men remained expressionless. The women didn't show a glint of feeling in their eyes.

Dark Glasses was standing behind the kid.

The kid was leaning over the machine.

Suddenly Dark Glasses attacked. He slammed the kid to the wall and punched him in the jaw. I got up. I wasn't thinking. I jumped on the man and shoved him to the floor. The kid saw his chance and ran out the door. Great. I couldn't handle this guy alone. I saw John getting up. I waved him away—he's no fighter. I backed toward the door. The man advanced. Behind him, two men stood up and unbuttoned their jackets.

I made it through the door and shoved it back. I was lucky. The door swung back and caught Dark Glasses on the chin.

He staggered but recovered. Before I could get away he rushed out. He lunged—caught my collar—swung me around. He raised his fist, tightened it—he was wearing a ring. The other two men stood right behind him. The scene —the three faces—locked into my mind. The fist was an inch from my nose. The ring was gold, with jagged edges.

While I was watching his fist, Dark Glasses kicked me in the groin. I fell to the sidewalk, doubled over. I heard the sound of cloth ripping and thought it was me. Then I looked up and saw the two men running away. Dark Glasses was falling. There was a shiv in his back.

I didn't understand, but I knew it was bad. I managed to stand up and limp into an alley. I heard voices.

'He stabbed Frank! He stabbed him in the back!'

I staggered down the alley. Already I heard sirens. I came out on a street. A bus was coming. I got on. I was shaking. I wanted to throw up. After a while I got off. I didn't know where I was. The street was dirty and lined with old brick duplexes. My balls ached and there was a dull thumping between my ears. I saw a police car. I panicked. I ran between two buildings and ducked down a stairwell. I sat on the bottom step and wondered what I could do. Before I decided, I passed out.

I woke up shivering. It was dawn. At the top of the stairs a little brown-haired dog was whining at me, wagging a bushy tail. My balls were swollen, aching. I gently touched them. They were hot, heavy—maybe something was broken.

I climbed cautiously up the steps. If somebody saw me here, they'd probably think I was a burglar.

The street was quiet. A few houses had lights in the windows. I walked to the corner and learned that I was at the intersection of Macklind and Odell. Which meant nothing to me. I walked a short block and came to an open cafe. I could see the doughnuts and smell the hot coffee.

The counterman was a stocky old guy whose face had been a punching bag for too many years. He poured a cup of coffee before he even asked what I wanted.

I sipped the coffee. 'Thanks,' I said.

'You want coffee?'

I looked up. Obviously I wanted it. I'd already started. 'Yes,' I said. 'I want coffee.'

'Okay.'

'And I'd like a doughnut.'

'You got money?'

Jesus. 'Of course.'

'Show me.'

'Look. I don't have to show—'

'You elope?'

'Huh?'

He nodded his head toward the front window. I looked out. For the first time I noticed the hospital across the street. The sign said State Hospital.

'Didja elope?'

'What do you mean?'

'ELOPE! DIDJA ELOPE?'

I stood up to leave.

'Elaine! Call the hospital!'

A girl came out of a back room, wiping her hands on a dish towel. 'What is it, Bumpy?'

Bumpy pointed at me. 'Eloped.'

'What is this?'

The girl—Elaine—smiled. Her eyes were alive. 'It's okay, Bumpy.' She started back toward the kitchen.

'You sure?'

She turned and studied me. 'I'm sure.'

'What *is* this?'

She asked me, 'You new around here?'

'Yes.'

'A lot of patients walk off the hospital when they aren't supposed to. The hospital calls it an elopement—don't ask me why. They used to come over here and order a big meal. Course they didn't have any money. Now we just give 'em a free cup of coffee and send 'em back.'

I sat down again. 'And how do you know I'm not one of them?'

She winked. 'You don't look crazy.'

'Ah.' I winked back. 'Little do you know.'

She laughed, which was nice of her.

'You want a doughnut?' asked Bumpy.

I took two and asked where was the men's room.

'Through the kitchen to your left.'

Elaine was in the kitchen slicing onions. She saw me and pointed at a door. I nodded. The sign on the door said 'Bathroom.'

It *was* a bathroom. It had a bathtub — the old kind, held off the floor by little iron feet — and there was a medicine cabinet over the sink. I guess the cafe was carved out of an old apartment.

I examined myself. My balls had swollen to the size of a fist. The skin was a deep red with purple splotches.

I pissed blood.

I was scared. When I walked back through the kitchen, I think Elaine saw my fear. I spotted a newspaper at an empty table and brought it to my doughnuts. I read the headline. Oh my God.

I was wanted for the murder of a policeman.

'What's new?' asked Bumpy.

'Nothing.' I hid the headline from his view.

'Gimme the sports.'

'Sure.'

I read the article. The cop was a hero with 'a long and distinguished record.' I was a 'drunken, vicious hoodlum.' John was 'held for questioning.' And here was an odd thing: nowhere in the article did it mention that the cop had attacked a kid and that I'd come to defend him. And nowhere did it mention the two men who'd followed us out of the restaurant. The police must have questioned the witnesses. Didn't anybody tell them what had really happened? According to the article, I'd become boisterous, the manager had complained, the off duty cop had identified himself as a policeman and asked me to leave, I had refused, the cop had tried to escort me out, and suddenly I pulled a knife. Weird. And I — 'a white, dark haired male wearing blue jeans and a tan jacket' — was At Large.

I was framed. And here I sat, chewing on a doughnut. How surprising. How amusing. I, a nice boy from the suburbs, had just gone blundering along, and suddenly I was a drunken, vicious hoodlum, a white, dark haired male wearing blue jeans and a tan jacket. I had no witnesses. The two men who'd done the real stabbing certainly wouldn't help me. Everyone else had been inside the restaurant. Even John and Lucy hadn't seen it — they probably thought I was guilty, too. I had a record from the Army. I'd been treated for drug addiction. I'd run out on my wife. Funny — I didn't *sound* like a nice boy from the suburbs.

My thoughts were interrupted by problems down below.

I was gagging.

I couldn't hold it down. I raced through the kitchen past Elaine and into the bathroom. I kneeled over the toilet. When I came out, Elaine was watching. She probably heard. She smiled at me quickly and then looked away. I felt that she wanted to say something but didn't know how.

I wanted to call John. There was a phone next to the door. I was walking toward it when two cops walked in. I turned right around and walked back past Elaine to the bathroom. I took out my wallet and flushed my driver's license and library card down the toilet. I had no other identification. I remembered the newspaper description of me wearing a tan jacket. I ripped it to pieces and flushed it in wads. It took a dozen flushes, and each time I had to wait a couple minutes for the tank to refill.

I was going to miss that jacket. It was an old friend. What's more, I needed something to keep me warm. There must be five thousand white, dark haired males wearing blue jeans and tan jackets in St. Louis. Why had I panicked? Sitting on the edge of the bathtub, I vowed not to be paranoid. Cautious — yes, of course — but if I was going to be paranoid I might as well go to jail. I made a mental list of immediate needs:

1. See a doctor.
2. Get out of town.
3. Replace jacket.

There. Now I felt organized. Life made sense again. Even fugitives must have order.

Elaine, washing plates, stared as I walked by. 'I can't decide whether you're sick or crazy.'

'Neither. Just weird.' I grinned. I couldn't tell whether I was pulling it off. In a half hour she'd seen me use the bathroom three times. She'd seen my fear after I'd pissed blood. She'd heard me vomit. And then she'd heard me flush the toilet a dozen times in succession.

The cops were gone. I called John.

Lucy answered.

'John there?'

'No. Willy?'

'Yes.'

'Where are you?'

'Kansas City,' I lied. Damn. Their phone wasn't tapped. Must not be paranoid. 'Lucy, I didn't do it.'

'What happened?'

I whispered: 'Those two guys—'

'What?'

The cafe was empty. Bumpy was busy with the coffee-maker—dumping grounds and changing filters. I spoke softly: 'Those two guys who walked out behind us. They did it.'

'Really?'

'*Yes*.' I was annoyed. She was doubting me. 'I read the newspaper. How'd they get that story about me being boisterous? Why didn't they tell about attacking that kid at the juke box?'

'Nobody talked. All the customers disappeared. The manager made up that story. We told the truth—about the kid, and how you tried to break it up. We said you must've stabbed him in self-defense.'

'I *didn't* stab him.' Jesus. What if Bumpy heard *that*?

'Okay.'

'How could I get him in the *back*?'

'Okay. Okay.'

'Do you believe me?'

'Sure.'

25

She didn't sound sure.

'Where's John?'

'They've still got him.'

What were they doing with him? 'I'll call later.'

'Okay.'

I didn't dare go over there. They could be watching for me. Or could they? Was that paranoia? Had I seen too many movies? Do cops really stake out buildings? What do cops really do, anyway? What are the rules to this game?

The image of the three men—just before the stabbing— kept flashing into my mind. Dark Glasses, a totally expressionless face, a fist inches from my nose, hairy fingers with bare knuckles, a giant gold ring with jagged edges. Behind Dark Glasses, the other two men. One man expressionless, dark jowled, deep-eyed—menacing and anonymous. The other man—strange, strange—the other man wore spectacles. His fair-skinned face had never needed a shave. His hairline was receding. His ears stuck out like little wings. His face was not expressionless. He was scared.

I was standing in front of the phone. I couldn't decide what to do next. I was still hungry. I didn't know if I could hold it down. I had to see a doctor. Could I? I didn't have to use my real name. It wasn't a bullet wound—he wouldn't be suspicious. How do I find one? Look it up in the Yellow Pages? I didn't know the streets. He'd have to be near. I couldn't walk far. In fact I'd better sit down. It hurt like—

My knees buckled.

Elaine took one arm. Bumpy had the other. They carried me back through the kitchen into a room with a bed, where they lay me down. Elaine peered into my face. 'You *are* sick,' she said. 'Are you from the hospital?'

'No. Not crazy. Just sick.'

'Bumpy, call an ambulance.'

'No!' I sat up. 'Please.' I was asking—begging for the first time. I would soon get used to it. 'Please. Just let me lie here a minute. I'm okay. I'll walk to a doctor. Just give me a minute.' I was scared of ambulances, hospitals—they'd want identification, verification.

26

'Well—' Elaine sat on the bed. 'I'll sit with you.'

Bumpy left.

I lay sweating. I was mad at my body. It wasn't performing. Then paranoia struck. Maybe they really *were* calling an ambulance. I tried to get up. The knees failed. I fell back.

'Elaine—'

'What?'

'Please don't call an ambulance.'

'We're *not*.'

'Is Bumpy?'

'*No!*'

All right. I closed my eyes. I said, 'How'd you know I'm not from the hospital?'

'You're too young.' She laughed. She seemed to laugh at everything. She began with a slow grin that eased across her lips until the whole face was Cheshire cat, and then the laugh would bubble up from way down in her chest—not the simple throat laugh, a joke laugh—but a deep laughter that grows out of happiness, contentment, satisfaction. 'They're all *old* folks. Most of 'em aren't crazy—just old. Bumpy used to be there. Nothing wrong with him—just nobody wanted him. He kept wandering over here—eloping. We got so used to him, finally we hired him. He lives here. This is his room. His bed.'

'Where do you live?'

'South Side.'

I didn't know where that was. I didn't care. I liked her. I just wanted to hear her talk. 'You in school?'

'Oh, no.' She was laughing again.

'What's so funny?'

'School.' And she laughed some more.

Her eyes had a life of their own. I was fascinated. I stared into them until she got embarrassed and looked away. 'I like your eyes. You speak with your eyes. Did you know that?'

'No.' She was looking at her fingers.

'I have this theory.' I launched into it. I believe that a man —or woman—reveals his soul through his eyes. I really do. Your eyes reveal your feelings. I believe that all the evil in the world is committed by people who don't reveal their feelings. The military and the police cultivate an expressionless face. They hold their mouths rigid. They hide their eyes behind dark glasses. Don't believe what you see in the movies. You can't inflict pain unless you keep an expressionless face. I learned in the stockade that if I could make a guard show a feeling—show his fear or frustration—he wouldn't beat me.

It's different with women. They have expressive faces. You rarely see an expressionless woman. I guess it's part of the culture. But some women stop their expressions just short of their eyes. And when their eyes show no feeling—watch out. But you—Elaine—you have sparkling brown eyes . . .

'You're babbling,' she said.

She went back to work. I lay alone. I stared at the ceiling, at the flashing vision of the three men. The one who looked scared. What was he doing there?

Elaine returned at eight. 'I'm off,' she said. 'Can you get up?'

I could, though I felt wobbly. And then I had to beg again. I was learning that fugitives have to do a lot of begging. Could she take me to a doctor?

'I'll take you to mine.'

'Don't go out of your way.' Hoping she would.

She had an old milk truck, painted yellow. She had to stand to drive it. In back it had a mattress, wood-burning stove, and a complete stereo system.

The doctor kept me waiting an hour and a half. The examination took thirty seconds. He was one of those self-important types. He never smiled. Doctors should smile.

'What happened?'

'Fight.'

'Who won?'

'Hard to say.'

'What did he slam you with? A baseball bat?'

'Just his knee.'

'Remarkable.' He shook his head.

'Bad?'

'You have health insurance?'

28

'No.'

'Then you'll have to go to Homer G. Phillips.'

'Who's that?'

'City hospital.'

'I don't want — I can't — what if I don't go?'

'Probably die.'

Elaine drove me. I lay on the mattress as the truck jiggled along. I was thinking up an identity. I decided to keep my first name. I'd never be able to get used to another one. But Willy what? Willy . . . Crusoe. Wilbur R. Crusoe. That sounded good.

'Elaine?'

'What?' She was throwing all her weight into turning the steering wheel.

'I'm your cousin. I came down from Minnesota to visit.'

'Why?'

'Can't tell.'

'What's wrong with you?'

'Never mind.'

When she parked at the hospital, she came back and stood over the mattress. 'If you're gonna be my cousin from Minnesota, I got to know what's wrong with you.'

'I broke something.'

'What?'

'My — uh — groin.'

'Your — uh — groin.' She giggled. She laughed. She was not sympathetic. She howled. She clapped her hand over her mouth and shrieked with joy. Her laughing shook the whole truck until the springs were squeaking.

Willy Crusoe had a little surgery and then lay five days recuperating. He learned from the newspapers that the police knew the name of the cop killer. He was William (Willy) Middlebrook. He was believed to be in Kansas City.

So. Either their phone was tapped, or Lucy had told. Either way, I couldn't call John. If the phone *was* tapped, I'd give away my location. And if it *wasn't*, then I couldn't trust Lucy and so I wouldn't dare say anything. John probably told them my name, but that was okay. He couldn't very well deny that he knew me, since we'd been eating together.

My ward — the indigent ward — was a catalog of human suffering. Half the patients were victims of violence: gunshot wounds, automobile accidents, family quarrels that ended with a butcher knife, attempted suicides. The other half were victims of alcohol, with poisoned livers and liquid minds. On the bed to my right lay Clarence, a fourteen year old who'd been shot in the spine by his older brother. He was paralyzed from the waist down. His mother visited every evening and kneeled by his bed and prayed for what seemed like hours. And when she was talking to the Lord, she didn't care who overheard. She shouted and sobbed. Before she would start, she'd ask Clarence if he wanted to join her. His response reflected an uncluttered view of life. It was the same response that he gave to doctors, nurses, therapists, hospital aids, and social workers: 'Shee-it.' While his mother was praying, Clarence watched television along with everybody else in the ward. Sometimes when she reached a high pitch a few of the patients would try shushing her, and once during *The Untouchables* even the kid said, 'Shut up, momma! Eliot Ness is in *trouble*!' She didn't hear. She was listening to the Lord.

The bed to my left was occupied by an old wino named Blacky. The name didn't make sense. Blacky was white. He had red hair. There was nothing black about him. I asked him about it.

'Blacky for my black eyes,' he said.

'But they're not black.'

'Was when they named me.'

He said he was in for his annual visit. Once a year he had to 'get the old liver cleaned out.' This was the third time. He'd stay for a week or so, and the doctors would warn him to stop drinking and tell him all the horrible things that were happening in his body, that he was rotting, that he was a sick old man, and then he'd check out and head for the nearest bar. 'I'll keep on gettin' dead drunk until I *am* a dead drunk,' he'd say with a wink and a smile.

Once, against my better judgment, I asked, 'Why do you drink?'

'Because I'm a sailor,' Blacky whispered in a hoarse, broken voice. 'I been around the world a hundred times. You know why I drink?'

'Why?'

'Because I'm a sailor in St. Louis.'

Blacky and Clarence held an ongoing circular conversation over my bed. The trouble was, Blacky couldn't speak above a whisper, and he was also hard of hearing. I ended up playing a human telephone between them. The conversation would go like this:

Blacky: 'How's it feel, boy?'

Clarence: 'Huh?'

Me: 'He said, "How's it feel?" '

Clarence would purse his lips: 'Shee-it.'

Blacky: 'What's he say?'

Me: 'He says, "Shee-it." '

Blacky: 'Well shee-it on you. You can forget about basket-ball.'

Clarence: 'Huh?'

Me: 'He says to forget about basketball.'

Clarence: 'Shee-it' (Clarence was tall for his age, and apparently he wanted to play pro ball when he grew up. Now that he was paralyzed, he refused to give up on the idea. His mother encouraged him: 'If you pray, Clarence, if you really talk to the Lord, he'll give you back your legs. I know he will.' His mother had brought him his basketball, and it never left his side. He slept with it cradled in his arms.)

Blacky: 'What's he say?'

Me: 'He says, "Shee-it." '

Blacky: 'You could run a cash register. You still got arms. You could run a checkout stand in a liquor store.'

Clarence: 'Huh?'

Me: 'You could work a cash register.'

Clarence: 'Shee-it.'

Blacky: 'What's he say?'

Me: 'He says, "Shee-it." '

Blacky: 'What's he want to be? He want to be a god damn astronaut?'

Me (not bothering to relay it): 'He wants to play basketball.'

Blacky: 'Well you can forget about basketball.'

Clarence: 'Huh?'

And so on. It passed the time.

On my second day Elaine and her rat boyfriend visited me at the hospital. I'll never understand it. Elaine had a sharp mind, a kind face, a good body. She could've had lots of men. Me, for example. But some women are drawn to rats the way some children love toads and snakes.

'Hear you all had an operation yesterday,' Elaine said. 'They wouldn't let me see you. Everythang all right down there?'

Thang. She said thang. I'd never heard it from the lips of a woman. I was in love from that moment on. Thang—wheat-fields and whippoorwills. The Kansas prairie, the gentle hills of Missouri. A rubber tire swinging on a rope from the old oak tree. Skinnydipping in the creek, sunning on a sandbar. Lovely, lovely thang.

I managed to answer: 'I hope it's okay.'

'Willy Crusoe, I'd like you to meet Loverboy.'

'Al,' Loverboy said. 'It's Al.'

'Hi Al.'

'Willy's my cousin from Minnesota.'

'That so?'

'I would've brought you flowers, Willy, but Loverboy spent my last seventy-five cents on a pack of cigarettes and a Hostess Pie.'

'That's okay.'

Al lit up. He didn't even offer me one. He surveyed the ward, grimacing. The ward looked back. Visitors—anybody's visitors—were public entertainment. Clarence and Blacky stared openly from their front row seats.

Al said to me, 'Couldn't you get a private room?'

'Didn't ask. What do you do, Al?'

'Nothing.'

Elaine leaned over and whispered in my ear: 'Sometimes he deals.'

'What do *you* do?' said Al.

'Nothing.'

'Ah.' That pleased him. He flicked an ash in my direction. 'How do you amuse yourself in this place? Just lie around and masturbate?'

Ears pricked up all over the ward.

'Al!' Elaine shouted. 'That's cruel.'

'Is it?'

'Yes it is. How could he masturbate when he just had an operation on his balls?'

'His balls?'

'Yes, his *balls*!'

'What's wrong with his balls?'

'He *broke* them. Now don't you think that was a cruel question?'

'Sorry. Hey. Willy. I'm sorry.'

But I couldn't answer. I was hiding under the sheets.

Two days later Elaine visited again. This time she didn't bring Loverboy Al.

'Hi, Cousin.'

'Hello, Elaine.'

I told her I'd be getting out tomorrow.

'Wonderful! You must be looking forward to going home.'

She must've seen my face fall. She sat on the bed. Neither of us spoke. Every eye in the ward was on her. Then she leaned forward and whispered something in my ear that practically made me jump clear out of the bed: 'You killed that cop, didn't you?'

'No!'

'Bumpy thinks you did. Something he heard you say on the phone. And that bit about being my cousin. And the way you turned around when those two cops walked into the cafe and went into the bathroom and flushed your jacket down the toilet.'

'You got a peephole in that john?'

'So you did do it.'

'No.' But there was no use playing games. 'They *think* I did it.'

'Same thang.'

How I loved that thang. I reached for her hand and held it between both of mine. At the same time I was judging the distance to the door and calculating how long it would take to leap out of bed and jump out of my gown and into my clothes and dash out of the ward.

'What about Bumpy?'

'Oh he's cool.'

'What about . . . you?'

She laughed. I saw the answer in her eyes even before she said it: 'Don't worry.'

'What about Al?'

'Won't tell him.'

'But he's your Loverboy.'

'Yeah but . . .'

Elaine asked about my plans, and I told her of my conflicting needs. I had to get out of town, and I was supposed to stay off my feet for a week.

'I'll pick you up tomorrow. We'll see what we can work out.'

'Elaine — why . . .?'

Her answer showed a mind that didn't bother with a lot of complicated moral constructions. She responded to immediate human needs: 'Nothing we can do for the cop. He's dead. But *you* need help.'

'Mighty pretty woman,' Blacky wheezed when Elaine had gone. 'Mighty pretty. When you get out, I want you to buy her a drink for me. Tell her it's for old Blacky.'

'Sure, Blacky.'

'Hey Clarence! Willy's gettin' out tomorrow. What do you think about that?'

Clarence was staring at the ceiling. 'Huh?' he said. He was holding the basketball at his side.

'I'm getting out tomorrow.'

Clarence glanced at me. He pursed his lips. 'Shee-it.'

I relayed the message.

'Boy,' Blacky said, 'I'm gonna get through to you if it's the last thing I do. I know you got feelings. You ain't all that tough.'

Clarence spun the basketball on his fingertip. He could hold it perfectly balanced that way. To Blacky he said, 'Shee-it.'

Blacky turned to me. 'Did he say shee-it?'

I nodded.

Blacky grabbed an empty vase from a table by his bed. He threw — and hit the spinning basketball, which bounced to the floor and under a bed.

'Hey!' Clarence shouted. 'Get it.'

Blacky laughed.

Clarence screamed, 'GIMME MY BASKETBALL!'

Blacky cackled.

'SOMEBODY HELP! HEL-L-L-LP!'

A nurse came running.

'GIMME MY BASKETBALL!'

When the nurse realized that all the commotion was over a basketball, she stood at the foot of Clarence's bed with her hands on her hips. She hit him with a glare that would have given most men blindness or a concussion. Clarence didn't blink. He screamed again, 'GIMME THAT BALL! GIMME THE GOD DAMN BASKETBALL!'

She had no choice. She had to shut him up.

Clarence embraced the ball in his lap, rocking back and forth. He turned to Blacky and pursed his lips. 'Shee-it.' He grinned.

That night Blacky died in his sleep. Nobody heard him die. Without any drama, without calling attention to himself, he very quietly stopped living. The next morning when the doctor came to give him a shot, he lifted a cold wrist. He pulled a stethoscope from the pocket of his white coat and poked it over Blacky's chest. He frowned and made a little ticking noise with his teeth. He flipped the sheet over Blacky's face and strode on to the next bed. 'Terminal,' he remarked to the nurse. That was all.

I heard a muffled sob from Clarence's bed. I looked over. He was huddled over the basketball in his lap. He was jerking his shoulders and upper torso, trying to make his hips and legs move. 'Lord,' he cried, 'don't make me work no cash register in no liquor store. Shee-it, God. Shee-it.'

I spent a week in Bumpy's room, sleeping in Bumpy's bed, eating meals that Elaine and Bumpy fixed in the cafe.

At night, after he'd switched off the television, Bumpy would lie on the rug and grunt answers to my questions. He didn't like to talk, but I fired questions at him — poking and prodding as if it was a cross-examination. I've always loved to get into the heads of old folks. Besides, I wanted to make sure I could trust him.

'How come you let me stay here?'

'Don't mind.'

'Why don't you turn me in?'

'Had it comin'.'

'Who?'

'The cop.'

'You like cops?'

'No.'

'You born in St. Louis?'

'No.'

'Where were you born?'

'Tupper Lake.'

'Where's that?'

'Adirondack Mountains.'

'New York?'

'Yep.'

'Um . . . how'd you end up here?'

There was a pause, and then a sigh at the impossibility of answering such a question.

'What did you do in Tupper Lake?'

'Messed around.'

'Work there?'

'Sure.'

'What did you do?'

'Paper mill.'

'Why'd you leave?'

'Closed.'

'Closed? What closed?'

A pause while he gathered strength. 'Mill shut down.'

'Was this in the Depression?'

'Guess so. *I* was depressed. Heh heh.'

'What did you do?'

'Heh. Left.'

'Where'd you go?'

'All over.'

Through the open window I could hear the sad moaning of a foghorn calling to the barges on the dark Mississippi. It sounded like a giant frog croaking an endless dirge. Sing on, oh giant frog. Mister and Mississippi is all you'll ever have.

'Were you in the war?'

'No.'

'Why not?'

'Hmph.'

'What did you do during the war?'

'Worked.'

'Where?'

'Californ'.'

'What did you do?'

'Built airplanes.'

'I was in the Army. I got drafted. I was in Vietnam. Then something happened,' I told him the story of driving the truck and six months in the stockade. I ended by asking, 'What do you think about that?'

'Huh.'

He wasn't cracking. I've often found that if you pester an old guy long enough, he'll finally break and reveal some gem that he's hidden from the world for years.

'How long were you in the hospital?'

'Couple years.'

'Why'd they put you there?'

No answer. I was being too nosy. You have to ease into

these things gently: 'Ever been out of the country?'

'Mexico.'

'Like it?'

'No.'

'Why?'

'Dirty.'

'Ever been in jail?'

'Sure.'

'What for?'

'Nothing.'

'Steal something?'

'No!'

'Drunk?'

'Vagrancy. Railroad bulls. About twenty of us stiffs in a boxcar. And a woman with a kid.'

Ah. 'Where?'

'Athol.'

'Where's that?'

'Athol, Massachusetts. I say it was named by a man with a lisp. Athol, Mathachutheth. And we were riding through on the B & M railroad. Figures.'

'Ha. And they arrested you all for vagrancy.'

'Something. Vagrants. Trespassing. Don't matter what they called it. We were stiffs. They had us.'

'And they put you all in jail? Why didn't they just let you pass on through?'

'The woman.'

'Was she wanted?'

'They called for two vans. They loaded all of us in one van —all the men, including the woman's husband, and the kid. And the woman—a young woman, pretty woman, dirty but pretty—they put her in the other van all by herself. Our van went straight to the jail. The other van didn't come till morning. When her husband saw her, he could see what they'd done. She couldn't look him in the eye. He went crazy. He rushed a guard and got him by the throat. Wouldn't let go. Two other guards were beating on him and he still held on. Finally one of them cracks him on the head with the butt of his rifle. Killed him. Cracked his skull. Couple days later they load us all in a bus and take us out of town. Everybody starts walking. They all go one way. I go the other. I'm going back to town. I'm gonna kill one of them bastards. I'll do it with my bare hands.'

He paused. I waited for him to continue, but nothing came. Finally I asked, 'Did you do it?'

He sighed. 'Nope.'

'How come?'

'I didn't know who done it. I might've picked out some guy who wasn't hurting anybody. He might've had a good wife and six kids at home. You know?'

'Yes.'

'You can't play God.'

On her breaks and before and after work, Elaine visited me in my hideout in Bumpy's room. I found out that she'd grown up in Excelsior Springs, Missouri. She'd been Home-coming Queen and graduated from high school still 'technically,' she said, a virgin. She was dating the son of the Superintendent of Schools, and other than working part time at the A&W Stand she wasn't doing anything except waiting around for her boy-friend to ask her to marry him. One night Al stopped at the A&W. He was driving a camper truck. He ordered a root beer and struck up a conversation. Something fell into place that night that had been hanging loose all her life. She didn't know what it was. She just knew it, felt it, as it clicked into the empty slot. She left with him that night and hadn't been home since. Al was on his way from Kansas to New York City. The camper truck was stuffed to the ceiling with marijuana that he'd picked in Kansas. He'd heard there was a shortage in New York, and he aimed to cash in on it. They stopped for the night at a Holiday Inn near Columbus, Ohio. Al parked the truck in the lot. They spent two nights in the Holiday Inn and never left their room except once to get some food down-stairs. They dropped acid, and Elaine lost her technical virginity and her nontechnical upbringing, at least for a while. When they returned to the truck, it was gone. Stolen.

There was nothing Al could do about it. Elaine decided right then and there that dealing was a lousy way to make a living. Al seemed to agree. They hitchhiked to St. Louis, where Al's father had a little shop where he repaired cameras. Al had decided to learn camera repair from his father, then go to some little town in northern California and set up a shop of his own. It didn't work out. Camera repair requires delicacy and patience, two qualities that Al didn't seem to have. He drifted back into occasional dealing. Elaine found the job at the cafe. Now they were saving up money, and soon they planned to join a commune in New Mexico and try their hand at farming.

'What do you see in him?' I asked her once.

'Al? Oh he saved me.'

'From Excelsior Springs?'

'All that.'

'But—'

'I *love* him.' The look in her eye was fierce.

I suspected that while in a sense Al had saved her, it was more accurate to say that she had saved herself. That night at the A&W Al had opened a door in a room of her mind where she felt trapped—where she had always thought there weren't any doors at all—but she herself had had the sense and the courage to walk out that door to the great darkness and mystery of the waiting night.

I wanted to buy her a drink for old Blacky since I'd promised I would, but I had no money. I'd entered the hospital with two hundred dollars in my wallet, but they took it all.

I tried Al. 'Could you spare a little money?'

'How much?'

'Oh—five . . .'

He searched his pocket and tossed me a nickel.

'I meant dollars.'

'I know.' He turned his back and walked away.

I needed more than five dollars anyway. It was time to see John.

I took a bus to the medical school and eventually tracked

John down to a dermatology clinic. The receptionist was not friendly.

'And what is the problem?'

'No problem. I want to talk to him.'

'Dr. Cline is busy.'

Doctor. He hadn't even graduated yet.

'Give him this.' I drew a double arrow on her note pad.

The waiting room was packed with walking specimens of acne and rash and rotting skin. Every seat was taken. I stood near the door and tried not to touch anything.

'Dr. Cline will see you now.'

I sat on the paper sheets of the examination table. John locked the door and lit his pipe. He wanted to talk about the stabbing. I couldn't work up any enthusiasm about the subject — I say what's done is done and the hell with it — but John wanted to play Perry Mason. He said that it must have been an assassination. He said that what struck him as odd was that the police didn't seem too upset about it. They questioned him for a half hour, and he told them about the kid at the juke box, the brawl, the two men following us out. They accepted the story. They didn't cross-examine or show in any way that they didn't believe it. And yet they held him for twenty-four hours and released the story to the newspapers about my being 'boisterous.' As far as John could tell, the police didn't want to know the truth or solve the crime. They'd kept him locked up so he couldn't give his story to the papers.

John had also done some research about Romey's, the pizza joint. It had a shady reputation. Gamblers hung out there. The people in the bookstore that was right next door to Romey's said that when they first opened, two goons from Romey's came over and mentioned 'security' and suggested who to order their posters from. Can you imagine? Mobsters in the poster racket?

I asked John how the police got the idea that I was in Kansas City.

'I told them. Lucy said she was sure it was a local call — it wasn't scratchy enough for long distance. So we figured — I

41

figured — you wanted them to think you were there.'

He sucked on his pipe. He was obviously proud of his logic.

I told John about my recurring vision. He wanted a description of the men. I told him what little I could about the expressionless man, and then I described the man who'd been scared — the fair skin, the spectacles, receding hairline, wing-like ears — he simply didn't look tough. He didn't look like a mobster.

'Then he was a gambler,' said John.

'And a loser,' I said. 'A scared loser. But what does that have to do with a stabbing?'

John sucked smoke. 'Paying debts.' Blowing smoke. Playing Sherlock. 'He owed money. Didn't have money. So they asked him to do them a little favor. In return for the favor, they'd cancel the debt.'

'Some favor.'

'Some debt.'

But it made sense. I once knew a man who gambled. Nicest guy you ever saw. Friendly, helpful — once he spent a whole day working on my car, showing me what to do. This was Boston. He lived in the apartment over me. His wife kept shouting. Every night, I heard shouting. Sometimes crying. Sometimes throwing things. He was compulsive. He was in debt. She kept shouting at him. About once a week, a big shiny green car would park in front of our building. No horns honked, nobody stepped out of the car. It simply pulled up and sat there like an ominous green wart on the pavement. My friends and I got so used to it, we'd joke about it: 'The green wart's back.' But it was no joke to my neighbor. Within a minute after it appeared, my neighbor would be in the car. Fifteen, maybe thirty minutes later he came back out of the car and went up to his apartment. The scene was so undramatic that it was eerie. And every night his wife would shout at him. One day, he came home with two broken legs. His wife moved out. The shiny green car appeared every week. No more shouting. I could hear his crutches clumping in the middle of the night. His grown daughter visited. I heard pleading. 'Daddy. *Please.*' She left. The shiny green car appeared. He sat in it for an hour. That night he got very drunk. I heard him singing. He sang 'Chattanooga Choo-Choo' at the top of his voice, but the words were all wrong and he slurred everything.

The next day he disappeared. A couple weeks later, a Boston cop knocked on my door. I didn't know anything. He said nobody knew anything.

I never heard about him again. I never saw the green wart again, either.

John wanted to know where I'd been hiding. I told him about the hospital, the operation.

'Can I see it?'

I didn't understand.

He rephrased it: 'Let me examine you.'

I started to unbuckle, then hesitated. I didn't want to do it. Something—a feeling I'd never had to deal with before—told me not to take off my pants. John and I had grown up together. We'd been closer than brothers. In a nonphysical way we'd been as close as lovers. That was the problem. A stranger could examine me impersonally. But when John touched me, they would be John's hands. What if something weird happened? Like what if I got a hard on? Which was dumb, of course. It wouldn't matter now. But back then, yes.

He fingered me gently. He prodded and asked if it hurt. He studied the scar. He held my balls, hefted them, told me to cough.

I wasn't betrayed. Body seemed to agree with mind. I coughed and waited for John to finish.

And waited.

I looked down. He was still holding on. The hand remained — one second — two — three — four — five — then withdrew. Five seconds too long. John wasn't meeting my eye. Was I reading it wrong? It was only five seconds.

I dressed. The rustle of clothes was deafening. Somebody had to say something. I asked, 'How's it look?'

'Okay.' He lit the pipe.

'Will I live?'

He didn't answer. He wasn't playing. Wasn't smiling. Dammit. Doctors should smile.

'Can I have some money?'

'Sure. Yes. How much?'

'Lots.'

Quickly he emptied his wallet — sixty-five dollars.

'Guess I'll go now.'

'Okay.'

I moved for the door. John was staring into the bowl of his pipe.

'Well . . . Good-bye.'

'Where will you go?'

'I don't know.'

I walked out, closed the door behind me. A nurse was bustling down the hall. I felt like everything was wrong. I took the money out of my pocket. I was afraid he'd given it to me for the wrong reason. I opened the door, walked back in. John was still staring into the bowl of the pipe.

'John . . .'

He looked up.

'. . . Double Arrow?'

He set down the pipe and put his hands in the pockets of his white coat. He was fingering the stethoscope.

'Look Willy. Cut the kid stuff.'

I was suddenly mad. I slammed the door and hurried down the hall and out through the room of acne and rash and rotting skin. As I left, I noticed the sign on the door that said DERMATOLOGY. Without even looking over my shoulder to see if anybody was watching, I ripped the sign from the door and walked away.

Two days later I mailed the sign to John. I thought about enclosing a note — something clever — like: 'Here's your sign, faggot.' But I didn't really know if he was one or not, and maybe he didn't know either, and as the time passed I realized that it didn't matter so much. In fact, it didn't matter at all. What had made me mad was something entirely different. Kid stuff, indeed.

What I ended up doing was drawing a single lonely arrow

on the back of the sign. Then I wrapped it and took it to the Post Office and insured it for one thousand dollars.

I told Elaine I wanted to buy her a drink.
She laughed. 'That's silly.'
I told her I'd promised a guy.
'What guy?'
I told her about Blacky.
She thought it was sad. 'I don't know,' she said. 'I don't think I want to drink for a dead man.'
'But I promised.'
'I didn't.'
And then — we were alone in Bumpy's room — I kissed her. Quickly. She was startled. She eyed me carefully. 'You want a drink or something else?'
'Something else.'
'Well, I think I'll take the drink.'
And so I learned that she wasn't totally impulsive. Almost totally, for sure, but she did have some reserve. Of course I probably didn't attract her very much. I'm not all that handsome. Not like Al.

She wanted wine. She said it was the only alcohol she could drink. She hated beer, and she hated hard stuff. She knew better ways to get high.

There was a bar right next to the cafe, but Elaine said she couldn't stand that place. We walked down the block to another tavern. Inside was gloomy darkness and the stale smoke of a cigar. The whole scene reeked of defeat. Without a word we turned and departed.

I bought a bottle of burgundy in a liquor store, and Elaine drove the yellow milk truck to a place on the river called Bellerive Park. We sat on the edge of the bluff and drank the wine and watched the barges haul up and down the deep brown water. We were alone in the park except for one man sitting in a car listening to a football game. The wind was cool. The barges blatted their horns. Across the river in Illinois was a bank of trees with bright orange leaves. The land was busy and beautiful and made me very sad.

'You all leaving soon?' asked Elaine.

'Tomorrow.'

I shivered.

'Dumbshit. Flushing a jacket down the toilet.' She held out one side of her coat. I snuggled in. She was warm. I put my arm around her shoulders. She put an arm around my waist.

We drank more wine. It was a gutsy burgundy—I could almost feel the grapeskins on my tongue—strong and hearty as only a cheap wine can be.

Elaine asked, 'You gonna be all right?' Her lips glistened with wine.

'Sure.'

'Where'll you go?'

'Don't know.'

'Balls okay?'

'Fine.'

She patted them.

I tried to kiss her.

She jumped away, pulling her coat off my shoulders. The wind was suddenly cold. I studied her face, her fearful eyes. I told her, 'I don't understand you at all.'

She stared glumly at the ground. Her fingers were ripping blades of grass into shreds. 'Come here,' she said. 'You're cold.'

I slid over, and she held out her coat. We finished the wine without speaking a word.

Elaine drove me to the university so I could check the bulletin boards for a ride. I didn't dare hitchhike or hop a freight—the police are always picking you up and checking identification. But I've never seen a university that didn't have a few good rides leaving every week.

I wanted to go to Wheeling. I figured the police had contacted Erica, or else she'd heard about my troubles one way or another. I had to tell her I was all right. I wanted her to know I didn't do it. And, most of all, I wanted to see if she was feeling any better, if she wanted me around again.

There was a ride going to New York which would pass right through Wheeling on Interstate 70, but it wouldn't leave for another ten days. I couldn't wait. Somebody was leaving for Chicago the next morning—not exactly on the way to Wheeling, but at least it was out of town. I called, arranged a pickup. The guy sounded goofy: 'Oh yeah . . . far out . . . I'll pick you up . . . wow . . . yeah man . . . outasight.'

I had supper with Elaine and Al. Elaine said it was the Last Supper. I didn't think that was funny. After we ate we all sat around the table in their one room apartment. Al produced a fat yellow joint. He said it was from a new source, and it was 'the best shit ever to hit St. Louis.'

Elaine asked, 'Is it Panama Red?'

'It's Guatemala Guano.'

'Hey that sounds good!'

Al exploded with laughter. He pointed at her head and said to me, 'She isn't too—uh—up here, y'know, she hasn't got it.'

'I guess I'm not too bright,' Elaine agreed.

It was strange. I knew Elaine was perfectly intelligent— probably more so than Al—and it seemed to me that she should know it, too. Why did she put up with him?

We passed the joint around, and soon we all were stoned in fine style. Then Al pulled a cigarette from his shirt pocket and lit up—again without offering one to Elaine or me. Soon the room was filled with a smell like burning tar.

I asked, 'What *is* that thing?'

Elaine laughed. 'They're his favorite ciggies.'

'What *are* they?'

'French ciggies. How do you say it, Loverboy?'

'Gauloise.'

'That's it. Gal-waz.'

'Get her,' Al said, rocking back in his chair, pointing his thumb. 'Gal-waz.'

Suddenly Elaine was shouting: 'Well I never had any French!'

Al rocked back. 'I'll french you.'

She stood up fast. She bumped the table with her thigh. A glass of water toppled and splashed onto my pants. Elaine didn't notice. She was screaming at Al: 'Don't gimme any of that *shit*. You ain't frenching *nobody*.'

I tried to mop up the water with my paper napkin.

'C'mere,' Al was saying. He stuck out his tongue and wiggled it between his lips. 'C'mere and learn some French.'

'GET LOST!'

'C'mere and eat a sandwich.'

Elaine suddenly calmed herself. With cool, with ice, she quietly said, 'I won't touch you, you little creep.'

I'd taken the other napkins and was busy damming the water, confining it to a puddle, but I was certain I heard every word. And yet I couldn't follow the logic of this fight. Now Elaine was in control. Al was saying, 'Aw baby, aw baby, I didn't mean it, please come here.'

Elaine sat down in her chair, crossing her legs. 'Creep.' She was trying to hold an expressionless face.

'Aw baby, please—aw baby, I'm sorry—please—come on—smile for old Loverboy. Aw baby . . .'

She resisted for almost a minute, but finally gave in to a constant stream of aw baby's. She smiled.

'Attagirl. Now gimme a kiss.'

She leaned toward him. They kissed—just a smack—from their separate chairs.

'Yeah,' said Al. 'Now. Another.'

This one lingered for a few seconds.

'C'mere. Sit on my lap.'

She came. She sat. They kissed. For a long time they kissed, and I had nothing to do. Their hands were roaming. I was getting embarrassed. I didn't want to sit there and watch Elaine and Al go through the whole routine. They acted as if I was invisible. They made me *feel* invisible. For a minute I wondered if I was really there.

I pushed my chair back. The leg scraped—a noise like a screeching cat.

Elaine broke from Al. 'Oh—it's *you*. Hey I got the screaming munchies. Anybody else got the screaming munchies?'

Al did.

'Let's get some ice cream.'

We piled into the yellow milk truck. Al drove. Elaine was

48

rolling another joint as we drove down a road called Hampton Avenue. It was lined with fast food franchises. There was so much neon in the air that at first Al didn't see the cherrytop. Elaine saw it and grabbed his arm.

'Al! Pull over.'

He glanced at the mirror. 'I'll beat him.'

'You *can't* beat him. This thing couldn't beat a *pogo stick*.'

'I'll lose him.'

'Would you *stop* the god damn truck!'

As Elaine was talking she'd kicked her leg, spilling marijuana all over the front of the car. I wanted to jump out. But then I'd just be calling attention to myself. Then they'd know for sure I had something to hide. Besides, I'd been reading the *Post-Dispatch*. These cops shoot to kill. I'd have to face them, bluff it out. But what if they recognized me? They had my picture — I'd seen it in the paper. My Army mug shot. What if they'd already recognized me? Maybe that was why they pulled us over.

Al had stopped on the shoulder in front of a Der Wienerschnitzel.

Elaine said, 'Get out, Al. There's dope all over the floor.'

'No. Let him come to me.'

'Get out you asshole!'

'Just act natural.'

'Natural!'

'He can't see the dope.'

'He can search.'

'He can't. Not without a warrant. Not if we act natural.'

'He can do anything he wants. Don't play lawyer.'

'Well act natural.'

'Asshole.'

'Shut up.'

'*You* shut up.'

I was shaking with suspense. So far nobody had emerged from the squad car. It was parked right behind us. From the light of the Der Wienerschnitzel I could see two cops. One was talking on the radio. Maybe they were calling reinforcements. Maybe they were calling the paddy wagon. Calling the

Army. The Navy. I was ready to believe anything. I couldn't bolt from here. One side was the highway—heavy traffic, moving fast. The other side was a big, well-lit Der Wiener-schnitzel parking lot—a perfect shooting gallery.

'Well Cousin,' Elaine said, 'what are you going to do?'

I shrugged. I couldn't speak. The mouth failed.

Al said, 'Do they want him? Is that why they pulled us over? If you get us busted, fella—'

'He's *all right*.'

'He really your cousin?'

'Yes.'

'It's yours, Elaine. The grass. Remember that.'

'It is not.'

'I'm on *probation*. I got three more *years*. You gotta take the rap.'

'I don't want to.'

'You got to.'

'They're mean, Loverboy. They feel you up. They make you strip.'

'What about me? You want me in the can for three years?'

'Course not, Loverboy, but . . .'

'Then it's yours.'

'Promise me you'll stop dealing.'

'Aw baby . . .'

'Promise! We're going to New Mexico. We're gonna farm.'

'Aw baby . . .'

'Then take your own rap.'

'I promise.'

'Love me?'

'Jesus Christ!'

'Do you love me?'

'Yeah baby.'

'Sound like you mean it.'

'I do mean it.'

'I'm going home, Al. No more of this shit.'

'We're all going home. If they ever get out of that damn squad car—'

'I'm going to Excelsior Springs.'

50

'You can't.'

'I am. I'm gonna go to college. I'm gonna study French. And art. If I'd never met you, I coulda gone to college.'

'You weren't going when I met you. You were just hanging around that A & W like some kind of big tit moron.'

'Al!'

'I got you away from all that.'

'I coulda changed my mind. I coulda decided to go to college. My daddy woulda payed for it. But *you* couldn't pay for it. All you want to do is boogie and ball. That's all. Just boogie and ball.'

'Aw baby . . .'

'And you can take your own god damn rap. You can boogie and ball all you want in that jail. And I know you got a brick in back behind the stereo. You said you were gonna keep this truck clean—*my* truck—and you put a god damn brick—'

'Aw baby—'

'Forget your aw baby crap.'

'Aw baby—'

'Asshole.' She turned to me. 'They're gonna get you.'

'Guess so.' I was beyond hope.

Al said, 'They *do* want him! What'd he do?'

Elaine: 'Killed a cop.'

'I did not! They *think* I did.'

Al: 'You killed Parkey?'

'Never asked him his name.'

'Get him out of here. Holy shit! Turn him in. Get him out and they won't search the truck. Go on. Get out. Run for it, you son of a bitch.'

'Al! They'll shoot!'

'I'll throw him out. Get out, you—'

'Look!' I said. The police car was backing up. It turned onto the road and passed us by. In ten seconds it was out of sight.

We sat.

Cars were whizzing by. In the Der Wienerschnitzel light I could see that Elaine was crying. Al was cracking his knuckles. I realized I'd been sweating—my shirt clung to my skin.

51

Finally Al said, 'Anybody for ice cream?'

I didn't answer.

Elaine wiped her nose on the back of her hand.

Al laid a hand on her thigh. 'Aw baby . . .'

Elaine dropped her head on his shoulder. She mumbled into his neck: 'Loverboy . . .'

Once again I felt invisible.

'Let's go home,' said Al.

One thing I had to ask Al: 'What did you call that cop? Parkey?'

Al looked away. 'I forget. What was his name?'

'Parker. Parkey a nickname?'

'How should *I* know? Come on. We're going home.'

They dropped me off at the cafe. I'd be leaving early in the morning.

'So long, Cousin.'

'Good-bye.'

'Stay out of trouble.'

'I will.'

The truck chugged up the street and out of sight. I stayed outside. I could see the light of the television in Bumpy's window. The air was crisp and cool. A searchlight from somewhere was sweeping over the stars. In the gutter were smoldering, dying ashes. The smell of burnt leaves. I was shivering. In the ashes I saw a glow. I crouched and warmed my hands over the embers. It wasn't much, but it was heat. As I crouched there, the coals flickered and seemed to grow, as if my presence had stirred them to a new life, a greater warmth. I had never felt so alone.

LEONARD AND CLYDE, *just out of jail*
Clyde picked his nose with a ten penny nail
Leonard read a Bible, said, 'Hear me, oh Lord,
Take me to Heaven in this Forty-nine Ford.'

Mother America
What have you done?
All of your children
Out on the run.

The back seat was empty, so when Leonard looks up,
He say 'Stop for those ladies, I think we're in luck.'
One was a gypsy, sat on Clyde's lap
Told him his fortune, gave him the clap.

Mother America
Red white and blue
She gave it to him
She'll give it to you.

—Tony's Dance Band

I 44

He looked intelligent, but I suspect that his synapses were permanently singed. He drove a yellow sports car shaped like a bullet. We shot down the highway at ninety, a hundred. KXOK was blasting out of the radio. He shouted over the barrier of music: 'Ever drive when you're tripping, man?'

'Any drive is a trip. By definition.'

'Huh?'

'Never mind.'

'So did you ever—'

'Nope.'

'Streets like spaghetti, man. Cars like snakes. People jerk around like an old newsreel. Funny? Horns! Too *much*. Neon. Wow . . .'

'You tripping now?'

'Naa . . .'

There was no place to put my feet. I suppose there was a floor down there somewhere, but all I could see was a rubble of beer cans, paper cups, hamburger wrappers, a necktie which I could not picture him wearing, plastic bags, a windshield scraper, a newspaper—*Los Angeles Times*, two weeks old—and a roll of paper towels. On the dashboard instead of a plastic Jesus there was a rubber Mickey Mouse doll grinning idiotically and holding an American flag.

'Hey man, you ever make it with a rose?'

'Make it?'

'Fuck it.'

'A rose?'

'Yeah.'

'The flower.'

'Yeah.'

'Nope.'

'Me, I did. Or they told me I did. I couldn't remember. That was some night.' He gazed nostalgically out the windshield, driving on instinct, seeing nothing I could see. 'Some long night . . .'

Seems like you're hardly out of the last outskirts of the St. Louis area before you're coming into Chicago. He let me out at Hyde Park. Before he drove away, I had time to read the decals on his rear window:

University of Chicago *Crescat Scientia Vita Excolatur*

University of Michigan *Artes Scientia Veritas*

U C L A *Let There Be Light*

Disneyland *Mickey and Minnie.*

US 45

The fields were brown and never-ending. Giant sycamores overhung tidy white farmhouses.

I'd had some good luck: I arranged a ride straight through from Chicago to Wheeling. Then bad luck: the car threw a rod before we'd gone fifty miles. Then again good luck: after work the gas station attendant was going to drive to Champaign-Urbana for the big football game. He was a grizzled old man driving a grizzled old farm truck. He sniffed the air and grinned, flashing more gum than teeth. Making sure I was watching, once again he nosed the wind. 'Mmm . . . Corn's in,' he said. 'Wheat's in. Looky thar! Punkin' patch. You like punkin'?'

'Pumpkin pie. Sure. You farm?'

'Naw.'

A flock of blackbirds swooped over the road and settled on the broken cornstalks of an empty field. Ahead, a giant crow flapped down to the shoulder of the highway and picked at a carcass.

'Would you like to farm?'

'Naw. Not me. My daddy farmed.'

He was constantly, methodically picking his nose. Carefully he swabbed out first one nostril and then the other. Whenever he came up with something, he examined it bemusedly and then licked it like chocolate off his fingertip.

He caught me watching. 'Recycling,' he said. 'That's what my kids call it.

'You got kids? How many?'

''Leven.'

'Eleven! Wow! How do you feed them all?'

'With a spoon. Haw haw.'

Haw haw. A good answer to an impertinent question. Of course the children would be fed. As we bounced between the fields of America in a dirty old farm truck, I had no doubt that the children of this land would always be fed.

CHAMPAIGN-URBANA

Three days after I left St. Louis, I found myself in a tavern in either Champaign or Urbana—I'm not sure which. In the window winked a blue neon martini with a bright red cherry. I was sitting at the counter between a young man in a blue suit and a middle-aged woman in a light blue dress. Not bad looking, the woman. Forty or forty-five, I guess.

The waitress suggested a cocktail before dinner. I declined. I ordered three hamburgers and a glass of milk.

I caught a chuckle on my right. The woman in the blue dress was laughing at my meal. When she saw she'd caught my eye, she announced, 'My goodness. I believe we have a farm boy here.' She sounded pleasant, midwestern, friendly.

I told her I wasn't a farm boy.

'Well you sure *eat* like one.' She slapped her knee and laughed—whinnying like a horse. She looked around to see if anyone else was laughing. I tried to smile.

'Don't you drink?'

'Sometimes.'

'Want a sip of my bourbon?'

'No thanks.'

'Come on. It ain't evil.'

'All I want is milk right now.'

'You *are* a farm boy.'

'Nope.'

She wore heavy makeup. It was like a mask.

I looked away, pretended to be reading the joke cards tacked up over the bar: YOU DON'T HAVE TO BE CRAZY TO WORK IN THIS— A hand grasped my shoulder. The woman.

58

She asked, 'What's your major?'

'Human kindness.'

'You putting me on?'

'I'm not going to school.'

'You don't live around here, do you? I don't believe I've seen you before. I'm pretty good at remembering a face.'

My hamburgers arrived just then; so instead of answering, I took a giant bite. She giggled. She thought I *ate* like a farm boy. Again, the hand grabbed my shoulder.

'Where you staying?'

I had to chew for half a minute and swallow three times before I could answer: 'Nowhere yet.'

She snapped her fingers. 'Here for the football game. I should've known.'

'No ma'am. Just passing through.'

'I believe they're out of rooms at the Holiday Inn. Matter of fact, I don't believe there's a room anywhere in town tonight. I ought to know.'

'You in the hotel business?'

'In a manner of speaking. Yes. In a manner of speaking.' She was laughing. Her makeup cracked when she laughed. She ordered another bourbon. 'Join me?'

I ordered an apple juice.

'Apple juice!' Hilarity. 'Cheers.'

We tapped glasses. She tilted her head back and drained the glass. All of her gestures were exaggerated.

The man at my left — in the blue suit — had finished eating before I'd sat down. During my whole meal he'd been sitting there, smoking cigarillos, staring toward a beer sign with a lighted waterfall.

The woman busied herself refreshing her lipstick and pushing her hair around. I attacked my hamburgers and wondered where I could sleep for the night.

The hand was back on my shoulder.

'So where are you going to stay?'

'I was just asking myself that same question.'

She leaned forward, as if sharing a secret. 'You won't find a room.'

'So I hear.'

'It's kind of cold for sleeping under a bush.'

'Guess so.'

'Are you clean?'

I shrugged. 'Sure.'

'I got a room you can stay in. I'll take pity on a poor wandering stranger.' Smiling. 'Since your major is human kindness.'

'Why thank you. That's very . . . kind. Thank you very much.'

'I guess I'm just a sucker for farm boys.'

'I told you —'

'I know. I know.'

'Where do you live?'

'Around the corner. Melody Motel.'

'Motel? You sure you got room?'

'Sure.' She laughed.

'I can sleep on the floor.'

'Oh no.' She laughed again. 'Well. What shall we do this evening?'

Whoops. I hadn't planned on some kind of date or something. I mean she was old enough to be my mother.

She saw my surprise. I saw a flicker of worry — or hurt — cross her face beneath the makeup.

I didn't want to hurt her, but I hadn't the slightest idea what to do with her. 'What — uh — what would *you* like to do?'

She looked me in the eye. She said, 'Let's go to bed.'

My fucking God. I was trapped. I'd blundered right into it. 'I — uh — I wasn't — uh —' Plucked eyebrows, pencilled over. There was no expression in her eyes. Why hadn't I noticed the eyes before? 'I really wasn't planning —'

'Now don't be bashful.' She patted my hand. 'I know what you want.'

What do you say when a woman lays it on the line like that, and you don't want to do it? I'd never been in the position of turning down an offer to sleep with a woman. I didn't have all that much experience with sex. I'm not so very . . . prolific, or whatever the word is. I stumbled for an excuse: 'I — uh —

listen. The fact is . . . You see—I won't waste your time. No sense beating about the bush. The problem is—uh—'

'You ever done it?'

'Sure, but—'

'With a woman?' She snickered. 'This ain't no sheep, farm boy. Or is it that—' And she laughed, but the laugh had a catch to it. 'Is it I'm too old for you?'

'Well . . .'

'You know how to pick a tomato? You don't pick the firm one. You want to squeeze it, feel it give a little. Maybe there's even some wrinkles on the skin. But when you bite into it . . . *Mmmm-yum*!'

The thing that confused me and put me at a loss for words was that I couldn't decide whether or not this tomato was a pro. If she *was* a pro, then I could simply dismiss her. She'd made a business proposition, and I could simply reject the terms of the contract. But despite the brash behavior, the plucked eyebrows, bright red lipstick, expressionless eyes—the eyes. That was the problem. They weren't entirely expressionless. Behind the hard exterior I thought I detected a core of fear, a glimmer of feeling, human emotion, a real person, a woman with pride, with desire, with . . . sideburns. No matter how many hours a woman spends fixing her hair, no matter how much shellac she dumps on her head to hold every hair in its assigned spot, if she has sideburns she can't control those suggestive little ringlets in front of her ears, those short dark curls mixed with tiny beads of sweat, sign of womanhood, of heat, of mons, of ticklish dark pockets and sensitive secret valleys . . .

'I got clap,' I said. I don't know where that idea came from. The words simply appeared in the air.

Her face fell. She curled her lip. 'Clap? That sheep give you *clap*?'

'It wasn't a sheep.'

'Thought you said you was *clean*.'

'I forgot.'

'Miss! Hey! A double bourbon! And bring a glass of milk for Casanova. Clap? You got a red wiener?'

61

'Red? No . . .'

'Does it hurt bad?'

'No . . . It's getting better.'

'Poor little thing . . .' She patted my thigh.

'Oh it's all right.'

'Don't it hurt?' Motherly-like.

'No.' I didn't want her sympathy. Her mothering. My fear of mothers. But I also didn't want to ruin my alibi. 'But it's still infectious. I mean I could pass it on. You know.'

She slapped her hand on the bar. '*Son of a god damn bitch.*' The more I tried to be inconspicuous, the more she became flamboyant. 'Who was it? Was it Gladys?'

'Gladys? No.'

'Some coed? One of those sorority sluts?'

'No no.'

'I'll be damned.' She threw back her head and downed the double bourbon. She wiped her mouth with the back of her hand. The lipstick smeared a red slash just below her knuckles. She hunched her shoulders and pursed her lips and sighed — and blew a blast of bourbony fumes into my face. If I held a match to her breath, there'd be a sheet of blue flame. She said, 'It really *was* a sheep, wasn't it?'

'Yes.' I confessed. 'A sweet little yearling. I thought she was virgin wool.'

'*Son of a god damn it to hell bitch.*' Another explosive sigh. 'You can't trust *nobody* no god damn more.'

'Yes. Well. I got to go.'

'You been *two-timed.* Betrayed!' She was waving her arms.

'Yes. Well. Good-bye.'

'The world's for shit, buddy boy. D'ya hear me?'

'Yes. Shh . . . It's all right.' I stood up.

She grabbed my arm. 'Take my advice.' She was half shouting. 'Don't trust no woman. *D'ya hear that?*'

'Yes. Okay. I've got to be going.'

She held on. Tight.

'Don't trust no-o-o god damn woman.'

Gently, I tried to pry her fingers loose from my sleeve.

The man to my left — in the blue suit — was watching with

dull eyes. He had a tattoo on his wrist—it looked like an anchor—half hidden by his cuff. I learned in the Army to beware of men with tattoos. And cowboy boots. Watch out.

Those fingers were really clamped on there. I tried to loosen one finger at a time.

I was the center of attention. Down the counter a big burly man in a T-shirt flicked his eyes over me coldly. His bare arm was all veins and muscles and hair. Some faded printing on the T-shirt said AL'S GARAGE.

Suddenly the woman was crying. A tear ploughed through the mascara. She let go of my arm and leaned over the counter with her face in her hands. Her shoulders shook. She sobbed. It was awful. I was confused. Maybe I could have walked out and left her there like that, but I was a bit apprehensive about the attention I was getting, especially from the man in the blue suit with the tattoo on his wrist. In fact, a second look at AL'S GARAGE revealed to me that he also had a tattoo. His was on the bulging upper arm, nestled among the veins and muscles and hair, a tattoo of a mermaid with breasts that expanded when he flexed his biceps. I quickly checked the other customers. I couldn't believe it. They *all* had tattoos. And a glance at the floor revealed an uncomforting number of cowboy boots. In the Army these people were the gung-ho killers, the sadists, the peasant-rapers, the bar fighters—and here in a tavern with a blue neon martini glass in the window in Champaign or Urbana, Illinois, who could say what a room full of tattoos and cowboy boots would do if I tried to leave a woman crying on her bar stool? And I felt sorry for her. I was sure now that she was a pro, but she'd lost the hard edge. She could feel.

'Hey,' I said, feeling stupid. 'Hey listen.' I shook her shoulder. 'Please don't cry.'

With her forehead still resting on her hands she scowled at me from the side.

The man from Al's Garage was slowly crushing a beer can in the palm of his hand while he stared intently into my eyes.

'Well,' I said. 'Let's—uh—let's go to a movie.'

'Oh goody!' She laughed and clapped her hands.

She wanted to go to the drive-in. I told her I didn't have a car.

'Thought you were "Just passing through." Didn't you say that?'

'I am. But I don't have a car.'

'Playing hobo. You kids. I swear. Well I have a car.'

She had a 1952 Studebaker V-8 stick shift. Two windows were missing glass. The seats looked like they'd been slashed. The passenger door was tied shut with rope, so both of us had to climb in from the driver's side. The floor was covered with Kleenex and paper bags. The clutch pedal had no footrest—there was only a sharp metal rod sticking up from the floor.

'You drive,' she said.

She snuggled up beside me in the front seat, one leg on each side of the transmission hump.

She directed me to the drive-in. When I stopped to pay for the tickets, she suddenly pushed away from me and hunched way over in the far corner.

The ticket seller peered in the window. He made no move to accept the money I was holding out for him. He leaned on the windowsill and stuck his head right inside. His mouth was three inches from my face, but he acted as if I wasn't there. He said, 'No use hiding, Claire. I know the car.'

Claire sat up straight. Suddenly she was extremely busy pushing her hair back in place. With a bobby pin clenched in her teeth she said, 'Take the money, fella. We're going in.'

He glanced at the money I was holding in my hand.

'I'm on a date,' Claire said. 'I got my rights.'

'You got no rights.'

I was leaning back, trying to put an extra inch between my face and his. 'What's the problem?' I said.

'Yeah,' said Claire. 'What's the problem?'

The man frowned. 'I ain't gonna argue,' he said.

Claire stopped fiddling with her hair. She leaned toward the man. Now all three faces were in a tight triangle. I wanted to slip out. Claire said, 'You ever heard of the Public Accommodations Act? Huh? Passed by President John F. Kennedy? Federal law? You heard of that?'

The man's face hardened. 'I got my orders.'

Claire folded her arms over her chest. 'I got my rights.'

'Not after what you done in here.'

'I done nothing.'

'I'll call a cop.'

'We're going,' I said. I threw it into reverse. Claire protested. I ignored her. In a minute we were back on the highway.

'Whatsa matter?' said Claire. 'You scared of cops?'

'Yes.'

'Where we going?'

'Your place.'

'Oh. Good.'

'I'm not staying.'

'Why?'

'Clap. Remember?'

'Let's have a drink.'

'You've had plenty.'

'*You* haven't.'

We continued in silence. Claire no longer snuggled against me. The wind thundered through the two missing windows. I searched for the heater.

'What you looking for?'

'Heater.'

'Don't work.'

I should have known.

'Don't you have a jacket?'

'I — uh — lost it.'

'Pull in there!'

'Where?'

'That drug store. I need something.'

I stopped. She ran in. I waited in the car. When we started up again, she snuggled up beside me with her head on my shoulder and her hand on my thigh. The hand moved, slowly.

'I'm trying to drive.'

'Uh-huh.'

It was a skillful hand. I almost ran a red light. I had to jam on the brakes.

'See what I almost did?'

'Uh-uh.' Rubbing in slow circles.

'You want us to have a wreck?'

'How come you're scared of cops?'

I didn't answer. I tried to ignore the hand.

Soon we reached the Melody Motel.

'Nice to meet you,' I said as I slid out of the car.

'Come in for a drink.'

'I gotta go. Got a ride tomorrow. Leaves early. Better catch some sleep before I —'

'Come in or I'll scream.'

'Remember I got —'

'I'll scream for a cop.'

'Just one drink.'

Two green plastic chairs. One Formica dresser. One knotty pine desk. One double bed with a Magic Fingers Vibrator — 25¢ for one hour. A shower, a toilet, a Dixie Cup dispenser. And clothes all over the floor. A hot plate and some liquor bottles on top of the dresser. *True Romance* magazines on the night table. A framed black and white photo of a young man in a Navy uniform. A potted cactus on the windowsill. A cuspidor in the corner — a small desert of sand dunes and cigarette butts.

'Bourbon all right?'

'Go easy.'

'Okay, farm boy.'

She handed me the drink and started unzipping the back of her dress. 'Scuse me while I slip into something comfortable.' She pulled the dress over her head and sat down on the edge of the bed. She didn't slip into anything. She was wearing a yellow slip.

'Drink up,' she said.

'I should really be going.'

'Guess what I got in the drug store.'

I didn't answer.

'Rubbers,' she said.

'Rubbers?' I was thinking of feet.

'Catch.' She threw a foil envelope onto my lap. 'Wasn't

66

that nice of me?'

I fingered the envelope.

'Bet you never even thought of it,' she said.

I sure hadn't.

'Now it's safe.'

'It is?'

'Don't you farm boys know *anything*? If you'd used one of these on the god damn *sheep* you never would've caught it in the first place.'

I closed my eyes, bracing myself. It was time for another lie: 'I haven't got any money.'

'Who asked?'

Maybe I could just walk out of there. She wouldn't really scream. She'd get in trouble herself. But she didn't seem to be scared of the law. And she was drunk. And getting drunker. She wasn't bad looking, really. She probably knew a lot of tricks. It was free. And I needed a place to sleep. But I was thinking of Erica, the smell of wool, the mountain pine.

I had a desperate idea. 'Enough monkeying around,' I said.

She nodded.

'The time has come,' I said.

She looked at me expectantly.

'Do you believe in Jesus?' I said.

'Come sit on the bed.' She patted the bedspread.

Louder: 'Do you believe in Jesus?'

She furrowed her eyebrows.

'Are you ready to let Christ into your life?'

She stopped patting the bedspread but kept her hand there, kneading it between her fingers.

'Would you like to read the Bible with me?'

Suddenly she lurched from the bed and poured herself a glass of straight bourbon. 'I don't *believe* this,' she said. She put the glass to her mouth and swallowed seven times. Another of her explosive sighs. 'Been preaching to those sheep?'

'Do you go to church?'

She put her hands to her temples.

'Do you read the Bible?'

She closed her eyes and shook her head.

'Why don't we read the Bible together?'

Opening her eyes. 'Go away.'

'I'm sorry you feel this way.' I stood up to leave.

Her eyes narrowed.

'Jesus loves you,' I said. I sidled toward the door. 'Jesus will comfort your tormented soul.' I had my hand on the door-knob.

'Stop.'

I studied her face. I couldn't read it. I opened the door. 'See you in church.' I was two steps from freedom. One step.

'HEY!'

I froze.

'COME BACK AND SIT DOWN!'

Door still open.

'POLICE! HELP! POLICE! POLICE!'

'Don't shout!' I slammed the door. 'Don't get excited.'

'SHUT UP AND SIT DOWN!'

I sat.

'You want to hear about God? *I'll* tell you about God.'

I did not want to hear about God.

'I've prayed to your God. You know what he gimme? He gimme multiplier skerosis. You know what *that* means?'

Yes. I knew.

She described the first symptoms—her eyes wouldn't focus, and she'd feel a sharp pain in the eyeballs, and then after a few days it would all go away—and then it came back, and then her hands and feet would lose their coordination—she'd be holding a glass of water and suddenly drop it for no reason at all—she'd stumble when there was nothing to trip over—it was like having demons—and then she'd get better, it all went away, she felt fine—and then it comes back, it always comes back. You never know when it will come back, only that it will come, and that it will keep getting worse. That's what God did for me. You want to talk about God? Tell me about His forgiveness. His mercy. But don't tell me He gave me this because of what I am. Don't tell me that. I wasn't always, you know. I married Jack right after high school. He had a job selling cars. Fords. He bought me a brand new Fairlane every September. He took a man out for a test drive, and the son of a bitch drove right into a truck. Insurance don't last forever, you know. I don't fancy starving. You saw that car. That's no Fairlane.

I said nothing. I drank the bourbon.

She said nothing. She crossed her legs, chastely tugging the hem of her slip down over her knees.

Headlights splashed over the curtains. A car without a muffler squealed away, burning rubber. A beer can struck concrete and rolled, clattering, clattering.

I was seeing auras. I hadn't seen any since my last acid trip, long ago, but suddenly they had returned. First the plastic chairs. A black, sinewy aura surrounded the chairs, pulsating, growing. The Formica dresser. The same black aura. The Saharan cuspidor, the Dixie Cup dispenser, more blackness, choking me, us. I could feel it. I couldn't breathe. I couldn't stand up. Sinking. Suffocating. I desperately swung my eyes about the room searching for a counteracting force of life. My gaze fell upon the pitiful little cactus on the window-sill. The cactus glowed in my eyes; it had an aura of emerald green. I looked at Claire. She, too, had the green aura. Our small auras were all that we had to hold back the formidable forces of death in this room.

I concentrated on the green. An uneasy truce. Gradually the auras receded.

Claire stood up unsteadily. She pulled off the slip. She paid no attention to me. She was unhooking her bra. I saw the long scar over the belly.

'What's that?' Pointing.

'Cesarian.'

'Oh. Where's . . .?'

'She died. Long ago . . . long . . . long . . . ago . . .'

The bra was off. She turned off the lamp. In the faint light that filtered through the curtains I saw her shed the rest of her undergarments and climb into the bed.

I listened to the squeak of springs, the rustle of sheets. I couldn't see her face, but I heard her soft words: 'You can go now.'

I remained in the chair.

I could tell by the sound of her breathing that she wasn't asleep. Then I heard her sigh. 'One hell of a seduction,' she muttered.

I finished the bourbon. The room hummed. As my eyes adjusted to the darkness I could make out the form of Claire under the blankets, breathing slowly. One arm lay above the covers.

Against the window I could see the tiny silhouette of the cactus. I slipped off my shoes. I moved to the bed, lay on top of the covers. I could smell her hair—a smoky odor, plus the metallic scent of some spray that turns a hairdo into a net of steel fiber. I wondered—if I squeeze it in my fist, will it crackle? Will it crumble through my fingers into a small sad pile of iron filings? I didn't want to know. I knew of the ringlets in front of her ears. I forced myself to think of those lewd, naked sideburns.

She rolled over. I reached out a hand, touched a heavy breast. She rolled again, pressing into me. Her mouth was in my ear.

'Ba-a-a-a-a-a,' she whispered.

She came like an earthquake. She was whimpering and wiggling and clutching my shoulders, and things were building up nicely on my half of the exercise and I was about to—
CRACK!

Like a kick in the balls. Like somebody had reached in with a hook and ripped out every suture, unknotted every vessel. I let go a scream and rolled off top of Claire and lay on my back, quivering and moaning. The doctor had neglected to warn me about something. Obviously.

Claire was gasping for breath. Sweat ran off her brow. Finally, still panting, she raised herself on one elbow and leaned over me. 'When you come,' she said, 'you really *come*.'

I guess an orgasm of pain looks and sounds very much like an orgasm of pleasure.

'So do you,' I said.

'Ain't it neat? It's my medicine I take for the—you know—multiplier skerosis. It's supposed to unblock my nerves. And does it ever! They ought to sell that stuff to everybody. I tell you, there's certain advantages to multiplier skerosis. It ain't such a bad life. You want to try some? The way you screamed last time, with this stuff you'll probably *explode*.'

'No,' I said. I'd already exploded. 'No thank you.'

She was sleeping so soundly, I thought I could slip out in the morning without waking her. I dressed quietly and—just before leaving—emptied my pockets onto her dresser. My last forty-eight dollars. It was a noble gesture, and probably a stupid one. I now had no money and a long way yet to Wheeling. But it made me feel good, and that's all the use there is to money.

I closed the door quietly and headed across the motel parking lot. I'd reached the sidewalk when I heard Claire's voice: 'Hey! Mac! Wait a minute!' She was hiding behind the door with only her head showing.

'I gotta go now,' I called back.

'Come here. I got something for you.'

I walked back to the door. Without exposing herself she held out one bare arm and handed me a heavy blue Navy jacket. 'My husband's,' she said. 'Been hanging in a closet fifteen years, but it'll still keep you warm. You're his size. Go on, take it.'

'Oh I can't.'

'Go on.'

'No. Really.'

'Go on, dammit. You're just as stubborn as *he* was.' She dropped it on the stoop and slammed the door shut.

I took it.

It wasn't until Ohio before I put my hand in the pocket and found the forty-eight dollars.

I 70

Somewhere in Ohio. He was the husband of a sociology professor. I never found out what he did himself. He had a habit of jerking his lower jaw back and forth so that his chin and lower lip wagged in time to some internal rhythm. He was tense as a steel coil.

He didn't speak a word for a hundred miles. The tires hummed. The day was dark with moody clouds. I was dozing off. Suddenly the words cracked out of his mouth: 'Let's stop.'

'Why?' There was nothing but grass, barns and fences.

The jaw jerked. 'Let's stop and fuck around for a while.'

There were no pinball machines out here, no drive-ins, no cafes or bars. Just wet brown earth. 'There's nothing to do around here,' I said.

He winced. He said again, 'Let's stop and fuck around for a while.'

I realized that he was speaking literally.

'No,' I said. 'I'm in a hurry. Let's not.'

'Okay.' His eyes darted to the mirror, as if somebody behind might have heard. 'Forget I ever said it.'

He drove on all the afternoon grinding his jaw, and he never spoke another word.

WHEELING

I had come for my mountain child. In the night I walked the streets—wet streets, after a day of rain—the slick sucking noise of tires on wet asphalt. I passed the B&O yards, busy with clanging and the rumble of diesels. I passed the mountainous sheds and belching smoke of Wheeling Steel. I heard the blat of a coal barge on the river, a sound that used to set my legs twitching when I heard it on the swinging chair with Erica, when I wanted to glide with the barge all the way down to New Orleans—but I had just finished ten days on a winding path from St. Louis to Chicago to Champaign-Urbana to Oberlin, Ohio, to Wheeling, scrounging up places to sleep, wheedling food, tired of begging, sick of anonymity, always a core of fear in my every move, fighting down panic every time I saw a police car, and the barge was only another noise washing over me in the night. I was climbing the steep streets into the quiet of the hills, the houses dark, water rushing down gulleys by the road, wet leaves dropping from trees with a splat. I stood on the porch of the old gray house. A light shone from the kitchen. Through the closed door I could hear a radio, WWVA. I knocked.

Erica's mother—Mrs. Patman—a wiry woman with tired eyes—came to the door in a bright red bathrobe. 'Willy! Hot dawg! Thought you wuz in jail.'

'Can I come in?'

We sat in the kitchen. Somewhere in the still house five children were sleeping, gathering strength for another day's bedlam, another chip in the erosion of their mother's life, her crumbling nerves. She turned down the radio, but left it on.

73

She'd been fixing some warm milk and honey, which she drank 'fer my dreams' every night before bed.

Erica was back in the sanitarium. She was down to a hundred pounds.

'Does she talk about me?'

'Not kindly.'

'Where's the fiddler?'

'Workin' nights now, too. Somebody's gotta pay for that child. Kin you help?'

'Not now.'

'He thinks yore no account. You better git fore he comes back.'

'I didn't do it. I didn't do anything wrong.'

'Oh yeah?'

'The cop was beating on me. Some guys came up behind and stabbed him in the back.'

'Oh yeah?'

'You think if we were fighting, I could stab him in the back?'

She considered the question. She was a skeptic, a hill woman, a fierce independent, and she knew all about the abuse of the law. 'Reckon not,' she said after a moment. 'But why ain't they lookin' for the other guys?'

'Nobody saw them. Nobody knows about them but me.'

'So *find* em.'

Wise words, I suppose. Maybe I should be searching for these men. But how could I find them? Would they still be in St. Louis? And what could I do if I found them? They wouldn't confess. I had no witness, no evidence. The power of the green wart. One was expressionless. One was scared, with ears like little wings. A gambler? A loser. And the dead man. Al had called him Parkey. Did Al know something?

'I'm going to see Erica. I'll help you out as soon as I can. She's my wife. I'll take care of her.'

'You? What kin *you* do?'

I had no idea what I could do for Erica. I just wanted to ease this woman's pain. Mrs. P needed more than medicine for her sleep, more than warm milk and honey for her dreams. She knew medicine. She made a salve out of wild ginseng to put on sores, and she rubbed polecat grease — skunk oil — on her children when they had a fever. She prescribed Kentucky bourbon for adult fevers, served piping hot with a peel of lemon. She believed a steady diet of sunflower seeds would prevent any ailment from sniffles to cancer. But one ache, no medicine could cure. She needed the hills of Kentucky, the cabin by the road, the land of her birth now washed away in mud, the child named after a magazine picture now grown to a wild creature. Would these people have been happier if I had never come into their lives? Would Erica be well now if I hadn't given her a bum baby? Was it all my fault? I was a 'furriner' — that's what Erica's mother called me once. When she said that word a strange feeling passed over me. I felt the ghost of her old Kentucky grandmother reaching out to touch me. I shivered: I remember the chill. I could see Mrs. Patman as a young girl sitting on the wide wooden planks of the front porch of the old Kentucky cabin at the feet of her own grandmother who spoke of a world divided into two kinds of people: hill people and furriners. I suddenly felt the strength of a tradition and culture that hadn't yet died and that still seeped down through the twentieth century into this house in Wheeling on a bluff over the river where a mother watched helplessly as first her daughter ran off to the furriners, the enemy, and then her husband went to work for them and took her from the beloved savage hills to live among them. And she became one. She was now a furriner. She was her own enemy. As we all are in our own ways.

A spider was weaving, dangling, scurrying, laying its trap between two cabinets that hung over the sink.

Erica's mother closed her eyes and nodded her head. Slowly she leaned toward the table. Soon she would dream.

I picked up her empty glass and lay it in the sink without disturbing the work of the spider. I wasn't going to disturb anybody's work or mess up anybody's life.

'I'm sorry,' I said. 'I'm going now. I'm sorry.' I felt as if I was apologizing for the whole twentieth century.

MUSHROOM MOUNTAIN

I stood on the shoulder of the road in a cloud of choking red dust and black diesel exhaust. The bus pulled away. I was alone. I heard a mockingbird. Beside the road lay the gray wooden walls of an old country store with its roof caved in and a fairsized sassafras tree growing inside. Out front the tall, narrow skeletons of two rusty gas pumps stood like the ghosts of the long gone hillbillies who once ran the place.

I walked two miles up a gravel road into a hollow. At the head of the hollow I passed a black shantytown where hounds barked and eyes peered from dark doorways.

I turned onto a dirt road and started up the mountain. Three miles later, I came to a fork. I'd been up this road only at night, in a car. I chose the left fork. Two miles later the road dead-ended at an abandoned quarry. I doubled back. By the time I reached the sanitarium I was so dusty I felt like a walking slag heap. I was afraid to go in there looking so beat, and anyway I was afraid the police might've warned them to look out for me. I walked up to the lake where I used to go with Erica, figuring to rest and plan my next move.

She was there. She was sitting on a log by the shore. A raccoon—an early riser, as the sun was just setting—was eating bread crumbs out of her hand. It spotted me first and scampered away.

'You!' said Erica. She stood up straight with her hands on her hips. 'Is it you?'

I walked to her, then hesitated. Was she angry? Wild? Frightened? Or loving . . .?

'You look like mud pie. Go jump in the lake.'

I think she meant it. 'Can't,' I said. 'These are my only clothes.'

'Take em off.' She waited. She tapped her foot. 'Go on.'

I just stood there. I wasn't going to take off my clothes.

'Where'd you get that Navy jacket?'

'Whore in Illinois. Said I reminded her of her husband.'

'You!'

'What?'

'You got to play on every fiddle you find.'

'It wasn't exactly—'

'Nucky.'

'She sort of . . . picked me up.'

'Nucky *nucky*.'

Somehow I'd imagined our reunion would be different. Here she was, my scrawny wife with the thin lips and apple-wide eyes. Brown hair, in spite of her name. She'd been born with three blond hairs on her head, and her mother had been reading the midwife's *National Geographic* when she stopped at the picture of a beautiful child with a lovely name. She still had that magazine.

'C'mere.'

I lunged for her.

She skipped back. 'Don't touch. Just c'mere.'

I stood before her.

'Yep. It *is* you. Set down.'

I stood, twitching my fingers.

'*Set!*'

I sat. She knelt beside me. Cupping her hands in the water, she gently washed my face. There was one spot on my cheek that she had to scrub with the heel of her hand. When she was finished, she kissed me once on the lips, a moist kiss with hard lips that sort of distractedly chewed on my mouth.

I tried to grab her.

She pushed me back. 'I'm better,' she said. She was still kneeling, hands on thighs, her face just inches from my own, every pore, every freckle, every downy hair big as boulders in my eyes. 'Just needed to be alone, I guess. Babies die sometimes. T'ain't your fault. T'ain't nobody's fault.'

77

She sounded better. She even looked as if she'd put on a little weight. I asked her, 'Did you talk to Dr. Bryant?' Bryant was the sanitarium's resident psychiatrist, a bald old man with strange black spots on his head where, rumor had it, he'd been the subject of highly experimental — and highly unsuccessful — brain surgery. All day long he spat tobacco juice into a paper cup in his top desk drawer. By the end of the day, it was seething with vile black liquid. That cup, according to the paranoid folklore of the wards, was added to the next morning's prune juice. Nobody believed the rumor, of course. Still, nobody, after the first visit to Bryant's office, drank prune juice for breakfast. Once I saw a note of Bryant's that described Erica as 'emotionally disterbed.' It's difficult to have confidence in a spot-headed, tobacco-spitting shrink who can't spell. I couldn't believe he had actually succeeded in helping Erica, and I soon learned that he hadn't. She'd been to a tent show.

'You mean a faith healer? Where?'

'Walleye.'

'But that's thirty miles—'

'Thirty by road. Two mile if you walk over the ridge. I found a trail. I just happened to wander over there one day, and next thing I knew I was in the middle of this old-timey revival meeting.'

'And the faith healing? It really works?'

'Wayell . . . You shoulda *seen* them people. I mean they're the kind of thing you expect to see when you kick over a *rock*. This one lady — she was *rolling* on the floor. She was actually foaming at the *mouth*. If she was a *dawg*, somebody'd take a gun an *shoot* her. And the men, they was wildeyed. They was all *crazy*. And I started wondering what happened to them, what made them that way? I mean people ain't born crazy. Something happens to em. Maybe that woman on the floor, maybe *her* baby died.' She took my hand. She looked into my eyes. My knees trembled. The dark depths of her eyes. 'I ain't gonna be like that. I don't wanna end up a burned out hillbilly. I'm only sixteen. I can *beat* it.'

I was sure she could. I was so happy I could sing to the hills.

What a change. When I'd left her, she'd been shaking and screaming.

I never knew what to expect from Erica. I grew up in the suburbs, the son of a scientist, and I believed in a logical and somehow benevolent universe where children are loved and protected, and money will magically appear when you need it. It wasn't until I left the suburbs that I learned that not only is the world not benevolent, it is sometimes downright mean, and it is rarely logical. Six months in the stockade were my final proof.

Erica's world had always been illogical and far from benevolent. She was the second oldest of seven children. She and her older brother as little children roamed the hills together until one day when they were gathering ginseng she looked up to see her brother's head explode. He'd been shot by a hunter who thought he was a bear. When Erica was thirteen, her school sent a letter to her pa, informing him that they suspected that his daughter might be suffering from emotional disturbance and would he mind if they gave her some tests. So he beat her. To him the message was simply, 'Your daughter is flunking.' After he beat her he locked her out of the house. She slept at a neighbor's. The next day she came home from school before her pa had gotten off work and locked *him* out. When he rattled the door and shouted to be let in, she spat at him through the mail slot. Finally she released the lock. When he opened the door she ambushed him with an electric carving knife. He wrestled it away from her. He held her hand by the wrist against a table top and threatened to slice off a finger unless she said, 'I love you, Pa.' She refused. He broke her skin, drew blood. She said nothing. He cut down through an eighth inch of skin. She could feel the blade vibrate across her bone. She said nothing. He hesitated. She said, 'Go on. Cut.' He threw the knife through a lampshade. She laughed. He bandaged her hand and locked her in her room—no food, no water, no bathroom. Thirty hours later he let her out. She walked calmly out of the house —she said she didn't even stop to go to the bathroom first— and she took a bus as far from Harlan as the money would take her, to her uncle's house in Wheeling. The uncle phoned her father, who came to fetch her. While her father was in Wheeling he just happened to hear about an opening for a Coca-Cola truck driver, a union job, a good job, and he went over and applied and somehow he got it. So instead of taking Erica back to Harlan, he returned alone and brought the rest of the family up to Wheeling. As soon as they arrived, Erica ran away. To Harlan. When the deputy sheriff sent her back, her pa pulled down her pants in front of the whole family and caned her with a willow branch. That night she menstruated for the first time. Now she says whenever she gets her period she has a sore fanny. To her that's logical. When Erica was fifteen she ran away again, this time with a boyfriend. They ended up in the Over the Rhine section of Cincinnati — a hill-billy slum — where Erica swallowed a tab of what was supposed to be LSD. Two days after she took it her body was still trembling and her eyes wouldn't focus. Her boyfriend delivered her to the hospital emergency room and then, without lingering long enough to explain what was wrong with her, disappeared forever. The hospital decided she was psychotic. They buried her in tranquilizers and transferred her to a mental institution. When her pa arrived, they wouldn't release her. They said she wasn't ready. Her pa didn't know much about mental health, but he decided that these doctors and nurses were 'too busy-busy.' He arranged to have her transferred to the sanitarium in the mountains. He couldn't afford it, but he did it. And Mushroom Mountain Sanitarium did the job. It didn't have a brilliant staff or a lot of high-powered, unsmiling doctors, but it offered clean air, cold nights, and the reassuring presence of pines. The cure took. Erica recovered, as she might not have if she had remained tranquilized and locked up in a big city institution. Somehow, her pa had done the right thing. Then when she returned home, Mr. Patman told her she'd have to pay him back. Every penny. I don't know how he really felt about Erica. He beat her sometimes, but other times he'd fiddle all night long just for her pleasure, with a stogie wagging in his mouth, plugging a hole where he was missing two teeth, filling the room with raunchy smoke.

I didn't have any question about how Mrs. Patman felt about Erica. She loved her, plain and simple. But loving Erica and knowing how to handle her were separate issues. Mrs. P believed, or said she believed, that 'nucky' was the root of all evil. 'That's all they want,' she warned. 'Give em your nucky and they ain't nothing left.' But the house was small, walls were thin, and doors were too warped to stay latched. Erica had seen and heard enough to decide that her ma wasn't exactly suffering from the nucky. In the same line of thinking Erica didn't believe her ma's warnings about 'psychadeelic drugs.' She wasn't sure what they were, but she figured if her ma didn't like them, they must be pretty good.

In fact, that was the key to Erica's mind: if her parents were against it, she was for it. She took to her parents like a cat to a dog. And if I tried to boss her around, she took the same way to me.

'Listen!' she said.

'What do you hear?' We were sitting side by side on a log by the shore of the lake.

'Train.' She cocked her head and studied the sound. 'L & N,' she said.

I listened. Over the whisper of the woods and the lapping of the waves I heard the low dull roar of a couple hundred coal cars. They must have been rolling down the valley way on the other side of the ridge. 'How do you know it's the L & N?'

'Sounds like it. Hey! Want to talk to you.'

'Oh. Yeah.' I'd forgotten. Amazing, that I could forget. What about my being a fugitive and my running away from her and what was the future for both of us? Plans. I prefer feelings. We're both good at feelings. I tend to fuck up plans, and Erica can't even make them. I took a long breath and plunged into it: 'I guess you heard about what happened in St. Louis.'

'No. What?'

'You haven't heard? About the cop? That I'm wanted?'

'Oh. That. Did you really do that?'

'No.'

'Good.'

'They *think* I—'

'I didn't. Never.' Shaking her head. Pursed lips.

'The police didn't see the—'

'Police. Don't let's talk about police.'

'But I'm—'

'Hush.'

So that was that. She didn't care. She didn't even want to hear about it. I asked, 'Well, what did you want to talk about?'

'Nothin' special.' She studied her thumbs. 'Just wanted to talk.'

'Can I hug you?'

'Not yet.' Clicking her thumbnails together.

'Do you love me?'

'Sure.' She shrugged. 'I guess.' She bit her thumbnail. As far as she was concerned, love isn't a question you ask and answer.

'What are we going to do, Erica?'

'Dunno. What're *you* gonna do?'

I told her I figured to lose myself in some big city—New York or Boston, probably—but first I wanted to visit my parents. I hadn't seen them in a long time and I knew they must be worried about me. Besides, they'd give me some money.

'Why'nt you stay here?'

'Here? What can I do here?'

'Foller me.'

She led me up an overgrown path, through briars and bushes, up a rise and across a brook. It was pretty dark by then and I kept stumbling and walking into branches, but whenever I complained she said, 'Foller me.' She practically danced through the woods. I could tell she had a big surprise waiting for me up there somewhere.

The brush got thicker. It was a jungle. What sky I could see was a deep dark blue, almost black, but I caught a glimpse of a big yellow moon poking up over the side of Mushroom Mountain. I hoped we weren't lost. Erica seemed to know

what she was doing. She led me into a small clearing and
pointed to the ground where some metal rubble was half
covered with vine.

'There,' she said.

'Where?'

'Right there! Can't you see?'

'That?'

'It's a *still*! A busted down still!'

So that was my surprise. That pile of metal was how she
expected me to stay here. Operating a still. Moonshining.
Me, already wanted by the law. I didn't even know how. All I
knew about moonshining was a song Joan Baez used to sing
about copper kettles in the pale moonlight. And I'd seen
Thunder Road. But this wasn't the thirties any more, not
even the fifties. You can't moonshine now. Not for a living.
They've got computers and wiretaps and grants from the
federal government. They'll get you.

'Erica,' I said. 'No.'

'Why not?'

'I don't even know how. And even if—'

'Everybody knows how. You just get you some good sour
mash, and—'

'What's sour mash?'

'What's— Why it's— Don't you know *anything*?'

'I don't know sour mash. Who taught you how to make this
stuff?'

'You teach a dog how to chase rabbit?'

'What about teaching a dog how to bring back a bird?
Some things take training.'

She frowned. She said, 'What I mean is, when all the other
dogs are lifting their legs, you're gonna lift yours. Right?'

'Aw come on, Erica. Lifting a leg isn't the—'

'If I lift my leg, you'll lift yours.'

'I won't.' How did I get into this?

'Lift it and I'll tell you a secret.'

'Tell me.'

'Lift.'

'For real?'

83

'Go on.'

It was insane. What was I doing here in the woods on Mushroom Mountain? I was standing in the moonlight, cocking my leg at a tree. 'Bow-wow,' I said. 'Woof. Bark. Barf. Snuckle snorf.'

She was delighted. She clapped her hands. 'Secret is,' she said, 'I don't know a goddlemighty thing 'bout moonshine.'

I couldn't help smiling. Erica had a nervous grin. We stood face to face.

I buried my hand in a warm spot.

She whispered: 'Nucky?'

'You want to.'

'You don't *know*.'

'I can smell it.'

'Go on.'

I unbuttoned the warm spot.

'Who said you could do that?'

'You said to go on.'

'I meant *go on*. You know.'

By that time I was unpeeling panties.

'What're you *doing*?'

'Going on.' She wasn't stopping me.

'I meant go on, you can't *smell it*.'

But now the panties were down, and there was no longer any doubt. I'm sure she could smell it, too. She really pours it out. Sometimes when we make love, it's like two kids playing in a mud puddle. I love it that way.

Erica pulled off her own shirt. She spread her clothes on the ground, and I added mine to make a rough blanket. As we lay down, naked except for shoes and socks, I settled the Navy jacket over us to keep warm. Actually the night was pretty cold—you could see your breath—but we were steaming.

We were well along the yellow brick road and nearing the Emerald City when it occurred to me that I might not be able to do it. That I might explode in pain once again, as I had only a week ago in Champaign-Urbana. In the excitement of seeing Erica I'd forgotten, even though I'd been brooding about it all week. I hadn't seen a doctor yet. I was planning to see my old family doctor when I visited my parents. Now that I had remembered it—now that I had jumped from Oz to Illinois—the memory of all that pain was too much. Erica's belly was quivering, jerking, she was right on the verge—and I popped out. Limp as a rubber band.

'Come back!'

I couldn't. Wouldn't.

'What'sa matter?'

I tried fingering.

'Want *maypole*.'

'Tongue.' I slid down her belly before she could argue. I lapped, swallowed, sucked, drank. She had a fine time.

So did I. I'd rather give than get with Erica. I'm weird that way. If I was ready to come at a time that would be bad for her, I'd just shoot off an indifferent load without even breaking rhythm and keep right on going. Afterwards, I'd feel satisfied in my mind but not always in my body. Not so with other women. Once I lived with a painter named Melinda who never had an orgasm, and I never tried to give her one—she didn't care—I fucked her in the shower, on the sofa, on the kitchen counter—she'd stare vacantly at the ceiling—chewing gum—she'd scratch an armpit—it was passive rape—I couldn't get enough—she drove me mad—one day I slapped her—she moaned—twisted her hips—I slapped her again—she was pumping her pelvis—I was amazed—'*Hit me again*'—suddenly I was furious—I beat her—she came—I beat her black and blue while she looked up at me with wide excited eyes—when it was over I knew I could never touch her again. I never told Erica about any of this. We never talked about sex, and we rarely spoke when we were making love.

Erica lay with her eyes closed, panting. I lay my head on her chest, riding its rise and fall. The chest was hard and bony—her breasts disappeared when she lay on her back. I listened to the lub dub of her heart. Gradually it was slowing down.

A whippoorwill was calling nearby. By my elbow, a torn sheet of metal made a dull gleam in the moonlight between two branches of Virginia Creeper.

The whippoorwill flew closer. It was deafening.

Erica stretched, pointing her toes, spreading her fingers, humming, smiling. 'So what was *that*?'

'I lost it. It just — uh — a bee stung me.'

I could never tell. I just couldn't. Sure she'd understand, but that was just the thing I couldn't face — her understanding, her concern — her mothering.

Besides, she'd be pissed. At least disappointed. She liked my maypole. Sometimes she liked just to hold it, to have it in her hand. She'd pretend it was a gearshift lever, shifting first gear, second gear, third. 'Vroom — vroom vroom — VROOM!' I'd tell her some trucks had twenty forward gears, but she'd never believe me.

She also didn't believe my explanation for why the lever had just popped out of gear. 'Bee didn't sting you.' She sounded disgusted. 'Night out. Bees are sleepin'.'

'This one had insomnia.'

'*Ha.*'

'Probably a sleep-walker.'

She snorted. 'Bees ain't fucked up like *people*. They're *workers*.'

'Maybe he was the night watchman, making his rounds.'

'*Boy.*' She rolled over, her eyes to the sky. 'I never know what you're gonna say *next*.'

'Funny. That's what I would say about you.'

'Nothin' *follers* what went before. It's . . . like we're a bunch of strangers.'

We two strangers lay side by side and stared at the stars. The woods were full of rustles. Soon our sweat disappeared, and Erica was covered with goosebumps. Still she didn't want to get up. She snuggled close and buried her face in my armpit. One of the rustles took shape as a raccoon. He hopped up cautiously — two steps forward, one back. I didn't move. Slowly he came closer. Erica was starting to shiver. The raccoon in one final decisive hop came right up to my face. We eyeballed each other, nose to quivering nose. Then, satisfied that we belonged, he skittered away to join the other creatures of the forest.

SUBURBIA

Same old broken doorbell. It hadn't worked since I hammered a nail into the button when I was seven years old. I knocked. Through the window of the door I could see the Hammond organ, my baby picture, my parents' wedding picture, a new color TV on a rollaway stand.

Erica cowered. For some reason she was terrified at the idea of meeting my mother. All she knew about her was that she saved ice cubes. I'd told Erica how my mother would empty the ice out of all the glasses after a meal, put them in a plastic bag and return them to the refrigerator. She had a mammoth Frigidaire with a gigantic freezer and enough room for a dozen ice trays — I think my father bought it with the idea of breaking her ice-hoarding habit — but the additional room only meant she could recycle more of the second-hand cubes.

How can anyone be scared of a woman who saves ice?

I heard shoes on hardwood floor. I knocked again. The footsteps came closer. Erica grabbed my hand and held it between both of hers. She looked as if she was trying to shrink, hiding behind me. Her cheeks were more hollow than ever. We hadn't eaten for a day and a half.

The door opened.

'Hi Mom.'

Her eyes flared. For a moment she said nothing. Her hair was all gray now. She'd cut it short. 'Willy,' she said. Her hand went to her breast.

I could feel Erica's hands tremble. I stepped aside. She looked like a cornered doe.

'Mom, this is Erica. My wife.'

Mom searched my eyes, then Erica's. 'Your wife,' she said. She picked some lint off the breast of her sweater, a neutral move that meant she was calling Time Out, as a cat will lick its paw when it is puzzled by a new situation.

The lint was gone. 'Well come in.' She smiled. 'Quick before somebody sees you.'

We came in. Mom closed the door, hesitated, and then locked it. I had never known our door to be locked before, not even at night when we were all asleep. It wasn't that kind of a neighborhood.

The three of us stood awkwardly in the living room. 'Welcome home,' said this woman who I called Mom. She held out her right hand. For a moment I was puzzled. Why was she holding out her hand? Then I realized. Reflexively I took the hand. It was an awful thing to do. I was shaking my mother's hand. I'll never forgive myself. I should have embraced her, thrown my arms around her and hugged her to me as I had when I last saw her two years ago. But I didn't, and because I didn't I realized that a line had been drawn across the paper of my life and from now on my story would be written on only one side of that line.

'Now let's see —' my mother said. She held a finger to her lips and touched it with the tip of her tongue. I grew up watching that gesture. It meant she was organizing ideas in her mind, and one of the synapses that the ideas must jump across as they raced along her nerves was the connection of tongue and index finger. Immediately, she was organized.

'Have you any luggage?'

'No.'

'Are you hungry?'

'Yes.'

'Good. How about some hamburgers and tomato soup?'

She flew into action. She told Erica where to find a bathroom. She told me to clear the newspapers off the dining room table. A role is a godsend in an awkward situation, and she'd just latched onto two of them: hostess and mother. She opened cans and molded patties and threw questions from the kitchen. Where had I been? When were we married? How was the wedding? Where is she from? How old is she? *Really*? How did we get here? Why didn't I write? What were the police—

She stopped in midquestion. From the kitchen came no more words, only the sizzling of hamburger.

While we ate, Mother went around the house closing all the curtains. Then she sat at the table and pumped Erica with a barrage of personal questions about herself and her family, which Erica answered vaguely and without enthusiasm. I could see that she was not warming to my mother. After lunch, I announced that we were mighty tired and would like to take a nap before Dad came home. Mother told me that my bedroom was just as I'd left it. She hadn't touched a thing, in fact she never went in there except occasionally to dust and vacuum, and—oh yes—my father had put a filing cabinet in there to store some papers from the office. Anyway, the bed was made, and Erica could sleep in the guest room.

'Hey.'

'Yes Willy?'

'We'll sleep together.'

Erica swallowed a giggle. For an instant my mother looked as if she had been slapped. I saw her eyes glance once again at my hands and then Erica's. Neither of us wore rings. The index finger went to her lips to be touched by the tip of her tongue.

'But Willy, it's a single bed.'

'After sleeping in cars, it'll be like a luxury.'

She started to cry. Erica squirmed in her chair. I ran my finger around the inside of my soup bowl, then licked it. I was calm. Let her cry.

I asked, 'Have any cops been here?'

She stiffened. 'Yes, Willy. Twice.' Her eyes begged me not to talk about it.

'How long ago?'

'When it first happened.'

Lines of tension, like leather.

'Think they'll come back?'

'Willy, your father knows a lawyer. When he comes home,

he'll take you to the lawyer and then the three of you will go to the police station. It's the only—'

'Shit.'

'Oh Willy.' Fresh tears.

'If I go to sleep now, will you call them?'

'For heaven's sake, Willy, I'm not that kind of a—of a—'

'Of a person?'

'Of a mother who would doublecross her own son.'

'Good. We'll go to bed now.'

'I'll change the sheets.'

'No. I'm sure they'll do fine, whatever's there already.'

'They're stale.'

'I'm sure they're immaculate.'

'They're stale.'

'Everything in this house is immaculate. I mean it's full of crap, but it's immaculate crap.'

'Is this why you came home?'

'I don't know why I came home.' And I doubted if I would ever come home again. Ever since I'd walked onto the front porch to encounter that same old broken doorbell, I'd felt out of control, pushed by the forces of family history, the stale emotional smoke of burned out childhood. That kid who lived here—that wasn't *me*. I was different now. Got to get out of here. Run. Live.

I stood and led Erica up the stairs to my old room. Sure enough, the old signs were still on the wall. The only way I could tell that the room had been entered at all since I'd left was the new filing cabinet, plus the fact that not a speck of dust had been allowed to gather.

I closed the door. Erica walked slowly about the room with her hands behind her back, examining the signs like paintings in a museum. Then she cocked her hands on her hips and shot me a look that was both a smirk and a dare. I studied those eyes. A gleam. A dare. I pulled off my shirt. She pulled off hers. Our eyes met again. A gleam like sun on water. Taunting. The hiss of breath. Beads of sweat on her chest. Sparks. The magnet. Soft. Quickly we stripped and fell on top of the bedspread. I could hear my mother clearing the table downstairs. With pleasure I noted the squeaking of the overburdened mattress. I didn't care about the pain. I wasn't going to worry about it. Two weeks had passed since Champaign-Urbana. I'd probably healed. Forget the pain. I had to do it. *Had to*. The mirror reflected a tangle of flesh. I no longer heard any sound from downstairs. Pungent odor filled the air. The mattress groaned. I heard footsteps start up the stairs, then stop and go back down. Signs over the bed — YIELD, SOFT SHOULDER, DANGEROUS CURVE, NO PARKING — old jokes, bygone days. Erica was moaning. I was gasping. The mirror peered over our shoulders. The smell was so thick you could rub it between your fingers. Our bellies slapped together and sucked apart. Squish. Juices guzzled along my thigh. The bed thumped against the wall in time with my thrusts. Erica made little chirping noises between her moans. I was grunting from deep in my throat. It was a symphony of lust.

Erica came first. She actually screamed with pleasure.

I came a second later. I also screamed. I rolled off the bed and hit the floor with a crash. I screamed again. Erica peeked over the edge of the bed. I was rolling on the floor, groaning, screaming, my hands clenched between my legs.

'Willy! What's the matter?'

I tried to form words.

'Willy! Blood!'

I looked down. Sure enough. Blood.

Now Erica was screaming. Panic was on the rise. Footsteps pounding up the stairs. My mother threw open the door. Her eyes took in the scene. Her nostrils flared. She choked. She stepped back. 'Willy, I— Are you— I—' Her hand went to her mouth. The tongue could not come out. I'd never seen her so pale. She stepped back again. Her other hand reached out for support, found none. She stumbled. She was standing at the head of the stairs. My God. She was going to fall — and tumble down the staircase.

Erica vaulted from the bed. Erica to the rescue! Lovejuice dribbling down her thighs. Such a lovely nymph. She took my mother's arm, tried to hold her up. Mother shook loose. Her

91

face—revulsion. She stepped back, away from the stairs. Again she reached behind for support. Again she found none. She was falling. Erica reached, lunged, missed. I'll never forget that lunge. Her hair swung in an arc, following the curve of her body's motion, sweeping through the air, the softest swishing sound, fine brown strands, sparkling in the light like a shampoo ad—striking my mother's face like a whip. Through the hair I could see my mother's outraged lips. Erica fell into my mother's lap, knocking her back. Their legs and arms entwined like brambles. Immediately my mother tried to raise herself up. Erica tried to disengage herself. The actions of one counteracted the efforts of the other. They writhed and squirmed. Neither of them could break loose.

I watched with interest. It lessened the pain.

Dinner was a disaster. My father didn't know what had happened in the afternoon. All he knew was that there were crystals of ice hanging in the air. My mother spoke not a word. Erica was nervous and clumsy—she must have dropped her spoon three times. I argued with my father about turning myself in. He's a reasonable man. He listened to my arguments. He understood my reasons. One idea he could not accept, however, was that if I was innocent, the courts would find me guilty. He believed in The Law. He believed in Justice. He still believed in a logical and benevolent world.

'What would happen, Willy, if everyone believed what you say? What would the world be like?'

'Chaotic. Okay. It's necessary to maintain the illusion.'

He loved to debate at the dinner table. 'And this illusion of justice, as you call it. What makes you exempt?'

'Because I'm in a *real situation*. I could spend the rest of my *life* in the Missouri State Pen.'

'But you say you didn't do it. If you're innocent, they'll find you Not Guilty.'

'But they won't!'

'Why?'

'Because there is no justice.'

'There *is* justice.'

'Justice is to law as truth is to advertising. Justice is a concept.'

'There. You said it.'

'Justice is not a reality. Justice is only a concept. Law is a reality.'

'And the law is just. Therefore, there is justice.'

'Aristotle would have you hanged.'

'What do you mean?'

'If a is b, and a is c, then b is c. That's what you just said.'

'Did I? Well wait a minute. If a is b, and a is c . . . B is c . . . That's right. Yes. Draw the circles. See for yourself.'

'It's *not* right. *You* draw the circles. Anyway, a is not c.'

'Which is c?'

'I said the law is reality. A is b. You said the law is just. A is c. Then you say, therefore, justice is reality. C is b. But a is not c, and therefore c is not b.'

'But a is too c.'

Erica dropped her spoon for the fourth time. My mother was sitting back with her arms folded, her face full of scorn. She hadn't touched a bite.

'A is not c, and neither is b.'

'C is a. B is a. B is c. A is b is c.'

'My God.'

'Consider the contrapositive. If c is not a, then . . .'

'I will not consider the contrapositive.'

'What, Willy?'

'I said I will not consider the contrapositive.'

Dad looked away. He raised the napkin to his lips, then set it down. He reached for a glass of water, fumbled, spilled a drop. He was hurt. He was embarrassed. I had cut him more deeply than I could have reached with a knife. I had refused to consider the contrapositive.

Early the next morning I visited Doc Bates, my old family doctor and the only one I trust. He smiles. He's a jolly fat man who happens to know about medicine. He's usually wearing a self-contained grin that shows that he is constantly and secretly amused by the absurdity of the human body. Besides being fat, he's a chain smoker who sometimes has to break off an examination and dash into his office for a drag on a cigarette. He's so jolly and friendly that it always seems natural to call him 'Doc,' but he won't allow it. He insists on 'Doctor.' He says 'Doc' sounds like Bugs Bunny, and he didn't go through twelve years of training to be a character in a Bugs Bunny cartoon. He set my broken arm after a playmate ran over it with a toy wagon. He explained birth control and reassured me about my nightly sin at an age when my parents kept such information under locked tongues. He treated my mysterious allergies that appeared around exam time every year during a certain stage of my youth, and wisely he treated them lightly. He gave me shots. He gave me checkups. He had probably peered into my ears, nose, and mouth a hundred times. He knew my body more intimately than I did. And now he was examining my poor old balls.

'Where'd they do this?'

'City hospital. Homer Something. St. Louis.'

'Jesus! Those guys—' He turned away.

I said to his back: 'What is it?'

He chuckled, turned. 'I could give you a long Latin word.'

'Don't. How is it?'

There was that grin. 'Shot to hell.'

That's what I like about him. A straight-forward diagnosis.

He fingered the sac. He wasn't examining me any more. He was just holding it up disgustedly, like an egg with a broken shell. I half expected him to heave it into the trash can.

'Doc Bates—'

'Doctor.'

'Will I live?'

'Sure.' That grin. 'You'll live.'

My father was sitting in the waiting room with a *Reader's Digest*. He had dropped me off at the doctor's office, and as planned he was meeting me after some errand he'd said he wanted to run.

He must have been aching with curiosity. He didn't know why I'd gone to the doctor. He hadn't asked. My mother

94

might have had some idea — after all, she'd seen me bleeding — but she saw a lot of other things at the same time which may have distracted her attention. The fact that neither she nor my father had asked why I wanted to see the doctor showed tremendous willpower. I had to admire them. Back in my brief college career, I'd once mentioned during a phone call that I'd been feeling poorly for the last day or two. Had I seen a doctor? No. Would I? If I didn't feel better soon. But Willy, you must take care of your— Anyway, two hours after the phone call I was sitting at my desk when there was a knock on the door, and in walked a doctor with his little black bag. A housecall! They'd arranged it, long distance, without even telling me. Such was their concern with my health. And now they were biting their tongues until they must have been black and blue.

As we were driving home, my father threw me a thick sealed envelope. 'Got you something,' he said.

The envelope said First National Bank. I'd been planning to hit him for some cash. I figured a hundred, tops.

'Can I open it?'

'Be my guest.'

It was a wad of crisp new twenties. A big wad.

'About how many you got here?'

'A hundred.'

A hundred twenties. Did I thank him? Did I follow my first impulse and shower him with praise? No. A second impulse immediately smothered the first, and I said, 'Do you want it back?'

'No.'

I stuffed the envelope into my pocket. 'I feel like a gangster,' I said, 'passing money in a car.'

My father smiled. 'Or a politician,' he said.

That's communication in my family. He knew I appreciated it.

My mother was sitting alone on the front porch in an aluminum chair, balancing a full glass of beer on her lap. I pulled a chair right up next to her and sat down. She glanced at me as she would glance at a moth batting against the window, and she resumed staring out at the night.

It was strangely balmy after a day of rain. The trees were bare—the streetlight sparkled through branches that were shiny with water. The rain had stopped, but heavy drops of water continued to fall from the trees to the porch roof, and from the roof to the ground. The gutters had long since ceased to function, clogged by ivy on the north side and trumpet vine on the south. My father refused to clean them. He preferred vines to clean gutters. My mother disagreed, and often let it be known. It was one of those running battles that had been going on for so long that neither party even heard what the other was saying any more, and the subject only came up when it was needed to maintain the rhythm of some other, fresher disagreement. At this moment, however, I don't think my mother was thinking about gutters. She hadn't touched her glass of beer. She was staring out over the sidewalk and across the street to some point in the blackness over the trees.

I was sorry I'd ever come home. I was two thousand dollars richer for it, but I was also one mother poorer. As I uneasily sat beside her and tried to think of something to say, I wished I could trade the money for the old mother-son relationship. Not that we'd ever been real close—I had always been something of an object in her house, a bottle fed baby, a son not a child, a duty to raise, an investment that would make his mother proud—but the market had crashed. I was sitting with the Great Depression.

'How's Nat?' I said. Nat was my older brother.

'Nat.' She shrugged. 'Nat.'

'What?'

'He's probably fine.'

'Probably?'

'How would *I* know?'

'He still in Vancouver?'

'Oh no. He and Ellen are separated. She's still in Vancouver with the kids. He's in Montreal.'

'What's he doing in Montreal?'

'*I* don't know.' She continued to stare into the dripping night.

My brother had always rejected me. He was several years older. I think the problem was that I was always entering a certain stage of growth just as he was leaving it, and rejecting it, and feeling a need to put it down, which led to his constantly putting *me* down. The only time he'd ever seemed pleased with me was the night I wrecked the family car at a local lovers' lane. Bad enough that I'd wrecked the car, but to do it at one in the morning on Piney Meetinghouse Road — there was only one thing I could have been *doing* there. He thought it was marvelous.

'What about Gretchen?' My sister.

'Gretchen's still in Cornell.'

'Graduate school?'

'No. She should graduate this Spring. She *promises*.'

'She drop out for a while?'

'No. This is her sixth year.'

'She flunk?'

'She changed majors. Five times. She's seeing an analyst. We told her we wouldn't pay for another year of school unless she saw an analyst.'

'You think she's crazy?'

'No. Just — you know Gretchen.'

'She's not crazy.'

'She's living with three men.'

'That's not crazy.'

'Well it's *something*.'

'It certainly is.' I scarcely knew my sister. We had been playmates until she reached the age of eleven or so — about the time we were no longer allowed to take baths together — and from then on her interests had been horses and boys, and mine had been baseball and girls. We'd had nothing in common.

Mother was stirring in her chair. For the first time, she looked at me. 'You know,' she said, 'some families . . . sometimes . . . *communicate*.'

I nodded.

'I could've taught school,' she continued. 'I didn't *have* to raise you kids.'

I was tempted to tell her about Sludge and the Battle of Barrack B-7. She wouldn't have understood my point; she would have heard only the swear words that are an inevitable part of the story. It was too bad. The Battle of Barrack B-7 was fought to defend her honor, and she'd never know. What happened was that for a while I was stationed in Saigon. I was in Company B, seventh platoon. My bunkmate was Sludge. Actually, he said his name was Sledge as in hammer, but we all called him Sludge as in sewer. He was a short skinny guy with spectacles — not exactly a ladykiller, and not a mankiller either — but he couldn't open his mouth without letting loose with a string of profanities. He cussed for punctuation. It was as natural as breathing. His home town wasn't Denver, comma, Colorado. It was 'Denver fart-cloud Colorado.' If you asked him if he had a match, he'd say, 'My ass and your face.' Then he'd hand you a match. It was insulting and yet so impersonal that you couldn't be insulted. It was simply a way of speaking, like a heavy accent. After a while you wouldn't even notice. Usually.

It was after taps. We were both lying on top of our bunks, naked, sweating into the muggy night air. I was half-heartedly trying to talk Sludge into trying out a joint I was smoking. He was half-heartedly resisting. The heavy air tended to make everything a half-hearted effort, including the war.

'Smells like thirteen-year-old gook pussy,' he was saying.

'Does not,' I said, or something equally clever. Arguing was an assertion of will, not an intellectual dialectic — and mostly just a way to pass the time.

'Fuckin' A,' said Sludge in rebuttal.

'Well if it smells like pussy, it smells like Raquel Welch's pussy.'

'Raquel! I'd eat a mile of that broad's shit just to get to her asshole.'

'Far out.' I giggled. I'd never heard that one before. He could be entertaining. 'Her asshole?'

'The little brown church in the woods.'

'Far out.'

Singing: 'O-oh come, come, come, come, Come to the church in the wi-i-ildwood, Come to the church in the—'

'Why the asshole? You got tendencies, Sludge? I never knew you had tendencies.'

'Tendencies? I'll have tendencies the day I menstruate.'

'Hey fellas! Sludge is on the rag!'

'*Sledge!* Dick-head! Peanut prick!'

'Well if you don't have tendencies, why'd you say asshole?'

'Why does a dead monkey fart?'

I giggled again. I was in a receptive mood.

'What was we talkin' about?'

'Marriage-you-wanna.' I rolled over on my side to face him, but I could only see his outline in the dark. 'I was telling you it's better than beer because it won't fill your bladder so you have to get up in the middle of the night. Right, Sludge? Pretty good reason, huh? What do you say to that?'

'Horse potwamie,' he replied sagely.

'What's the matter? Scared?'

'No, turdblossom.'

'You're afraid it'll lead to hard stuff. Right?'

'Wrong, ass-wipe.'

'You smoke tobacco, don't you?'

'Fuckin' A.'

'Well then—'

'Sombitch.'

'You know what tobacco does to you—'

'Pussyhead.'

'Give me a reason.'

'Touch-hole. Cocksucker.'

'Don't get personal.' Of course everything he said sounded like a personal insult. After a while it could get on your nerves. I was smoking my third solitary joint, enough to make the room sway and the darkness burn. Enough to let him get on my nerves. I was losing interest, anyway. Let him rot his liver. He wasn't worth saving.

Unfortunately, Sludge did have one sensitive cell in his brain: he could tell when he was pricking the shield. I'd told him not to get personal.

'Whatsa matter, shit-for-brains, can't you take it?'

'That's enough, Sludge.' I was too stoned to think straight, or I would have ignored him. The grass made me more sensitive to the ugliness at the core of what he was saying.

'Name's Sledge! Jerk-off!'

I said nothing. Through the hum of my mind his sounds were like the buzzing of a horse fly.

'Fart-face! I shit on your father's grave.'

'He's alive.' I shouldn't have answered.

'I shit on your *mother's* grave.'

'Her, too.'

'I shit on your *grandmother's* grave. Old Granma Middlebrook! I come on her headstone. I piss on her bones. She was a whore and when she ran out of men she crawled to the barn. Your grandfather was an ass. Your father's half-assed. Ha! That's good! And you—'

'Sludge,' I said, and I was getting annoyed, 'you're a motherfucker.'

'Yep.' I could hear the grin through the dark. 'Yours is next.'

That's when I jumped him. He'd done it. He'd made it personal. I landed on him with a knee in the belly. I tried to belt him in the jaw, but missed in the dark. He rolled out from under and kicked at my face. I swung again and connected with his nose. He picked up the bed and heaved it on its side, and I fell off to the floor. Next thing I knew he'd grabbed his rifle. Blam! Then again. Blam! Then twice more. Blamblam! By this time the rest of B-7 had mobilized, and they overpowered Sludge in a heap of sweaty bodies. Somebody turned on the lights. MPs rushed in the door. A sergeant. A lieutenant. There was going to be big trouble. 'What happened? Who's shooting? Anybody hurt?'

Nobody was hurt.

Slowly, Sludge emerged from the bottom of the heap, still clutching the rifle. He stood, naked, leaning on the gun. Calmly he drawled, 'Did they get away?'

'Who?'

'Charlie! Fuckin' A Cong!'

'Where?'

'Sneakin' in the screen! He woulda slit every bastard's throat in here if I hadn't—'

Sludge was led away to account for the battle, and I was left to wonder why that one particular insult, of all the stream of insults, had reached through the protective armor of indifference.

'Yep. Yours is next.'

Mother finally noticed the glass of beer by her hand. She raised it to her mouth, sipped absent-mindedly, and set it down. It must have been warm and flat by then. 'You know, Willy,' she said through the drip of the trees as she continued to stare out over the lawn, 'I've been sitting here trying to think of something I've done right in my life. Something I've done *well*.' She raised the flat beer to her mouth, but didn't take a sip.

'You know, Willy, I can't think of *anything*.'

LEONARD AND CLYDE, *just out of jail*
Clyde picked his nose with a ten penny nail
Leonard read a Bible, said, 'Hear me, oh Lord,
Take me to Heaven in this Forty-nine Ford.'

    Mother America
    What have you done?
    All of your children
    Out on the run.

Clyde was a carpenter, Leonard a Jew
Clyde liked to hammer, Leonard to screw
Clyde built a house without windows or doors
Construction was perfect, concept was poor.

    Mother America
    Save me from sin
    Life is a game
    Only cheaters can win.

                  —*Tony's Dance Band*

I 95

We took a night bus to New York. As we rolled over Maryland in a river of headlights—on the John F Kennedy Memorial Highway, for heaven's sake—Erica started badgering me again to explain that bloody sexual opera we had performed for my mother. I couldn't hold her off any longer. I explained that Doc Bates had ordered total abstinence for at least three months.

'Ab—who?'

'I can't come.'

'The blood?'

'Yeah.'

She grinned. 'Fiddle break a string?'

I got annoyed. I didn't see anything funny about it. Elaine, shrieking with laughter: 'Your—uh—groin.' Now Erica. Grinning.

'I'm no fiddle,' I said.

'You shore ain't,' she cackled.

I fumed.

'Yore a faucet. Got a leak?'

'All right. Look. It's not funny. The faucet works. You can still turn it on. But the pipes were repaired. They have to set for three months. The putty has to dry. If you turn on the hot water now, you'll blow up the heater.'

'Aw,' she cooed, 'don't be mad.'

'I'm. Not. Mad.'

'Yore upset.' She ran the palm of her hand gently over my cheek.

Without thinking—though later I would ponder it endlessly

103

—I slapped the hand away.

She bolted. She sprang into the aisle and dropped into the window seat on the opposite side of the bus. She stared fiercely out the glass.

Stupid, stupid, stupid. She was only trying to help. She was understanding. And that's what I abhorred: understanding, sympathy. Control. Dominance. *Sympathy is dominance.*

I slipped across the aisle and sat next to Erica. I touched her arm.

'Leggo.'

I let go. The bus rocked. The engine whined.

She was still staring out the window. I could only see the back of her head, a slight vibration of her hair when she spoke: 'Three months?'

'Yes.'

'You fixin' to run away on me?'

'No.' It hadn't even occurred to me. 'I swear.' I touched her neck.

She shook me off.

'I ain't no plumber,' she said.

'*You're* not broken.' I touched her shoulder.

She shrugged. My hand fell. 'The bathtub's dirty,' she said.

'You mean—?'

'There's a ring around it. And the drain's clogged.'

'I'm Roto-rooter.'

'You're a broken toilet.'

I loved her so much at that moment—I couldn't tell you why.

PHILADELPHIA

When I awoke, the bus had stopped, and Erica was gone.

'Is this New York?'

There were three passengers: a tired old black man, a greasy teenage white boy, a fat Puerto Rican mama. None of them answered, or even met my eyes.

I stepped down from the bus. It was parked in the bay of a terminal—a cavern of noise and diesel exhaust and broken faces. The decor was Early Modern Rest Room: yellow-tiled walls, cement floor, not quite enough light. The driver was standing by the door.

'Is this New York?'

'Philly.'

'When do we leave?'

'Five minutes.'

'Did you see a girl get off—about seventeen, brown hair, skinny?'

'Nope.'

She could have been buying candy or going to the rest room or just stretching her legs, but somehow I doubted it. Five minutes later, my doubts were confirmed. The bus backed away. I was in a city I knew nothing about. I'd never even met anybody from Philadelphia. I'm sure Erica didn't know anything about the city either.

I searched the bus station. I asked the attendant if she was in the ladies' room. I asked an old man at the newsstand if he'd seen her. I walked outside. Surrounded by faceless boxy buildings. Down the street was a castle—a bizarre white stone monster of a building with a gigantic tower rising from one corner—undoubtedly with rat-infested dungeons—missing only a moat and a drawbridge. Had I stepped into the Dark Ages? I walked on. I found myself on Market Street. Every city has a Market Street, and it is always sleazy. Philly was no exception. I walked around the block. I passed two girlie-movie theaters, a tattoo parlor, three bars, one condemned building, two cafes and one used furniture store. On the door of one of the cafes was a handwritten sign:

NO

SHUT

CLOSED!!!

I started wandering aimlessly. It was midnight. By dawn I had learned something about Philadelphia. I learned that nothing—absolutely nothing—is open after midnight. I'll bet they even turn off the telephones. I learned that strangers walking down a dark street will cross to the other side to avoid you. I saw that every inch of wall space from the ground to about eight feet up was covered with graffiti—worse yet, *boring* graffiti. It was all names. The kids here had been reduced to the level of dogs pissing on lampposts.

Then just at dawn as the dirty gray light began filtering down to the streets, when I was exhausted and hopeless and ready to abandon my search, my Philadelphia education began in earnest. I was stopped by a gentleman in blue. He was patrolling alone in a squad car. He pulled up where I was walking and rolled down his window.

'Hey fella.'

I froze.

'Where you going?'

'Nowhere.'

He heaved himself out of the car. He was chewing gum. His face was pink as bubblegum.

'Lean against the car, spread your hands and legs.'

'I haven't done anything.'

'Shut up.'

He pushed me against the car and frisked. I panicked. I had almost two thousand dollars in my pocket. How would I explain? I had no identification. I'd been wandering

106

aimlessly through this neighborhood of rowhouses for an hour. Somebody had probably thought I looked suspicious, and I suppose it *was* suspicious behavior. But if I got booked for loitering or something, if they checked my fingerprints, I'd match my old Army prints which were now in the possession of the St. Louis police and, I suppose, the FBI and all the other expressionless men.

I happened to glance over the roof of the car and noticed that a kid was leaning back on a front stoop across the street. He was about sixteen, sitting with his arms folded, watching out of the corner of his eye. An early riser. I checked up and down the street. Nobody else in sight. A pop bottle at my feet. Royal Crown Cola.

The cop said, 'Let's see an ID.'

I hated this man. I hated him so much I was shaking. This disinterested cud chewer was about to destroy my life, and he didn't even know it. I was an object to him, a function to perform. My hatred turned him into an object for me as well, not a human being but a situation. And only because he was a situation could I treat him as I was about to do.

I turned and faced him. Adrenalin was pumping. I reached in my pocket and pulled out a twenty dollar bill and pretended to lose my grasp of it just as it left my pocket. It fluttered to the sidewalk. Quickly I bent down to pick it up. The cop didn't stop me. Maybe he thought I was going to bribe him. Maybe I should have, but I never even thought of it. Instead I grabbed first the twenty and then the pop bottle. I exploded from my crouch and smashed the bottle as hard as I could into the side of his head, just above the ear. It made a noise like 'thwack!' and bounced — actually bounced — off the side of his head. The bottle didn't break, and the head didn't bleed. Bulging eyes stared at me stupidly. He didn't fall. Before he could recover I hit him two more times and then — it seemed like poetic justice to me — I kicked him in the balls. He went down. I ran across the street, turned to the left, hesitated just for a moment to look for an alley, an escape. A hand grabbed my arm. It was the kid. 'Come on' he said. He pulled me into a basement. I followed. I ran full speed into

107

a washing machine, bounced off, and kept right on following my leader. He seemed to know what he was doing, and things were happening so fast that I certainly didn't know what to do.

'Out the back. Move.'

We were in the alley now.

'Follow me.' I followed him running down the alley between garbage cans and broken ladders to another rowhouse where he opened a padlock and led me into another basement. He locked the door. We caught our breath. I looked around. There were three ratty sofas and a table covered with *Playboys.* The walls dripped. On the floor were painted five names in the angular style of the graffiti I'd seen everywhere. Beneath the five names, in the same script, were two words: 'The Judges.'

I studied my host and savior. His face was tight and cool — no expression except a hardness of the streets. In spite of the hardness, I knew from what he'd just done that I could trust him — for a while. His hair was short — which was unusual now that bushy Afros were the style — and his scalp was pocked with hairless scabs — which I assumed were from ringworm.

The kid switched off the one bare light bulb that had illuminated the room. 'Keep it dark,' he said. 'You'll be safe here. I'm gonna check the action.' He left. I heard him bolt the padlock. I was locked in. I heard his footsteps fade down the alley.

I couldn't believe it had happened. It was so sudden. One minute I'm walking down the street, five minutes later I'm locked in a dungeon-like basement and I've beaten a cop. Me. I'd never beaten anybody before. I didn't know I had the power. I was stunned. *I'd beaten a man.* I had — for a minute, at least — been an expressionless man.

The basement had one dirty translucent window. It let in enough light to keep me from tripping over anything. I could see that there were no other doors at my level, but there was a staircase that led to the first floor of the house. I tried the knob of the door at the top of the stairs. Firmly locked. I sat down on a sofa and, a doubly wanted fugitive now hostage of a stranger, I thumbed through the old *Playboys* by the dim light of the window. What else could I do?

I must have fallen asleep because the next thing I knew five kids were sitting on the other two sofas, and the kid who brought me there—with the ringworm scabs—was saying, 'Let's take a vote.'

I sat up.

Nobody looked at me. Ringworm continued, 'Everybody on my side, raise their hands.'

Three raised hands, plus his own.

'Okay. Good.' He turned to me. 'I'm Chief Justice. Okay? That's my name. We're The Judges. Okay? That's our gang. We gonna help you.'

'Thanks.'

'They didn't want to help, mainly cause you're—'

'White,' said the one kid who hadn't raised his hand.

'—but I told 'em how you busted old Pinkey up side the head, and that's cool.'

'Pinkey?'

'Lucky for *you* it was *him*. My great gramma coulda laid him out. He scared to touch us. Sometimes we throw fire-crackers at him. He can't do nothin'. He don't come around here too often. He *scared*.'

Lucky me.

'Okay,' said Chief Justice. He leaned forward. 'Who re you?'

The interrogation. A beam of light glared into my eyes from the window. 'Willy. Willy Crusoe.'

'What's your bag?'

'Nothing. I'm lost. I'm looking for my old lady. I got to stay way from cops.'

'You done something?'

'Yes. No. They *think* I did.'

'Do you *think* you did?'

'No.'

'What do they *think* you did?'

'Killed a cop in St. Louis.'

They whistled and cheered.

'All right,' said Chief Justice Ringworm.

They quieted immediately.

'Okay. Where's your old lady?'

'I don't know. We were on a bus to New York. She got off in Philly.'

'When?'

'Last night.'

'What's she look like?'

'White. Seventeen. Brown hair—long, down her back. Skinny. Freckles.'

One of the other kids—with enormous pouty lips—broke in: 'What's a freckle?'

'Aw Clarkie. Jee-zus.'

Clarkie flashed a finger.

'Whatsat? Your IQ?'

'Hey,' said the Chief.

They were still.

He continued: 'What's her name?'

'Erica.'

He sat back and folded his arms. The interrogation was over. 'We'll ask around,' said the Chief Justice.

'Great!'

They exchanged looks. One of them—Clarkie—whispered to Chief Justice, who nodded and turned to me. 'We done you a favor,' he said.

'I know and believe me I—'

'Maybe you can do us a favor.'

He explained. They were a gang. Not a big gang—just the five of them. They were surrounded by other gangs. Philly had about two hundred gangs—black, white, brown. The city was tough. The Judges' territory was two blocks long and one block wide. If any member of any other gang set foot in their territory, there'd be a fight. If they entered any other gang's territory, the same thing would happen. Hence the graffiti— it marked boundaries, ownership, dominance. Other gangs would sometimes sneak in and paint their names in your block. It was a dare. And on neutral ground everybody

painted everywhere. The subways were neutral. Broad
Street. Market. Business areas. Schools. Parks. But if you
were alone on neutral ground, you might get jumped. They
always travelled together. This wasn't a game. They had
guns. Kids were shot all the time.

It sounded claustrophobic to me, not to mention dangerous. But I guess they had no choice. They were born into a
feudal system of a city broken into hundreds of tiny fiefdoms.
I had an absurd vision of Ringworm mounted in armor,
perched on a stallion, pointing a lance. With graffiti sprayed
all over the armor.

Anyway, I could go anywhere. I was older, and I was white
and shaggy. Nobody would think I was working for a gang. I
could run errands where they couldn't go. I could see what
the other gangs were doing.

'What kind of errands?'

'When we think of something, we'll let you know.'

'How can I spy? What do I look for?'

'We'll tell you when we want to know.'

These kids looked tough. They projected an air of bravado
and cool. Underneath it all I know they were scared, but still I
wouldn't want to confront them in an alley. I had to admire
Chief Justice Ringworm. He'd acted without a moment's hesi-
tation to help me, putting himself in danger without knowing
anything about me, and I wasn't even black. I didn't mean to
belittle him when I thought of him as Ringworm — but it was
such an obvious mark, it stuck in my mind.

'You better lay low,' Chief Justice said. 'They be lookin' for
you.'

'Can I stay here 'til dark? I need some sleep anyway.'

'Okay.' He scratched his head. 'You know what you need is
a disguise. Too bad you ain't a nigger. Pinkey don't know one
from another.'

I agreed. But I didn't think I could get away with putting
blackface on. That would only call attention to me. Then I
had a thought. I asked Ringworm, 'Would you get me some
peroxide?'

'Huh?'

'Peroxide. Bleaches hair. Blond.'

'Oh. Yeah.' He nodded approvingly. 'Good idea. My mama got some. Upstairs.'

Clarkie chuckled. 'Yo mama?'

'Shut up.' Ringworm turned to me. 'Okay. You can use our bathroom. Just go up the stairs. Here's the key. Nobody home. We'll go look for your old lady. Okay?'

Fine. They left; I became a platinum blond (I found the peroxide on a shelf in the bathroom under a picture of Diana Ross, above a shelf containing nine different colors of wigs, from silver to red—I guess his mother was capable of using peroxide, too); and then I slept. Like a baby.

The Judges returned at dark. Of course they hadn't found Erica, but they said they'd keep an eye out. I thanked them. Profusely, excessively, I thanked them until they became embarrassed. I was trying extra hard because I wasn't sure how well we were communicating. I had a fear in the back of my mind that their sudden unsolicited friendship could just as whimsically turn to hostility.

As for Erica, I couldn't be sure she was even in the city. She could be on her way to Wheeling at this very moment, or she could go anywhere else she wanted. I had a hunch, though, that she was still in town. Wheeling meant her parents, and I doubted she'd want to see them. And why go to another strange city when she was already in one that was, to her, new and exciting and big enough to hide in, if hiding was what she desired right now. Her last words to me—'You're a broken toilet'—gave me the feeling she just wanted to get away from me for a while. But if she was hiding, when she cooled off she wouldn't be able to find me. I couldn't exactly advertise where I was or where I would be at any given time. As a fugitive, I had to maintain a low profile. I couldn't trust anybody enough to give them an address—not even my parents. This fugitive nonsense was becoming a nuisance.

I was starving.

'Okay men,' I said, 'now that I'm a blond—'

'Boy! Is you ever!'

'Hee-hee!'

'Is it true blonds have more fun?'

'Now that I'm blond, and it's night, I should be pretty safe outside. Is there a place to eat around here? Hey — why don't you join me? I'll treat.'

An uneasy look passed among them.

'Um — no,' said Chief Ringworm. 'You go on. Okay. Come back in a couple days. Just come to our block. We'll see you.'

I decided to go downtown to eat. From now on I would seek the anonymity of crowds.

I didn't *feel* anonymous. I felt ridiculous. Every time I caught my reflection passing a store window, I cringed. I looked absurd. I have a dark, heavy beard, and I hadn't shaved in a day. The contrast of my dark complexion and my fluorescent hair made me look like one of those haunted city freaks — the kind you find in any city hanging around any Market Street — the borderline psychotics, the pimps and hustlers and given-uppers, the studs, the flaming faggots, the runaways, the peddlers of chemical marvels whispering softly as they walk slowly by, the Jesus freaks, the Hare Krishna freaks, the ever present winos, the cripples and beggars and penniless old men. And me. I was a nice boy from the suburbs.

I ate in a place called Stanley Greens. Then on an impulse I called Elaine's cafe in St. Louis.

Bumpy answered. I asked for Elaine.

'Uh — who's calling?'

'Willy.'

'Willy. Hey. How are yuh?'

'Fine. Where's Elaine?'

'Where are *you*?'

'I'd rather not say.'

'Oh. Yeah. Elaine ain't here.'

'When will she be back?'

'I mean she *ain't here*. She's gone.'

'Where?'

'Said she was going to New Mexico, but then I got a post-card from New Orleans. Gave an address. Sounds like she's staying there.'

113

'Why?'

'Wait a minute. I got it right here. Lemme read it. It's got a picture of some street car on the front. On the back it says, "The St. Charles Street Car Line. One of the oldest and most pic— uh— picturesque—" '

'What did *she* say?'

'She says, "Dear Bumpy. Slight detour. I'm a cocktail waitress. Little old me. You should see the tips. Big spenders on Bourbon Street. I'm practicing to be a stripper. Come down and see." "See" is underlined. I think it's a joke.'

'What else?'

'The address.'

'Can I have it?'

He read it to me, and I wrote it down. Dauphine Street.

'Why'd she leave?'

'Al's in jail.'

'What happened?'

'Busted. Sold a bag of stuff to a plainclothes cop. But he might get off because it wasn't the real stuff.'

'What was it?'

'Parsley.'

That sounded like Al.

'Elaine was so mad, she just flew out of here. Said she never wants to see him again. She don't mean it.'

'Wish she did.'

'You better hope he gets out. He said he knows something. About that guy.'

'What guy?'

'The cop you killed.'

'*I didn't kill him.*' I glanced around nervously. I was in a phone booth, alone, safe.

'Yeah. That's right. You didn't kill him. You should talk to Al. He knows.'

'What?'

'He knows who did it.'

'Really! Hey—' But what a mess. I couldn't go talk to Al. Not while he was in jail. I might go for a visit and stay as a permanent guest. I didn't even know whether I could trust

114

Al's information, or even whether he'd give it to me. And what if I did know? What could I do? Hire a lawyer? I was in no position to take it to court, the forces of 'justice.' But still my curiosity burned. 'Did he tell you?'

'Naw. Won't even tell Elaine. Just said he knows. Said the whole town's tight because of what happened. Said that's why he got busted. Said it's heavy right now. He's scared. He ain't gonna talk. Not unless he can get out of town. Can't blame him. Those guys are mean.'

'Yeah. Well. Can you tell Elaine I called if you see her?'

'Sure. Any message?'

'I'm in Philadelphia for a while.'

'Philly! What for?'

I didn't know what for. It just happened. I said good-bye. I had some things to think about. Like Elaine. It was hard to imagine her as a cocktail waitress, even harder as a stripper, but then it's hard to imagine any stripper. Once I met a fresh-faced girl who was a coed at the University of Texas. She wanted to be a doctor. She studied medicine all winter, then spent her summers bumping and grinding on Bourbon Street. If she could be one, anybody could. It's just a job, like any other. As for Al and his information, I decided to wait and see. I sure wasn't about to risk a trip to St. Louis any time soon. But I wouldn't mind a trip to New Orleans . . . But I wasn't going anywhere until I found Erica.

I was walking down Broad Street when I noticed the old lady. She had hair like a mushroom and a wart on one eyelid. Her dress hung from her hips like a hotel bedspread. She waddled.

I was walking toward her.

She waddled in front of me.

I moved to walk around her.

She blocked me. She stared up at my face. She reached out a hand that was dripping with age and touched a lock of my now golden hair.

'Quack,' she said.

'Excuse me?'

115

'Quack quack.'

And then she moved on.

I took a room in a run-down hotel. For two days I wandered the streets of this crumbling old city. The people wore grimaces and looked like they were being pinched. Without Erica I felt like my spirit was a pie with two slices removed. I missed her finger in my belly-button. I missed her smile like hot steaming apples.

I called her mother.

'Willy? Hey boy! Is that you?'

She shouted into the phone. She was one of those people who panic at a long distance call, trying to holler over the miles of wire, her mind boggling at the expense of it all, trying to say good-bye as soon as she says hello. I asked her if she'd heard from Erica.

'No! Ain't she with yew?'

'She ran away in Philadelphia.'

'Way out *there*? Where're yew?'

'Philly.'

'Let us know if you find her. Got to ring off now. Got a bill from Mushroom. Nine thousand dollars. Got to go now. Thanks for callin', Willy boy!'

'I'll call in a couple —'

'Bye!'

She hung up.

I checked with the Judges. I hadn't walked half-way down their first block before Chief Justice popped out from between two buildings.

They hadn't seen her, either.

'Anything I can do for you?' I asked.

'No man. Everything's cool.'

The next afternoon I was loafing by the pool in JFK Plaza when the sailor sitting next to me got up and left his newspaper behind. I turned to the want ads. One caught my eye:

COMPUTER OPERATOR. 2 years exp. $7-8k.

Just that and a phone number. Nothing special. But suddenly I felt the need to keep my hand in, to prove I could still do it. And it would pass the time.

I called for an appointment. A female voice, bored, asked could I make it tomorrow afternoon. Two o'clock.

'I'm sorry. I can't make it tomorrow. What about today?'

'We aren't seeing anybody until tomorrow.'

'Tomorrow is impossible. I could make four this afternoon.'

'We won't begin interviewing until tomorrow. Perhaps you could come in the day after—'

'That's impossible.'

'Well why don't you call us when you—'

'Four today is almost tomorrow. I tell you what. We won't have an interview. I'm a salesman. This is a sales appointment.'

'What are you selling?'

'Myself.'

'Look. I—Hold on.'

Click.

I held on. Feeling good. I could still do it.

Click.

'Still there?'

'Right here.'

'All right. Four o'clock. Good luck.'

Easier than I expected. Off and running. Now where's the phone book? Ah. Yellow Pages. Hmm . . . Yes. There were eight stores within two blocks selling used furniture, used clothes. Now just where is this Lancaster Avenue? A map at the beginning of the Yellow Pages. Lancaster. There. And the subway goes . . . There. Good.

Not unlike Clark Kent, I emerged from the phone booth.

At Fortieth and Market I climbed from the gloomy screeching cave into a wasteland. There could have been a nuclear attack while I was under the streets. Whole blocks were level as prairies. What wasn't level, should have been. Buildings boarded up, graffiti of course, weeds, wine bottles, shattered street lights, even shattered traffic lights. The kids here threw rocks at traffic lights. All I ever did was steal signs.

Prudent shopping and a little friendly haggling produced a

wardrobe of light green slacks, dark green suit (nice fit except an ounce too tight at the shoulders), white shirt with button down collar, smashing royal purple tie, and (the one weak link) frayed leather shoes that a good hard shine just might cover up for an hour or so. Acceptable. Quite. After all, I wasn't applying for president of a bank. And I'd only invested five dollars and eighty-nine cents. Then as I was returning to the subway, resplendent in my new duds, my eye fell on the *coup de grace* in the window of the Salvation Army store. A gold leather briefcase with the initials MBB. It cost me six bucks, more than all the rags and worth every penny. So what if I was a peroxide blond? I had a green suit and a gold leather briefcase. Nobody would know it was me.

Somebody knew.

It was the duck lady. She was waddling up Fortieth Street as I turned the corner. Our eyes met. I'd know that mushroom hair anywhere. And she recognized me. I swear she did. She waddled right up to me and, just like before, she stared up at my face and reached out one decrepit hand and touched a lock of my hair.

'Quack,' she said.

I spun around and started to retreat.

'Quack quack,' she called after me.

I doubled my pace.

'Quack,' she said indignantly, plaintively, positively.

I ran.

At four o'clock sharp I marched through odorless antiseptic air-conditioned halls into the office of Janet D. Seeger, Personnel Manager, Ace Supermarkets (still a small chain, but they had Big Plans). She handed me an application, which I immediately returned to her fingers. I withdrew from my briefcase (hiding the initials from view) one resumé, a string of lies I'd dictated at a print shop just one hour before. Her eyes studied it from top to bottom, and then she said, 'Do you have any experience?' (indicating that either she couldn't read or her memory was remarkably short).

'Yes,' I said. 'As it says on the resumé. Five years.'

118

'Very good.'

Apparently that was all she needed to know. She asked a few personal questions and sent me to the office of the Operations Manager, Walt Parker.

Ms. Seeger introduced me and departed.

'Hiya Willy.' Smiling. Cigar. 'Sit down.'

'How do you do, Mr. Parker.'

'Walt.'

'Walt.'

I could see that Walt Parker was an Affable Man.

'What kind of machine do you have, Mr. Parker?'

'Walt.'

'Walt.'

'Just a little old 360/30. But we—'

'Ninety-six K?'

'Sixty-four. But we—'

'But you have Big Plans.'

'Exactly.' He laughed. 'I think you know us.'

I thought I did.

'Now let's see what your resumé—'

'DOS shop?'

'Yes.'

'POWER?'

'No.'

'Just background?'

'We spool off some tapes to print in F1.'

'Mostly BG.'

'We're thinking about bringing in GRASP if—'

'Don't. Try SPRINT.'

'You know GRASP?'

'Unfortunately. And POWER. Bugs. Both of them. Hard waits. Loops. Jobs mysteriously disappear from the queue. Drive your systems man crazy.'

'What's this SPRINT?'

I bantered with him. I didn't care about SPRINT. I was just displaying the jargon, showing him I knew multiprogramming, I knew JCL, I knew batch processing, I knew the hardware, the software, the whole silly bundle. The

119

important thing was to keep him off the resumé. I scarcely remembered what was written on it. And if he checked any of those references . . .

'Well sir,' Walt Parker finally said. 'You seem to know computers. Now about—'

'What sort of work do you do here?'

'Inventory, mainly.'

'Payroll?'

'Bi-weekly.'

'Package?'

'In-house.'

'Uh-oh.'

'You said it.'

'Data base?'

'TOTAL.'

'Ah.'

'Yes. Well.' He checked his wristwatch. 'I see by your resumé that you—'

'How many shifts work here?'

'Just two.'

'Weekends?'

'Rarely.' He smiled at that.

'What shift did you want me for?'

'Days.'

'Well.' I settled back in my chair. 'It sounds pretty good. You see, what I'm looking for is an Opportunity to Grow with a Growing Company.'

Walt smiled. 'We could certainly use an Aggressive Young Man. You took the words right out of my mouth. We think what we offer is—as you say—an Opportunity to Grow with a Growing Company.'

Walt Parker tapped his cigar and glanced at his watch. We had been talking for a half hour. 'Well sir,' he said, 'it's time for me to make like a tree.' He grinned. 'And leave.' A thunderclap of laughter. 'Oh by the way, would you like to see the computer room before you go?'

Victory. They only give you a tour if they think they're going to hire you. And he hadn't asked one question.

Sure enough, I was hired. Not because I'd dazzled Walt in the interview, though. I was the only candidate who accepted the crummy salary they were offering. Right off I worked three seven-day weeks — twenty-one consecutive days. I wasn't surprised. Managers usually lie about how much overtime they're going to require, but I couldn't be angry considering the lies I'd told in order to get hired. We were both in the same game, Walt Parker and I. The business game. Testing the limits of deceit.

I had a supervisor named Elliot. He had been promoted from the job I was now holding. I ran the machine, Elliot supervised me, and Walt Parker managed Elliot. He was just a kid, but he was the Ambitious Young Man. He was twenty. He wore hexagonal spectacles. He was constantly combing his heavy black hair. He kept every hair in its assigned spot on his head — it was an exercise in discipline. As we were leaving after my first day at work, his first as a supervisor, he held the door open for me to go out and said. 'Wilbur, all I can say to you today is, be careful with what you do. That's all. Just be careful with what you do.' He actually said things like that. Another habit of his was to speak in numbers. Every computer message has a number that prints out with it. The number is for reference, but the meaning of the message is in the words. For example, the computer might type out:

1I60A READY FOR COMMUNICATIONS.

This is a standard message, one that an operator sees hundreds of times a day. It always has the number 1I60A, but not one operator in a hundred could tell you that that's what the number is. Elliot, however, would say, 'Now, Wilbur, when you receive a one eye sixty a, the response is —' Of course I would say, 'A what?' 'A one eye sixty a. Ready for communications.' 'Ah. Ready for communications.' 'The response is —' Elliot took it all seriously. He had a little office behind the air conditioning unit that had originally been intended as a closet. The air conditioner provided a steady cold draft and a constant throbbing hum. On his desk Elliot kept shorts, tennis shoes, a T-shirt, and a coffee mug with 'Elliot' glazed onto it. In a drawer marked 'Emergency Medical Kit' he stashed a pile of porn magazines. The cover story of the top magazine was entitled 'The Pleasure of Cocksucking.' There were three women in his life, and he scheduled them with computer-like precision. He had a fiancée; he was living with his mother; and he was having an affair with one of the keypunches. Every Sunday morning he attended the Baptist Church with his mother. Every Tuesday night he went bowling with his fiancée. Every Monday and Wednesday he left with his keypunch amoureuse. He spent his lunch hour working out in a gymnasium. In my first twenty-one days there, I think he wore twenty-one different neckties. I knew all these facts, and yet I knew nothing about him. Elliot was an expressionless man. Elliot was a mystery. His was a foreign culture to me; he might have been an Amazon headhunter. And in many ways, Elliot was The Enemy.

Elliot and I came to terms—sketched out the boundaries of our relationship—on my first weekend of overtime. On my first day at work, I'd worn all the secondhand duds I'd worn to my job interview. On my second day, I shed the suit and tie. On the third day I wore tennis shoes and forgot to shave. On Saturday I wore blue jeans and a work shirt, and I brought a six-pack of beer. I was alone all morning. In the middle of the afternoon I was sprawled in the swivel chair with my bare feet kicked up on the computer console. I was working on my third can of beer.

'Crusoe! Jesus Christ!'

It was Elliot.

'Who turned off the air conditioner?'

'I did.'

'Why?'

'It doesn't breathe right.'

'Doesn't *breathe*! Crusoe—Where are your shoes?'

'Over there.'

'Beer! For God's sake, Crusoe, we don't pay you for—'

'I finished BBX60.'

'60? Didn't you do 40?'

'Sure did.'

'What about 20 and 25?'

122

'Done.'

'What time did you start?'

'Eight.'

'That's impossible. BBX20 and 25 take four hours, and 40 takes three. 60 takes three more. You can't finish 60 until six o'clock.'

'It's done.'

I showed him the console. I'd run multiprogramming—two jobs at once.

'That's impossible, Crusoe. It isn't catalogued relocatable.'

'I catalogued it.'

'You!'

'Why waste all that time?'

'You're not authorized. You're not a programmer. You can't—'

'It's done.'

'I'm gonna go balance those reports. And you just better hope they balance.'

I knew they balanced. I'd already checked.

'And turn on the air conditioner.'

I turned it on. I knew I'd have to. But I'd made a good trade—without saying it, we'd just agreed that I could wear blue jeans and bring beer to work on weekends, if I promised not to turn off the air conditioner.

The next Monday, Walt Parker called me to his office. He was talking with a salesman. I took a seat in the corner under a sign that said, IF IT IS NOT WRITTEN DOWN, IT IS NOT A PROBLEM. I recognized the salesman. His name was Jimmy Lareeno, and I'd seen Walt Parker leave for lunch with him every day for the last week. They took a two-hour lunch. Jimmy Lareeno had a nickname for Walt Parker. He called him Ollie. It was based on some old joke involving Laurel and Hardy.

'Well Ollie,' Jimmy Lareeno said as I sat down, 'I see you're gonna pretend you really work here—'

'Most people think *you* do, Jimmy.'

'Maybe I do. Maybe, indeed. If I get that contract—'

'Dream on.'

'I'm dreaming, Ollie. I'm dreaming, indeed. What did Moore bid?'

'Now you know I can't tell you—'

'How can I underbid him if I don't know what he bid?'

'I don't get the bids, Jimmy. The whole thing's in the Procurement Office.'

'But you know, Ollie. You know, indeed.'

'And you know I can't tell you.'

'You don't have to, Ollie. You do not have to. You don't even know the bids. How can you tell me when you don't even know the bids? All you know is what you print on that little computer. And one of the things you print is a daily report for the Procurement Office. And on that report, on a certain page, there is a list of numbers. The numbers are in order. My number's on that report. My number is four dollars and eighty-nine cents per. My number is not on the top line, Ollie. Moore is on the top line. What number is on the top line, Ollie?'

'Jimmy . . .'

'Don't give me a bid, Ollie. I wouldn't ask that. I'm just asking about your computer printout. Just a certain top line. And don't forget who bought lunch today, Ollie. Who always buys lunch. But don't think about that, Ollie. Think about a printout. Think about the top line of a certain re—'

'Three dollars and ninety-two cents per. Jesus, Jimmy. You don't have to be so heavy-handed as all—'

'Holy shit. Ollie. Holy fucking shit. That's a dollar a box. I can't meet that. I can't come near it.'

'That's why I told you. So you'd shut up. You're gonna lose the contract, Jimmy. There's no way.'

'One thing I offer, Ollie. Service. I give you service. I change delivery dates when nobody else can. I go a lot farther. Remember that Saturday, Ollie? Remember when I brought over three boxes of paper in the trunk of my car? Is Moore gonna do that for you? You know what kind of trouble you'd of been in if I hadn't brought that paper? You know how it looks when you don't meet a payroll because you forgot to order enough paper? That's what I can offer, Ollie.

Service. And it wouldn't hurt you either, Ollie. You know it wouldn't exactly hurt you if I won the contract. As a matter of fact, you just might—'

'Hold it.' Walt Parker's eyes swung around to me. 'What do you want?'

'You called.'

'Oh. Yeah. What about the Trial Balance?'

I told him that the Trial Balance Report was out of balance because somebody had switched the labels on a tape. The input tape would have to be recreated. I was working on it, but the report couldn't possibly be finished until the next day.

'Switched labels! My God! What can we do?'

'I told you I'm recreating the—'

'I said what can we *do*?'

'I'm regenerating the—'

'What can we tell the Director?'

Ah. Walt Parker's approach to a problem was how to hide it.

'Tell them it was a data check.'

'No good. They'll want to know why we don't have a backup.'

'Tell them the machine broke down.'

'They know it didn't.'

'Tell them the Business Office sent up some bad data that we had to correct.'

'Hey . . .' He held up one finger. 'Not bad. Let me work on that. Not bad.'

I waited for him to dismiss me. I noticed another sign to the right of my chair: TO ERR IS HUMAN, TO REALLY FOUL THINGS UP TAKES A COMPUTER.

Walt Parker was jotting something on a note pad. He looked up. 'Oh. You can go, Willy. You too, Jimmy. Time to make like an orange. And peel.'

Jimmy Lareeno got the contract. Walt Parker teamed up with Elliot for a meeting with the Procurement Office. Walt explained to them about how important it was to get good service from a vendor and what a lousy reputation Moore had for service and hey—if you want an example of good service, Lareeno gives the greatest service in the world. Elliot said he didn't know about service himself, but he did know about paper and Moore's was cheap stuff. It didn't stack well, whereas Lareeno's folded perfectly. And when you ran it through a burster or a decollater—well, Lareeno's special forms just had it all over Moore's. The Procurement Office was impressed by this unsolicited testimony. In fact, they were so impressed that they signed a three year contract with renewal options for paper that was going to cost them an extra dollar a box. Jimmy Lareeno was likewise impressed. He often treated Walt Parker to lunch after getting the contract, and he even gave Walt a stereo set. To Elliot he gave a transistor radio. I thought the radio was kind of cheap, but Elliot seemed satisfied. Anyway, Elliot had other problems on his mind. Seems his fiancée was pregnant. What's worse, when his keypunch found out about it she exploded with jealousy. She'd always known Elliot was engaged, but apparently it hadn't occurred to her that he might sleep with his fiancée as well. Anyway, Elliot announced that he would marry his fiancée right away. The keypunch told him that if he married, she'd tell everything to the fiancée. Elliot said that's too bad because I'm going to do right by her—after all, he'd gotten her into the situation. Are you sure, said the keypunch, and Elliot said he thought so. Well, Elliot arranged to elope with his fiancée. He was to come to her house Tuesday night, their bowling night so nobody would suspect anything, and instead of bowling they'd go to a Justice of the Peace somewhere. Monday night, as usual, Elliot went out with his keypunch, planning one last fling. Tuesday morning he was married. To the keypunch. She'd told him *she* was pregnant, too. She quit her job and they moved into an apartment, and a couple weeks later she announced that the doctor had run another test and guess what. She wasn't pregnant, after all. Elliot took to smoking a pipe. He stopped exercising at the gym on his lunch hour and sometimes stepped out with Jimmy Lareeno and Walt Parker. He'd return from lunch with whiskey on his breath. Sometimes he'd wear the same tie for two whole weeks. The Emergency Medical Kit bulged with a larger and larger stack of magazines. He was no longer a mystery to me. And he was no longer the Ambitious Young Man.

I didn't learn all this from Elliot, and I certainly didn't observe it all first-hand. My source of gossip was Billie. She was the scheduler—that's the person who sets up jobs so they're ready to run on the computer. She knew everything about everybody. She was like a human tape recorder. Apparently nobody could resist speaking into her microphone. She wouldn't start out being nosy when she talked. She'd let her prey carry the conversation for a while until he let slip with a morsel of personal information—and suddenly she'd pounce. She'd latch onto that one morsel (like: 'Oh really? Your father's dead?') and yank out a whole string of questions ('How long ago? How old was he? Where was this? Were you close? How'd your family take it? Oh, you have a brother. Where does he live? What does he do? Does he like it? Is he married? Do you visit?'). She got away with it because she could cluck and sympathize like a pro, and she knew how to laugh and when to do it. Which all makes her sound like a horrible person but she wasn't, really. I thought she was wonderful company. I took her out to lunch on my third day at work and practically every day thereafter. I didn't tell her anything about myself. She didn't even know where I lived. I figured that's why she kept going to lunch with me—I was her toughest case. I found it easy to avoid giving her that one morsel she needed before she'd strike. Instead of telling her about myself, I let her feed *me* all the gossip. After all, there was no point gathering all this information if she didn't tell somebody. I met a need. I also got her to tell me a lot about herself. I even managed to embarrass her once. She had the blackest skin I've ever seen, so black it was like negative color, like a color vacuum that sucks the hues from the air around it. All I did to embarrass her was ask, on the Monday after she'd returned from a weekend at 'The Shore'—Atlantic City— 'Did you get a nice tan?' It was a dumb question and I'm the one who should've been embarrassed, but for some reason the

127

question made her so nervous and giggly that she had to excuse herself and go to the ladies' room. She was a city woman and an office girl. In the office any man could give her orders and get a 'Yes, sir. Right away, sir.' On the streets no man would dream of giving orders to such a woman. Her hair was a gigantic Afro bundle—a massive wiry globe in which a hand could disappear up to the wrist. Sometimes she kept pens and pencils up there. She could just as well have kept a typewriter. I was fascinated by the smell. Hair like that holds on to a little of every odor that passes through it. Some days it smelled of incense and perfume, other days it was bacon and smoke. If she went shopping, she came back carrying the scent of Wanamaker's and Macy's. And always there was a background smell, a mixture of body and city as the oils and sweat of her own flesh blended with the dirt of Philadelphia—the paint fumes, the gasoline, the roofing tar and plaster dust and cigarette smoke, the smog and yesterday's garbage—filtered and refined—not overpowering and not unpleasant, surprisingly, but a nice smell, a comfortable smell, one you could move in with like an old but well-tended house. Billie was a young woman, younger than me. She lived with her mother and father in a rowhouse somewhere in North Philly 'in a neighborhood you wouldn't want to go to,' she told me. She hated her mother, a woman who believed in gospel religion and whose singing could drown out the church organ, according to Billie. Her mother also believed in chaperones and had forced them on Billie for a while until on one of her dates the chaperone got mugged, at which time her mother forbade all dates entirely. Billie continued dating, *sans* chaperone, and that was the end of that. I think it was the only act of rebellion she had committed in her whole life.

'Why don't you move out?' I asked her once.

'Where to?'

'Anywhere. Just to get away from her.'

'I don't like living alone.'

'Then don't.'

'I can't live with a woman. I just don't think I'm capable of it.'

128

'Then live with a man.'

She snarled. 'Like who?'

I couldn't answer that. She asked the question with a sudden flash of bitterness that made me disinclined to probe any farther. I guessed that men had hurt her before. But I suspected that maybe there was another reason she didn't leave home. Maybe she was scared to. She'd never been away from home, she told me, except occasionally her mother dragged her down to some itty-bitty town in North Carolina where she was born, and she'd languish there for a week of utter boredom. She was tuned to a city rhythm. She couldn't enjoy the country. One time she was all set to go to college — she'd been accepted by a school in Virginia — but she didn't want to go because she would have had to leave her best and dearest friend. She cared about this friend so much that in the month of August before she was supposed to set off for school, she came down with a strange lingering illness that caused a slight fever and kept her bedridden for weeks. The mysterious disease just stayed and stayed, and finally in consideration of her health she had to cancel her plans for college. A couple of weeks later, the illness disappeared.

'And your friend. Was she glad?'

'Oh yes.'

'Are you still friends?'

'Sure.' She lowered her eyes. 'Course she's married now, has a couple of boys. Don't see her so much any more. I mean . . . You know. I was dumb. I coulda been a college girl. Now what am I? Scheduler. What am I gonna do with myself?'

'You could still go to college.'

She shrugged.

I asked, 'What do you want to do?'

'What does any woman want to do?'

'Beats me.'

'Well, when you figure it out, then you'll know what I want to do.'

At the time she said that, we'd been lunching steadily for over a month. In fact, our lunches had become something of an office joke. Elliot teased me about this red-hot romance I

129

was carrying on. I couldn't explain to him. He wouldn't understand how two people could be happy just talking to each other.

Christmas was a lonely time. I was still living in the same run-down hotel. It was near the subway, I could walk to work from there. I felt completely anonymous among the pensioners and traveling Bible salesmen. I worked nearly every day and went to movies nearly every night. I ate mostly in the coffee shop downstairs. About the only thing I needed the room for was to sleep and watch television. And sleep I avoided as much as possible. I had nightmares. It was that same vision: three faces in St. Louis, a giant gold ring, a fist — beckoning me to join them, to sink into their pit of evil — I will not join them, I must not — Dark Glasses, an expressionless face, a man who was scared. A gambler? A loser.

Movies were a way to put off sleep. There was just one problem. I'd walk out of the theater and forget where I was.

What city?

From inside a theater, all cities look the same. I went to movies for escape, and the escape for me was total: a placeless state of mind, surrounded by dark walls and dim ceiling. I sat in the same folding seat, ate the same buttered popcorn, and when the movie ended I was walking through the same lobby passing the same candy stand and the same tired ushers in the same Edward Hopper scene as I had been passing all my life in so many cities at so many times . . .

I panicked. When I reached the door I would be entering the streets of a city again and I had no idea which city it would be. The panic would pass; I would remember: Philadelphia. But which theater? Was I downtown at the Fox, or had I taken a subway out to the Terminal, or was I in Germantown at the Bandbox, or had I walked over to South Street and the TLA Cinema? Another panic, another re-orientation. Perhaps traveling salesmen have the same occupational hazard when they step out of office buildings. Perhaps they learn, make notes ('This is Tucson. Tomorrow is Phoenix. Important — this is *not* Albuquerque.'). I never seemed to learn. I think it was because I wouldn't admit to myself what my life had become. I was losing my bearings. I missed Erica. I didn't know if I'd ever see her again. Most of the time — especially in daylight — I felt confident that she'd pop up when she was ready. She could get in touch with her parents any time she wanted. Unlike me. I couldn't go home. I was just killing time. In the black of night I lay in bed or sat sleeplessly staring out the window at the deathly silent streets — cut suddenly by the flashing streak of a police car or the lonely errand of a taxi — streets washed nightly by rain beating at my glass or dripping monotonously on the sill — and I would shake with the fear that I would never see Erica again. That my life would be a never-ending winter of rain, an endless insomniac night in a pensioners' hotel. Because I could not share my troubles with a woman I loved. Because she ran away from her troubles as I ran away from mine. We both would run from problems that clung like shadows. No matter how fast we could fly, or how far, our troubles would follow, for our troubles were ourselves.

When I wasn't brooding on Erica, I was brooding on anonymity. I was unplugged from the vast interconnected electronic communications grid of the country. I felt unplugged from the people themselves. As Willy Crusoe I could not validate myself. I couldn't get a driver's license or a credit card or a social security number. (I used Willy Middlebrook's number at work. So far nothing had come of it. My checks included a deduction for social security which, I presumed, was being added to Willy Middlebrook's account.) I couldn't even open a checking account. I had to cash my paychecks at a Pantry Pride grocery store. I couldn't vote. And for fear of what the postmark would reveal, I couldn't send Christmas cards.

One snowy night a week before Christmas, I bought two rolls of dimes and settled myself in a phone booth downtown on Walnut Street. The snow fell relentlessly; a mob of bundle-toting shoppers flowed over the sidewalks before my eyes. Crippled beggars sat on stools or leaned against walls, shaking cups. A loudspeaker played 'Deck the Halls' over and over and over again.

I called my parents. The phone rang fifteen times. They were probably out shopping, too. They couldn't send me a present, not even a card. They thought I was in New York.

I called New Orleans. They had no listing for Elaine on Dauphine Street.

I called Bumpy in St. Louis. He didn't seem surprised to hear from me. He said Elaine had left New Orleans and headed out West in her yellow milk truck. When she'd written him, she thought she'd go to Montana — she had an uncle in Butte — but said she'd stop anywhere on the way if she found something interesting.

'And Al?'

'He got a year.'

Good, I thought, though I didn't say so.

'What's new at the cafe?'

'Nothing.'

'You still get — what do you call it — elopements?'

'Yeah. Sure. You know how it is. Nothing ever changes.'

Nothing for him, maybe, I said to myself.

I tried to call John. His wife Lucy answered the phone.

'Could I speak to John?'

'Who wants him?'

That was hostility, loud and clear, coming over eight hundred miles of wire. I was suddenly suspicious, and I didn't want her to know who I was.

'You don't know me. My name's Fitzpatrick. It's a medical matter. I've got to discuss it with John.'

'He isn't here.'

'When will he — ?'

'He isn't here any more.'

'Oh. I . . .' I couldn't think of what to say.

'Well?'

I hung up. I didn't even say good-bye. Some psyches merge and others seem to collide for some reason, and mine and Lucy's were certainly a collision. The only other time I'd phoned her I'd also lied, telling her I was in Kansas City when I was really in Bumpy's cafe. She brought on paranoia. But what of John? Were they separated? So soon? Why?

132

I called Mrs. Patman in Wheeling. Once again she panicked, shouting over the wires.

'Hey boy! We ain't seen her. You got her?'

'Nope.'

'The fiddler bought a truck! How do ya like that?'

'Really? What—'

'He saved up all the money to pay off Mushroom, then he thought he could use it better on a truck. They're plenty mad. They cain't find him.'

'Where is he?'

'Out on the road somewheres. He's an independent. Goes anywhar.'

'Don't you ever see him?'

'Shore. But he keeps his money in a bank in Cincinnati. Mushroom cain't find it.'

'I bet he's happy.'

'Shore. Ain't yew?'

'Nope.'

'Cheer up, Willy! Merry Christmas. She'll come back. And hey—happy New Year.'

I wished her a happy New Year in return, and many happy new years to come.

That was it. I'd gone through all my contacts in the world. I scooped up the remaining dimes and emerged onto the sidewalk expressway. On the corner an old blind man wearing one blue sock and one green one was selling a box of bruised apples. His seeing eye dog slept at his feet, oblivious to the surging shoppers. I took an apple and dropped a handful of dimes onto the little tin plate.

The blind man smiled and nodded.

My pocket was heavy. What the hell. Burrowing into my pants, I extracted every last coin. Raining dimes. They clattered onto the plate. One coin bounced, escaped, and rolled by a dozen clomping feet before it disappeared over the curb. The blind man seemed startled—he jumped. The dog perked up its head, yawning. Giant teeth like ivory icicles. The blind man faced me. He knew exactly where I was standing. 'Thank you,' he said. 'Hey—thanks a lot.' And then he winked.

Christmas day I woke up depressed. It was snowing again. The coffee shop where I usually ate breakfast was closed. I ambled along the quiet streets, the only prints on the fresh snow of the sidewalks. Everything was closed.

I walked along Walnut Street, then turned back down Chestnut. It was a wet snow, falling in fat flakes that felt like little pebbles against my face. The slush was two inches thick on the sidewalk. Water seeped into my footprints so that I left a trail of puddles as I walked.

I gave up on breakfast. It was getting more toward lunch time, anyway. I turned up 16th Street to JFK Plaza and then ambled along the Benjamin Franklin Parkway.

I found myself passing through other people's Christmases. I passed a young man with a spider monkey on his shoulder, the monkey's tail wrapped around the man's neck. The monkey wore a ski sweater and a bright green stocking cap. He kept brushing the snow out of the man's hair and beard. He was obsessed with his job, muttering monkey curses as more snow kept settling where he had just brushed it clean.

I passed a boy carrying a radio the size of an attaché case, blaring music you could hear for blocks.

In Logan Circle I passed a young woman setting up a tripod and camera. She was working on a picture of one of the giant bronze frogs in the fountain. Normally, the frogs are spouting great streams of water from their mouths. Today the water was off. An icicle hung from the frog's lower lip like a giant herpes sore. I walked behind her so as to keep the snow fresh in her field of view.

I was feeling better. An old man was hobbling along in big black galoshes. He was bent over a cane, half-way collapsed, shoving his feet through the snow. 'Good day, sir,' I said to him. He looked up, surprised. 'Why good day to you,' he said. 'Merry Christmas.'

On the Parkway a Pontiac was spinning wheels on a slick of ice. I gave the man a push. He waved, and fishtailed up the street.

Kids were sledding on the hill by the Art Museum. I stood with some parents at the bottom. There were about a dozen white kids, one Puerto Rican and two blacks. My eyes were drawn to the Puerto Rican. A dead cigarette butt was hanging from his lips. He was only about nine years old. Acne already, sprouting on his chin. All the parents were white. They were sharing thermoses of coffee, chatting, paying no attention to the kids. When a little incident occurred, I was the only one who noticed. Two white kids were sharing the same sled. One was about eight years old, the other maybe thirteen. The older one was easily the biggest kid there. He had red hair. Apparently this big red-head got tired of sharing a sled with his little brother. The redhead walked up to the Puerto Rican and—without a word—snatched the rope from the little kid's hand and started pulling the sled up the hill.

The little Puerto Rican didn't say a thing. He stared. The cigarette butt drooped.

I walked over. 'Hey,' I called. 'Hey you.'

The red-haired kid stopped and turned around. He pointed at himself in a 'who me?' gesture.

'That your sled?'

No answer. He simply let go of the rope. The sled drifted gently, noiselessly to our feet.

The Puerto Rican kid picked up the rope and started up the hill. He hadn't even *looked* at me. His only reaction that I could see was a tightening of the lips so that the cigarette butt poked out straight under his nose. I felt like the umpire in a baseball game, only spoken to if I made a bad call.

'Hey.'

The kid stopped, turned. Big silent questioning eyes.

'Can I have a ride?'

He grinned. The butt wagged. I followed him up the hill.

'My name's Willy.'

He nodded. We reached the top of the hill.

'Why don't you sit between my legs.'

Wordlessly, he settled in. Down we went. One of the adults pointed a thermos at me. Somebody laughed. I steered with my feet. Damn kid wouldn't say a word. '*Habla usted Espanol*?' I asked. No answer.

At the bottom I climbed off. 'Thanks for the ride. Much obliged.'

The kid turned, eyes avoiding mine. I watched him pull the sled back up the hill.

Suddenly he turned. 'Hey bro.'

Words. Hey. 'What?'

'Pow-ah.' The fist.

'Right on.' Returning the fist.

The kid grinned, wheeled, and raced away, tugging the sled, shrieking with laughter.

It was still snowing. I was still hungry. By now I was sure some places would be open, so I hurried toward Market Street.

I didn't make it. A bus stopped. Out of its door lurched a bearded man. Middle-aged, messy hair, a suitcoat over a sport shirt. He marched right up to an oil drum garbage can that had been sitting peacefully in the snow minding its own business. He attacked. He pounded and kicked that oil drum for all he was worth. Oh he was savage. Merciless. And he had the advantage of surprise. The garbage can never had a chance. It banged and reverberated in pain. Finally it sank to its side in defeat. The man beamed. Then he squatted over the can, reached in and tossed handfuls of garbage into the air. Cans. Bottles. Newspaper. A circle of litter grew about him. He paused, wiped his brow with his sleeve. He was out of breath. Suddenly the can settled an inch into the snow. The man pounced. He applied karate. He applied jujitsu, kung fu, taekwondo. At last the oil drum was thoroughly subdued.

'*All right*,' the man shouted.

He started walking. Weaving. Lurching. He overtook another man and started talking in his ear. The man ignored him. He continued to talk into the man's ear until his attention was caught by a cement ball on a post at the bottom of a stair railing. It was bigger than a cannon ball. He boxed with it, feinting and ducking and landing some good punches. Then as a woman passed by, he broke off boxing and walked beside her, mouthing words in her ear. She too ignored him. Suddenly he stopped. The lady walked on. He began pissing into a water fountain. He was standing in front of a picture window, an elegantly restored rowhouse with a gas lantern burning on the porch. A long piss. Cars passed along the street; a couple of teenagers walked by, whispering, sharing secrets. Only I was watching. Finally he zipped and continued along the sidewalk. He walked like an ant—up here and over there, suddenly stopping, reversing direction, zigging and zagging. Once he stopped and shouted 'Hey!' Nobody paid any attention. He pulled a bottle from his back pocket, drained it into his mouth, tossed it into an alley. He crossed a street against the light. I followed when it turned green (couldn't risk a jay-walking ticket). He crossed Penn Center and City Hall and worked his way over to 13th Street.

Another man was sitting on the sidewalk with his feet in the gutter. He wore a shabby gray overcoat. He was old and black and fat. He was conversing eloquently and thoughtfully with a soggy pile of newspaper. 'You talk about God,' he was saying. 'What you know? I tell you 'bout God. He ain't. That's right. God ain't. You better believe it.'

'Hey Frank,' said the boxer. 'Wait up.'

Frank—the mournful theologian—looked up. 'Buster,' he grunted.

'Wait up, Frank,' said Buster the boxer.

'Does it look like I'm leaving?' Frank had a carpet of snow on his shoulders and shoes.

Buster stepped up to Frank, slipping and regaining his balance on the soggy papers that Frank had been entertaining. 'Dumb coon,' said Buster.

'Creamface,' said Frank without looking up from the papers.

'Hottentot,' said Buster, as he stroked his beard.

They traded insults with about as much passion as they would put into trading social security numbers. Buster hunched his shoulders. A suitcoat and a sport shirt weren't enough in this wet snow. He asked, 'Where's Nicolo?'

Frank pointed a thumb over his shoulder.

'He open?'

Frank shrugged.

137

Buster walked up to a window and pounded on the iron grating. 'Nicolo!' he shouted. 'Hey Nicolo!'

Frank resumed his discussion with the newspaper.

I was leaning against a car on the other side of the street. 'Nicolo!' Banging on the grating.

'You know how I know?' Frank was saying. 'I got proof. I was sabed. Yessir. I was sabed at the mission.'

The window opened. A head appeared. A fat man in a red shirt. White stubble of beard.

'Merry Christmas, Nicolo,' said Buster with a big bright smile.

'Beat it,' growled Nicolo. He had a voice like a reindeer's fart.

'We need a jug, Nicolo.' Buster was slapping his sides to keep warm, dancing on his feet.

'Side door,' said Nicolo, and he spat through the grating into the snow.

The window closed. Buster walked around to the side of the building. A door opened. Buster held out both hands, palms up.

'Two dollars,' said Nicolo.

'Uh-huh. Well. You see. Yes.' The big bright smile.

Nicolo narrowed his eyes. 'You got two dollars?'

'Aw. Nicolo. My buddy. My pal. Only one day a year would I ask —'

The door slammed.

Shoulders hunched, hands in pockets, Buster returned to where Frank was holding forth with the newspaper. Snow was sticking to Buster's hair and beard.

'I coulda to-o-old you,' said Frank.

I decided it was time to move on. I pushed off from the car. I sneezed.

Four eyes swung my way. Buster pursed his lips. Frank nodded. Frank made an effort to raise his immense body from the curb, but gravity won out. Buster sprinted up to me.

'Mister,' Buster began, 'I wouldn't ask this of you except I got a daughter she's got cancer and I need —'

'All right.'

138

'She's got cancer you see and if I don't—'

'Here.' Two dollars.

'If I don't pay the doctor they might amputake her arm or something so you see I need—'

'Take it!' Frank shouted from the curb.

Buster took. He purchased an unlabelled gallon jug. He grabbed Frank by the arm. 'Scuse me,' Frank said to the newspaper. Buster pulled him up. I watched. They'd walked two car lengths when Frank noticed I was still standing right where they'd left me. 'C'mon,' Frank waved with a heavy arm.

Buster chimed in: 'Drink to my poor daughter's cancer.'

I didn't mind if I did.

'Say, who *are* you, anyways?' Frank asked.

'I'm Willy.'

Frank leaned toward me sympathetically. 'Ain't you got no friends, Willy?'

'I have a wife.'

Buster and Frank exchanged a look.

'Where?' said Frank.

'What happened?' said Buster, and he handed me the jug.

'She ran away.'

'When?' said Frank.

'Drink,' said Buster.

'About a month ago. Or two. I don't know.' I drank. The stuff was awful.

'Bitch,' said Frank.

'Naw,' said Buster. 'He deserved it. Din't you deserve it, fella?'

'No. Yes. Maybe. Well. I don't know.'

Frank guffawed, 'I think he don't know.'

'She got a problem?' said Buster.

'Buster got a problem,' said Frank. 'He beat on things.'

'And I *pulverize* 'em,' said Buster, smacking his fist into his palm.

Frank clutched his stomach. 'I don't fe-ee-el so good,' he said.

'That's cause you're hungry,' said Buster. 'You got more *room* to be hungry than most folks.'

139

'Keeps me warm.' Frank patted his sides. 'Cold's got further to go fo it touches my heart.'

'Okay,' I said. 'Let's find some food.'

Awe framed Buster's face. 'You got *money?*'

'A little.'

We found an old Horn and Hardart's with tall ceilings and plush booths and real mahogany panelling. We piled our trays with turkey and dressing and mashed potatoes, muffins and salad and Jell-O, milk and apple pie and coffee. We were all so hungry we didn't talk much for a while except to grunt 'Good' or 'Pass the salt.' On the music system, over and over, came Perry Como Christmas carols. Hundreds of them. From where we were sitting, I could see through a window to the kitchen, where an old stoop-shouldered cook with a gigantic chef's hat scooted about and shouted orders to two young assistants. The old man accompanied his orders with a fast chant:

> *Gimme a turkey*
> *Gimme a dressing*
> *Gimme a rummmba rummmba rummm-mmm-ba*
>
> *Gimme a peas*
> *Gimme a gravy*
> *Gimme a rummmba rummmba rummm-mmm-ba.*

Frank was the first to stop eating. He set down his fork with half the food still on his plate. 'I don't fe-ee-el good,' he said.

'You drink too much,' said Buster through a full mouth.

'You talk.' Frank shifted uneasily in the booth. 'Sammy Davis, Junior,' he said calmly.

'Where?' said Buster, chomping and smacking.

'That's the man.'

'Where?'

'Sammy Davis, Junior. That's a man for you.'

'*Where?*' Buster craned his neck, searching the cafeteria.

'Is he *here?*' Frank said, suddenly excited.

'Din't you just *say* he was?'

'I ain't seen him.'

140

Buster resumed eating. 'Dumb coon.'

'Creamface.' Frank picked listlessly at the turkey. 'Sammy Davis, Junior. He can *sing*.'

'Izzat who's singing?'

> *Gimme a bacon*
> *Gimme an omelette*
> *Gimme a rummmba rummmba rummm-mmm-ba.*

Frank sighed. 'I don't fe-ee-el so good.'

'Can I eat your taters?'

'Fo a price.'

'For what?'

'Fo fi minutes wit yo wino mouth shut.'

'Deal.' Buster snatched the plate.

> *Gimme a cranberry*
> *Gimme a squash*
> *Gimme a rummmba rummmba rummm-mmm-ba.*

Frank looked mournfully about the cafeteria.

I followed Frank's gaze. We looked over the wild-eyed woman who lived out of a shopping bag; the saggy-faced man who couldn't speak without coughing and gasping for breath; the shuffling half-wit with rags in his shoes; the woman with skin as gray as shirt cardboard, incontinent, known to the busboy as 'Old Puddleseat,' deaf, her mouth twisted sideways by poor-fitting dentures; the coffee and doughnut man going back for seconds today, because it is Christmas and near the end of the month and he has an extra fifteen cents; the old one-eyed man slowly masticating, open-mouthed, smacking, yellow balls of food rolling over his tongue; the soup slurpers, the finger lickers, the sniffers and coughers and snorters and farters. I felt right at home here. We were all common as potatoes. We would never get a Master Charge card. We would never go to Disneyland. We would never be kissed by a cheerleader.

A woman walked in the door — a young woman, blond, in a white coat.

Frank slapped the table. 'An angel!' He stared.

Buster looked startled. 'Easy, Frank.'

> *Gimme a santy*
> *Gimme a reindeer*
> *Gimme a rummmba rummmba rummm-mmm-ba.*

Frank was struggling to get up. 'Buster! An angel!'

The blond woman in the white coat was filling a styrofoam cup with coffee.

'Buster! Lemme go!'

Buster was holding Frank by the arm. Buster looked at me, shrugged, then shot his eyes up to the ceiling in a what-can-you-do gesture.

'Buster! She's getting away!'

The woman had paid for the coffee and was walking out the door.

'An angel! A fucking angel!' Frank was shouting. People were staring.

The door swung closed. Buster let go.

Frank slid out from the booth. He lumbered for the door, buttoning his coat. 'Hey! Angel! You there! Stop!'

The woman was hailing a cab.

'Frank. Wait.' Buster sighed. He slid out. 'Thanks for saving my daughter.'

'My pleasure.'

'See yez.'

The woman sped off in a cab. Frank tottered to the curb. Buster pulled at his sleeve. I looked down at my cup of coffee, and when I looked up again, they both had disappeared.

On my way back to the hotel, I sensed that I was being followed. I peered over my shoulder from time to time, but nobody was there. Somehow, though, I couldn't shake off the feeling that I was being watched. Considering my legal situation, it was not a comfortable feeling. I tried to tell myself it was a simple attack of paranoia—an occupational hazard of us fugitives. I knew the cure: go to a movie. *Dr. Zhivago* was showing at the Tower. That was the perfect movie for reminding yourself that if you think *you* got problems, buddy, look at the rest of the world. I headed for the subway.

A hand clutched my arm.

I spun around and clenched my fists (Willy Crusoe, street-fighter).

Oh.

It was the duck lady. Her mushroom hair was topped with snow. She was holding a package wrapped in newspaper, tied with a pink ribbon.

'Quack,' she said.

'What?'

'Quack!'

She thrust the package into my hands.

'Huh?'

'Quack.'

'Is this for me?'

'Quack.' She nodded.

'Thank you. I—hey wait.'

She was waddling away.

I walked after her.

There was a policeman a half block away. She walked right up to him. She certainly knew my weakness. I turned and descended to the subway. On the cold gray platform of screeching echoes, standing in front of a giant graffiti reading COWBOY DOLLAR NICK HERBIE DEATH TO THE BETRAYOR, I untied the pink ribbon and tore away the newspaper wrapping. Inside was a plunger. What my father called a Plumber's Friend. To which my mother would always say, 'Drano is the Plumber's Friend.' To which my father would always say, 'The plumber needs all the friends he can get in this house.' To which my mother would always say, 'Amen.'

Amen.

Inside the cup of the plunger was the message: 'Merry Christmas to a Broken Toilet. E.P.M.'

My social security payments finally bounced. I received the news in a crisp telephone call from Ms. Seeger, the personnel manager. She expressed surprise at the fact that I didn't carry my social security card in my wallet. I told her I'd search for it that night and give her the correct number the next morning.

Was she on to me?

At lunch I found out just how deeply Billie was rooted into the grapevine. She leaned across her Low-Cal Fruit Plate with that gigantic tumbleweed of hair spread like an umbrella over the table (smelling of books today, of musty old paper and ink, of the dust that settles on the spine), and she asked, 'What's this about your social security? Elliot was wondering . . .'

And more so was she. It was her first frontal assault.

'News gets around,' I said.

She placed her fingers on my arm. Gently, coaxingly, confidentially, she said, 'Willy . . . What are you hiding?' Her eyes probed. She smiled softly. Fingers lightly touching my arm. I felt the strange pull of her power to suck information from the secret corners of the soul.

But I didn't answer. I reached up with both hands and sank them into that library of hair—thrust them into that warm and intimate explosion of wool. My hands disappeared up to the wrists. There were ears in there. *Ears*.

'Hey—*what*?' She jerked back. She was embarrassed. Flustered. I had invaded her personal space. In a restaurant, yet.

My hands had returned to daylight. I bet mine were the first fingers ever to touch her ears. It was almost like seeing her naked. Entering her. *Knowing* her. I was mesmerized.

'I love your hair.'

She frowned. 'It's ugly.' Nervously she patted the hair where I had touched. Her eyes scanned the restaurant.

'Ugly! My God! It's *fantastic*.'

'Ex—excuse me.'

She ran off to the ladies' room. I had deflected her assault. I was puzzled, though. I'd always assumed she was proud of her hair. I should have known. I was always meeting women who carried themselves as if they knew that they were beautiful and loved to be the center of attention, but who secretly were convinced that they were ugly.

When Billie returned, she made no more mention of social

security. What she did say, though, surprised me: 'When you gonna take me out, Willy?'

I laughed. 'As soon as I check out your reputation. Do you put out?'

'I'll put *you* out.' She smiled.

I studied that silent smile. I couldn't read beyond the lips. Did she mean it? Should I ask her out? I couldn't tell, and I knew I didn't want to do it, so I didn't.

That night I walked through fresh snow to the territory of The Judges. Nobody met me when I entered their block. I searched out the back alley basement clubhouse where Chief Justice had taken me after my encounter with Pinkey the cop. It was dark. I walked around to the front of the house and knocked on the door.

A woman in a golden wig opened the door a chain's length. 'Yeah?'

'Does Chief Justice live here?'

'Yeah.' She disappeared. I heard slippers flopping down a hall. 'Danny! It's a white man.' I heard a muffled reply. 'Yeah. Blond.' More murmuring. 'Well don't bring him in *here*.' Shoes striding toward the door. Chief Justice Ringworm himself.

'Okay, man. The basement.'

He led the way.

Inside the walls still dripped. The table was still covered with *Playboys*. I sat on the moldy sofa.

'What's happening, man?'

I told him I was wondering—I should've thought of this long ago—did he happen to know any way I could get a fake ID?

'Whatcha need?'

'Something. Anything. With a social security number.'

'Social security card? Anything else?'

'Is it that easy?'

'Uh-huh. What else? Driver's license?'

'That would be nice.'

'What name?'

'Willy Crusoe. Wilbur R. Crusoe.'

'Write it down. Pennsylvania license okay? That's the easiest.'

'Fine.' He reminded me of a shop clerk taking orders for a catalog sale. All he needed was a white shirt and a pencil behind his ear.

'Any special number? That costs extra.'

'How long will it take?'

'Usually 'bout a week.'

'Then I need to order a number. I gotta tell somebody tomorrow.'

'Write one down.'

I made one up out of the phone number and street address of my hotel.

'Where do you get them?'

'Po-leece.'

'*Really*?'

'Hey man, this is Philly. Don't you know 'bout Philly?'

I was learning.

'Every time you hear a si-reen, that just means more money changing hands.'

Speaking of money. 'How much is this going to cost?'

Ringworm quoted the rates: 'Fifty for social security. Hundred for the license. And twenty-five each for the number. Least that's what it was last time. In advance. How much is that?'

'Two hundred dollars.'

'How long you need to raise that kind of scratch?'

'Two seconds.' I peeled ten twenties from my pocket.

Ringworm snatched the money and tucked it inside his pocket. I watched the bills disappear and wondered if I was doing the right thing. Could I trust this guy? Sure. He'd already proved himself. Of course I could.

'Okay,' said Chief Justice. 'Now do me a favor.'

'Sure.' Feeling suddenly uneasy.

'Go to Fortieth and Walnut. There's a McDonald's. Okay? See if there's a kid in the McDonald's wearing an orange headband.'

'Is that all?'

146

'If he's there, come back and tell me. Then there's more.'

'Who is he?'

'A Spiderman.'

'Oh.'

I went to Fortieth and Walnut. What a silly errand. These kids were playing games. Territory. Spies. Spidermen. Judges. Comic book games. Rules that go back to the Dark Ages. Welcome to modern civilization. Welcome to McDonald's.

At a table in the corner sat six kids with orange headbands. They weren't eating. Just hanging out. The place was packed — people were eating standing up — but the table next to these six kids was empty. A buffer zone. Nobody wanted to sit there. And it looked like nobody at McDonald's was going to tell these kids to buy something or move on. They reigned supreme, joking and laughing in the corner. Two of them were arm wrestling. Another was folding napkins into paper airplanes.

So they were there. That was all I needed to know. Mission accomplished. But as long as I was there, I decided to buy a hamburger. And fries. And a vanilla shake. And — hey — an apple pie.

I sat at the empty table in the buffer zone next to the six Spidermen. They paid no mind to me. I ate the hamburger. A burly black kid wearing a green varsity jacket sat down at my table. He had a fish sandwich. He seemed aggressive and alert. His muscles were taut. His gaze was steady. A sudden hush had fallen over the crowded room. I saw some children edging toward the door. I heard a sound like the growling of a dog from the table of Spidermen behind me. My varsity companion eyed them coldly. A napkin airplane glided over my shoulder and struck Mr. Varsity on the temple.

'Hey,' he said.

Softly from the Spider table: 'Huh muhfuck?'

The next thing I knew, two tables had overturned, blood was flowing from one eye and three noses, and I was running as fast as I could down Fortieth Street while a siren screamed down Walnut. They hadn't touched me. I felt like a protected species. Like I'd been in the eye of a hurricane — momentarily — and then without lingering for the full weather report I'd made one sideways leap and two running steps and I was out the door.

I breathlessly reported my adventure to Chief Justice. He listened attentively. He reached into his pocket and pulled out a slip of paper. 'Go back tomorrow. Okay?'

'Will they be there?'

'If they ain't daid.' He handed me the slip of paper. 'Give this to the big one.'

'They're *all* big.'

'One's bigger. Okay? He's got a red *and* an orange headband.'

'What'll he do when I give it?'

'He'll take it.'

'What'll he do to *me*?'

'Nothin'.'

'You sure?'

'Uh-huh.'

'What if he does something anyway?'

'He won't.'

'How do you know?'

'He just won't. Okay? You chickenshit?'

'No.' Yes. He seemed sure. He seemed to think it was out of the question that any harm could come to me. 'What is this?'

'Take a look.'

One side of the paper was blank. On the other side was nothing but a solid black circle, crayoned.

'So?'

'It's the Black Spot.'

Then I remembered. The Black Spot. Yo-ho-ho, and a bottle of rum. I wondered if their teachers knew what use was being made of the literature they forced these kids to read.

I returned to Fortieth and Walnut the next day. I was terrified. I had no faith in any code of honor among these gangs. I only went because I owed Ringworm a big favor. It occurred to me how odd it was that I was so scared of some kids and not of the police. Police were something to be avoided. They were

148

the interface between freedom and bureaucracy. Gangs, though, now gangs were something to be scared of. No bureaucracy there. Just knives and chains and guns. Or just hands, when you know how to use them. Me, I didn't know, except how to hold a pop bottle. And somehow I figured it would take more than a bottle of Royal Crown Cola to hold off six Spidermen, even more than a bottle and a Black Spot combined. Fifteen men on the dead man's chest—yo-ho-ho and a bottle of Royal Crown. The dead man's chest. The dead man.

When I reached the McDonald's, I gave myself no time to think. I marched right up to the table of six headbands. Sure enough, one was bigger, and he had a red and an orange band. He was tearing a Big Mac box into tiny pieces. He had a spider drawn on the back of one hand.

'Uh . . . Excuse me.'

Twelve eyes swung up at me. The big one spoke: 'Huh, muhfuck?'

I held out the paper, folded in half. 'For you.'

He took it.

Good. I was afraid I'd have to force it on him.

He opened it.

My knees shook.

He scowled, flipped the Black Spot onto the table.

'You better go,' he said.

I went.

A week later I returned to Chief Justice. In the basement he gave me my cards and told me that Clarkie was dead.

'Who?'

'Clarkie. Okay? They got Clarkie.' He seemed annoyed.

'Who got him?'

'Spidermen. We got two of them. One in the spine. One just in the leg.'

'You *shot* them?'

'Uh-huh.'

'Is this some kind of a *war*?'

'I think it's over.' He looked very tired. Without looking

149

grateful, he said, 'Thanks for your help.'

'Sure. Any time.' Never. I'd been planning to ask Ringworm if he could help me find the duck lady—I spent every night looking, since Christmas—but I decided I didn't want to owe any more favors.

'Come around if you need anything.'

'Sure.' I went to the door. I was thinking of John, of sign-stealing. Little teen-age pranks. *Gang war*. Shot in the *spine*. I guess it depends on the neighborhood.

'So long, Blondy.' He grinned.

'Hey. Speaking of hair.' I couldn't resist. I stood at the door.

'Huh?'

'Why do you keep it so short?'

He scowled. 'What's wrong with it?'

'Nothing. Nothing wrong with it.'

'You meddlin'.'

'No. I—Yes. Right.'

'We don't allow no *meddlin'*.'

'Sorry.' I started to leave.

'It's my scars. Right?'

I stopped again. 'You had ringworm.'

'Nope. Fight. Some guy busted my head.'

'Jeez.'

'That's all right. You shoulda seen what happened to *him*.'

I didn't ask for details. I put my hand on the door. 'Well. Thanks for . . . everything.' We both knew we'd never see each other again. 'Let me know if I can do anything for you. And have a—' I opened the door. 'Have a nice life.'

It had been a mistake to give Ace my real social security number. Even though I now had a new number, the damage had been done. For all I knew, my name was already buried in a stack of computer printouts lying on some desk in the FBI office. Sooner or later, they'd track me down. Besides, my new number would bounce eventually, too, and then there would be more questions than I could answer. A curse on these numbers. If I have children—if I find Erica—if she

150

wants to try again — a thousand ifs — she will give birth in her own home, her own bed. There will be no hospital record, no birth certificate — no numbers — even if we can't register the kid for school without them (small loss) — even if we can't claim a tax deduction (smaller loss) — even if the kid has to fight all his life to prove his existence . . . But that's just the problem. The poor kid would have to battle all his days. He would be more free with a number than without it.

At lunch Billie was recounting how she had been searching for a folder in Elliot's filing cabinet. The drawer was marked HARDWARE SPECS. Inside were wrestling magazines, a jar of decaffeinated freeze-dried coffee, a Western Auto catalog, Jimmy Lareeno's transistor radio, a framed glossy eight by ten color photo of Elliot and his wife in their wedding clothes, and the folder labelled 'Update — Accounts Payable.' She opened the folder and out fell a bloodstained lady's nylon panty. 'I picked it up off the floor and was holding it between two fingers — like this — wondering what in the *world* — and in walks *Elliot*! I like to died. And he says — he just looks at me calmly — he says, "Accounts Payable is in the top drawer." And out he goes. I swear. What's in that man's head. He won't be around too much longer. I heard Walt saying. Elliot's in the squeeze. You're next. You'll get the promo.'

'I'm quitting.'

'*When*?' Her eyes shone like headlights. She leaned across the table. Her face was taut. Her hair carried the smoke of Walt Parker's cigar.

'Soon.'

'*When*?' She was not to be deprived of her scoop. Her eyes sucked at my knowledge.

'Maybe right now.'

'Leaving town?' Sucking.

'Might.'

Calmly she announced: 'Willy Middlebrook.'

I think I jumped two feet.

'Thought so.'

'How'd *you* know?'

She grinned with pride.

151

'The social security thing?'

She nodded. Victorious.

'And *they* know?'

'No. They don't add two plus two. Me, I'm the suspicious type.'

'I'm definitely quitting right now. Tell Walt I'm going to make like a banana. And split. What *else* do you know?'

She grinned, white flash of teeth shining in that incredible blackness:

'I don't think you know any more.'

'I know you take yourself mighty serious.' She was pointing a finger at me. 'I know you got something to hide. I know you white boys don't grow up with enough troubles, so you got to make some of your own. Yeah, I know that. You think it's exciting. It's *romantic*. It makes you feel like you're really doing something. Troubles are a *game* for you. You know any time you want you can stop playing. You can get a good lawyer. You can go to Canada. Your skin is your ticket. You can get back on the train any time you want. You're a Weatherman, aren't you?'

'No.'

Her eyes widened. But she came back. 'You're a draft-dodger.'

'No.'

'Deserter.'

'No.'

Her eyes narrowed. She whispered, so softly I had to read her lips: 'Symbionese Liberation Army?'

Whispering back: 'No.'

'Then why are you hiding? You got too many parking tickets?'

'I haven't done anything.'

'There. See?'

'I'm wanted. For killing a cop.'

'But you didn't.'

'Right.'

'See? It's a *game*. You *love* it. You want to ride boxcars—you want to huddle in a shack with sleet pounding

152

on the roof—hide in shadows—hide and seek—use passwords
—be *scared*—when you're scared you know you're alive—like
a kid in a haunted house—you want to get *dirty*—you wish
you were *black*. Touch it. Feel it. Go on. Touch my arm.'

I fingered the skin.

'Is it different?'

Actually, it was. I rubbed up and down the inside of her
forearm. It was more . . . tight. Amazing. I was absorbed,
fascinated by this skin, and was totally unprepared when she
pulled her arm back and spoke again.

'Guess you aren't gonna marry me.'

'Marry!'

'Thought so.' She wound her hands deep into her hair—
where I had once touched. She caught my eye and held it in
an unbreakable gaze. She smiled. Softly, almost tenderly, she
said, 'You stupid idiot.'

I never returned to work after lunch. I went to my hotel. I
took a bath. I shaved. I washed my ridiculous hair. I clipped
my nails. I sat on the toilet for an hour and a half. I went out.
Took a walk. Went to a movie. Ate three pastrami-on-rye-
with-coleslaw-and-russian-dressing sandwiches at Stanley
Greens. Took another walk. The sky was clear. Even through
the glow of the city I could see Orion and Cassiopeia and even
the Pleiades. I went to my room. I slept. Woke at dawn. Went
down to the coffee shop fifteen minutes before opening time.
They let me in anyway. They knew me. I gave big tips. Over-
tipping, some call it with a sneer. Snobs. I feel sorry for
waitresses. It's an awful job. So I tip twenty, twenty-five
per cent, buck minimum. Whatever. I had an omelette and
scrapple and silver dollar pancakes and two cups of coffee. I
started walking. A slushy day. Rush hour. Faces of pain. The
Philadelphia grimace. Roaring buses. Howling trucks.
People who honk. Everybody honks. Kids. Catholic uni-
forms. Pimply girls. Pretty. Hoods. Vandals. Endless graffiti.
Shouts. Running. Fight. Sudden quiet. Rush hour over. The
day begins. The hum of work. The smoke of factories. The
shuffle of women with shopping bags. The raw hatred of men

153

in cars. The pulse and pattern of a city. The city. This city. Streets named Passyunk or Moyamensing, Isseminger or Mole. Red brick rowhouses for block after block, white wooden porches, white sunrooms, white window frames, white mounds of snow piled on the curb. Drawn curtains. Some people live their lives behind drawn curtains. Here on the street you can see your breath. Your ears get cold. You sink your hands deep into the pockets of your Navy jacket. You slip on ice. You smell the wind off the Delaware River. You watch a freighter — a giant wall of black and rust — slipping through the water toward — where? Where would you like to go?

In a cheese shop along the Ninth Street Market I bumped into the duck lady. Literally bumped. She blinked. Wart on her eyelid.

'Excuse me,' I said automatically.

'Quack,' she said. She turned to go.

'*Where's Erica?*'

She was walking, bobbing away. I followed. She walked. She paid no attention to me. She weaved among stalls, buying nothing, peering into the eyes of fish on ice, squeezing apples, sniffing spices. She walked on. Her breath appeared in little puffs. She wandered up Ninth and down South Street by little antique stores, little galleries, an ice cream factory. She stopped at every garbage can and quickly peered inside as if glancing over a table of contents. Occasionally her eyes would rest on an interesting title, and her hand would dart into the can and flip to the page and extract a broken umbrella or a woman's left shoe or a sweater with half a sleeve. These she stashed in a blue shopping bag. She ambled through the quiet of Independence Mall, crossed the madness of Market Street. Under the Reading Terminal, the heavy still air of the market, the rumble of trains, a booth selling jugs of cloudy apple cider, jars of honey labeled Wildflower, Safflower, Orange, Buckwheat, Clover. Back to the street. Stores selling bins of can openers and paperweights. Adult movies. Bars. Adult books. Kelly's Restaurant — a glance in the window — booths jammed with shoppers and office girls — a glass of wine

154

and a sea food lunch. Not for us. She walks on. Under the lunatic arches of City Hall—fitting symbol of government—useless columns under flower-sculptured pedestals and cornices, statues of cherubs and eagles, lightning rods, coats of arms, bizarre engraved mottoes—all form and no function—heavy with stone, unadaptable, slow-witted, but permanent, stubborn and strong, impervious, weathering wave after wave of lashing storms, violent protest, blatant graft, incompetence, corruption, indifference. Over the Schuylkill River, the creeping grumbling expressway. Suddenly down to the subway. I run to follow. Darkness underground. My home. Silver cars, torn seats—they've been slashed, then covered with graffiti. Swaying listlessly. Daylight. Above ground. Off at Sixty-third Street. Walking under the tracks, deafening screech of trains, over Cobbs Creek, by a monolithic Sears. A dead pigeon lies on the sidewalk, one wing torn completely off. The town of Millbourne—one block wide and six blocks long—fiercely white. A doughnut store. She goes in. A young woman behind the counter, blond hair in a bun, smiling, missing one front tooth. She knows the duck lady. She gives her a bag of day old doughnuts. 'Don't tell the boss. Hear?' She winks. The duck lady nods. I buy a bag and follow her out. Chocolate doughnuts. Cream-filled doughnuts. Jelly doughnuts. Sugar and cinnamon and plain doughnuts. A baker's dozen. One is covered with coconut. I throw it to a funny-looking dog—like a cross between a skunk and a beagle. Sixty-ninth Street. Upper Darby. She boards a bus. I follow. We ride. I eat doughnuts. Over the Schuylkill again, and Wissahickon Creek. Off the bus. Wandering the streets of Manyunk. Old river town. Sun-washed houses. A cat in a window. Grape Street. A corner grocery. The duck lady enters. The door swings, a bell rings. An old lady smiles and nods. The duck lady nods. The old lady babbles. She smiles and nods and babbles at the duck lady. She speaks words but not sentences. She is an idiot. Her breasts hang down like sacks of flour. She is pleasant. The duck lady passes time with her, nodding at intervals, folding her hands over the loop of the shopping bag. I read the backs of boxes of cereal. Finally

155

we leave. We board another bus. I'm lost. Then we transfer to a streetcar. We are in Germantown. Slowly we jerk downtown. The city spreads endlessly away from us—teeming, rotting, boarded, brown—millions of human souls—living and dying and fucking and watching television—sinking into the oblivion of this decaying festering uninspired city, medieval Philly, sinking and sucking us down, sapping our energy, our will to survive, the forces of life . . .

Suddenly we step off the streetcar. The duck lady is going down steps to a basement room in a row house on a street called Naudain. She unlocks the door. I am standing right behind. As the door gives, she turns to face me. She looks sadly into my eyes. Raising an unsteady hand, once again she touches my hair (now dark at the roots). We enter. A single room. Piles and piles of sheets and blankets and clothing and rags. Smell of damp cloth. In a corner, amid a pile of blankets half under and half over, lies the face of a girl with electric eyes and long brown hair.

'About time,' she says.

I sit on the bed. She offers her hand. I hold it between both of mine.

'I ain't crazy,' she says.

'I know.'

'I ain't burned out, either. But . . . sometimes . . . I just feel . . . kinda . . . low down . . .'

The duck lady gives her the bag of day old doughnuts. Erica pushes them aside. She's lost weight. Maybe twenty pounds.

'Kin you flush?'

'Not yet.'

She pulls her hand away.

'Is that why you're hiding? Is that the only reason?'

I think she shakes her head. I'm not sure. Her cheeks are hollow. Hands bony. Eyes sunken—but charged with fire. No matter how crazy, how sullen and withdrawn she becomes, there is always the fire somewhere deep in her soul, and once I have met her eyes and glimpsed the fire I know she will come back, she will shake off her demon, become Erica once more.

The fire is Erica. The fire is the woman I love. The mystery in the flames, the benevolent warmth, the flashing intensity, life-giving heat and skin-searing danger, burning independent and alone and yet consuming its fuel, its own source of life — and the brighter she burns, the faster she destroys her own source of life. I hovered over my fire, warming my hands and suddenly realizing that I had been babbling my thoughts, speaking my love to Erica as I analyzed it to myself.

She was regarding me with detachment. Barely listening. She is not burdened with the need to know about love, to talk about it and define it.

I asked, 'Will you talk to me?'

She nodded.

'Will you tell me why you're here?'

For a moment she turned within herself, and then came back with what she had found: 'Cuz . . . I want . . .' She abandoned the struggle. 'Cuz of the bus.'

That was not the reason. I had slapped her hand away on the bus. For that she didn't run away and hide and stop eating for a month. But the slap had started something. Perhaps it had given her a glimpse of the vast separation between our souls, between everybody's souls, between her and her father and mother, between her and her brothers and sisters living and dead, between her and the boyfriend who dumped her in Cincinnati, the doctors who treated her and mistreated her, the duck lady who sheltered her. We are all alone within ourselves.

'I'm sorry for the bus.'

She nodded. 'It's okay.'

'Will you come with me now?'

She shook her head. 'Not yet.'

'When?'

'Soon.'

'Can I come back again?'

'Gimme a while.'

'Can I have a doughnut?'

She handed me one from the bag.

'Would you like one, too?'

She smiled sheepishly. She took one for herself, though she only nibbled at it.

I was elated. And I was proud of my self-control. When I had visited her at Mushroom Mountain, when she'd had the relapse after the baby died, we only fought with each other. It was so easy for us to get mad. One wrong word. Control is the key.

I finished the doughnut. I took her hand. 'I'll see you later.' Squeezed her hand. 'Maybe in a week.' Knowing I couldn't rush her. 'Maybe two.'

I leaned over and met those eyes and kissed her on the lips. The eyes closed. She kissed back. Then the eyes burst open. A hand pushed me away.

'Quit yer kissin' on me.' But she smiled. 'Now go tune the fiddle.'

I went. Self-control. I walked the wintry streets as night fell on the city. I felt alive and hopeful and full of possibility. And also, as city crowds surged about me, as people ran for buses and lined up for movies and glanced at me from warm windows, I felt alone. I felt restless. I felt . . . something else. Something for which there is no word because it is so fleeting that no one can catch it long enough to name it. I stared in a window at a man tossing pizza dough. I walked on. If I'd been a smoker, I would've lit up. If I'd been a drinker, I'd have ordered a stiff one. I guess I'm a walker. I walked to the docks and along the river and back through Society Hill.

I ate at a cafe.

I went back to my room and masturbated.

It is probably the stupidest thing I've ever done. I had not healed. Now I was back where I had started, if not worse. I wiped up the blood, moving gingerly with shooting pains. As I rubbed a towel over the sheets, my head was clear and thinking of ironies—how pleasure brings pain—love brings hate—obstacles beget love—romance, the death wish—how I had just committed—temporarily at least—symbolically—self-inflicted—sexual suicide. It all ties in. Miss Putts would be proud.

* * *

No jobs. While my back was turned the bottom had fallen out of the economy. I'd been too busy with my own life to care about Mideast wars, oil prices, recession. Suddenly it mattered. I couldn't find work. No listings in the want ads. I tried an agency. They sent me to Boeing, but when I arrived at the gate, there were a hundred and fifty men and women in line already. I couldn't compete with that kind of a situation. I needed to lie, to deal on a personal level, to snow the employer. I couldn't even use Ace for a reference, or I'd risk tipping off the FBI.

I tried some nearby towns. No jobs in Norristown. None in Lancaster. None in Harrisburg, Wilmington, Newark. I still had a lot of the money my father had given me, but I didn't want to fritter it away. I tried to find some other type of work. I applied for a fry cook opening. They wanted somebody with experience. I told them I'd been a fry cook for three years on the West Coast. They told me to put on an apron. In ten minutes it was obvious I had no experience. A seasoned cook is a skilled worker.

After two weeks of fruitless jobhunting, I decided to see Erica again. I felt calm. I felt controlled. I could handle it. The night was overcast, foggy. Haloes around streetlights. Car headlight beams spread into a cloudy glow. Naudain Street. I crouched before a basement window to peer between parted curtains. The duck lady was stirring a pot of stew on the stove. Erica was sitting on the edge of the bed, giving herself a sponge bath. She was picking some lint out of her belly button. She was scrubbing her knee. She was flicking hair off her shoulder. An old radio was playing the Chiffons, the Shirelles, the Orlons. So fine. So fine. Yeah babe. Your love's so doggone fine, sends those chills up and down my spine. Oh she was lovely, sponging a soapy thigh.

The duck lady answered my knock, bowed stiffly, and motioned for me to come in. The room was steam hot.

'Hey there,' Erica said from across the room. She was sponging her little tennis ball breasts. Raspberry nipples. Tart memories. 'Thought you'd be back. Come set a spell.'

I set. It was an old wicker rocker that squeaked and

groaned and fairly screamed in agony when I rocked back. I sat and rocked and held my tongue. There were a hundred things I wanted to say, but I wanted to let Erica control the situation. I knew I couldn't force her to come with me. If I tried to push, she'd just dig in her heels. Most important, I had to hold my temper. Remembering conversations with my mother. Family insanity. Watch out. Trouble was, I'm not exactly a master of diplomacy. I can't be subtle. But then, neither could Erica. First thing she did was part her thighs and point at her soapy thicket. 'Kin you make babies?'

'I did something stupid when—'

'Don't wanna hear it.'

'Why is it so important? What does it matter if—'

'Why does it matter! Are you a man or a whadoyacallit?'

'I'm still a man.'

'You're a whadoyacallit.'

'You want another baby?'

Pouting. 'I want yourn.'

'You'll get it. We just have to wait.' I wanted one, too. Several. Not babies—I'm not wild about babies—but children. Little friends. I wanted progeny. I don't know why.

Crossing her legs. 'I'm waitin'.'

'Can't you wait with me?'

'You went and 'bandoned me.'

'*I* abandoned *you*?'

'You 'bandoned me and got some job and been makin' all this money and livin' in some fancy hotel—'

'It's a dump!'

'And eatin' fancy food and makin' all this money and all your rich friends—all the horsey set—you been playin' polio and drinkin' their bourbon—'

'Polo.'

'Yeah. Playin' polio and drinkin' their bourbon and makin' love to their women—you got some colored woman with hair like an atom bomb—drivin' them fast cars and makin' cocktails—'

'How do *you* know?'

Erica nodded her head in the direction of the duck lady,

160

who was standing at the stove with her back to us.

'Can she *talk?*'

'She don't need to.'

'How does she—'

'She kinda . . . explicates . . .'

Explicates?

'How does she—I mean what does—why . . .'

'Ferget how. Ferget why.'

'But I mean what does she . . .'

But Erica wasn't listening. She was kneeling on the floor, extending her fingers and making clucking noises at a rat that was edging toward her, sniffing, whiskers twitching. She coaxed it up to her fingers and into her hand. She placed it on her shoulder. It ran under her hair.

'That's Ron. Ronny Rat.'

It was an ugly old Philadelphia rat, fat and gray with white blotches on the tail. I shivered to see it run over her naked skin.

'Wanna meet him?'

'Nope.'

'City boy.'

Even in the city she could tame the wildlife, talk to the mourning doves. And the duck lady. Mourning dove of Philadelphia.

Erica removed the rat from her hair, quickly towelled herself, and pulled a cotton dress over her head.

'Dinner ready?'

The duck lady was ladling the stew into three bowls. She wiped her hands on her dress. She spoke to Erica: 'Quack-quack.'

'Wanna eat with us?'

We sat at a table that was missing one leg. I had to be careful not to lean on it, or the whole thing would come tumbling down. The duck lady chewed slowly and thoughtfully, shifting her eyes from me to Erica and back to me again. I found myself telling Erica about something I hadn't thought of in years: how John and I used to walk over Volkswagens, back when they were new and strange and 'foreign.'

161

When we saw one coming down the street, we'd stand in the middle of the road to force it to stop, and then we'd simply step from bumper to hood to roof and off. Really shook up the drivers. We'd walk away without looking back. I don't know how we got started. It was just something we did during a certain phase of our lives.

'I had a phase,' Erica said.

'What?'

'Immortality.'

'You used to be immortal?'

'Wanted to be. I useta write my name, age, height and weight on a slip of paper and stuff it in a chink in the wall or a crack in the floor boards, or I'd go out and stick it in the holler of a tree or under a boulder. Once my uncle visited from Michigan, and I hid one in his car. Probably still in Detroit somewheres.'

'And that made you live forever?'

'Sorta. Somehow.'

'That reminds me of something I believed when I was little. I don't know how but somehow I got it in my head that I had to stand naked for one minute in every room in my house — and that no one could know about it. So I'd sneak into a room, strip, and stand there for a minute. Every room and every closet. And the basement and the attic.'

She snickered. 'I can just see you standing there with your little pecker.'

'There's some weird forces driving our lives. I don't have any idea why—'

'To make you live forever?'

'No. Nothing like that. No reason at all that I can figure out.'

'I don't ever want to die, Willy.'

'You know what else I used to think? I used to think water towers were full of applesauce. That's one of my earliest memories.'

'*Don't ever let me die, Willy.*'

'I won't.'

'We'll have a baby.'

'Uh-huh.'

'You dumb fuck.'

'We will. We can.'

'Look what happened last time.'

'That was . . . bad luck. It won't happen again.'

'It was you. I thought it was me, but it weren't. It was you.'

'It wasn't either of us. It wasn't anybody's fault.'

'Go play polio. Lookit us. Lookit how she lives.'

'*I don't play polo! I don't have a girlfriend! I don't live in a fancy hotel!*'

'Git.'

'Will you come?'

'No.'

'Let's go to the mountains. Let's talk to the doves. Remember the doves?'

'No.'

So. She denied the doves. She *couldn't* deny the doves. 'I'm bringing you with me.'

'I'll fight. I'll run away. I'll scream. I'll git a cop. I ain't going. You cain't make me.'

'Remember the tent show? The woman rolling on the floor? Is that you?'

'No. It's you.'

I hated her.

'I hate you,' she said. *Damn her.* Reading my thoughts.

I wasn't thinking. I was feeling. There are times when our actions are inevitable. There is no control. No thought. I had to get away. I had to get her away. I hated her. She hated me. We were in love. If she wouldn't leave, I would. If you don't run, you don't live.

Erica was laughing. 'Go buy some balls.'

'What are you trying to—'

'Lookit this dump.'

'Here. How much do you want? I've got seventeen hundred dollars. How much?'

'You cain't buy me.'

'I'm not *buying* you! I'm *giving* you *money!* Here!'

I threw the whole wad at her. Snowing twenties. Suddenly I

163

felt free and lightheaded. I went to the door. I could have flown.

'I'm coming back.'

'I'll call for the cops.'

'You drive me crazy.'

'That's cuz I *am* crazy.'

'You're *not* crazy.'

'*Some*body is.'

'I'll buy that.'

Penniless, furious, I walked out the door. Penniless. Not a penny. Yet somehow light and unbonded like a leaf suddenly dropping, drifting in the wind over golden autumn fields I'd yearned to cover during all the green summer— drained of sap—wrenched from the branch in a sudden gust of wind, a flurry of twenty dollar bills—the stem popped from the pocket—the fresh breeze—sunlight—swirling—crisp air—flying—a mad plunge . . .

LEONARD AND CLYDE, just out of jail
Clyde picked his nose with a ten penny nail
Leonard read a Bible, said, 'Hear me, oh Lord,
Take me to Heaven in this Forty-nine Ford.'

   Mother America
   What have you done?
   All of your children
   Out on the run.

A long distance call come from Heaven one day
Saint Pete calling Clyde, 'Boy I'm comin' your way.'
Clyde say, 'Hey Pete, you know I'm doin' just fine
Baby you just go your way and I'll just go mine.'

   Mother America
   Oh say can you see
   Life is so short
   We got to be free.

— Tony's Dance Band

THE HIGH WAY

I ran. I lived. I was now a card-carrying American. I had a driver's license and social security card. A citizen of the City of the United States. Son of Mother America.

A housepainter in paint-splattered coveralls drove me in a paint-splattered station wagon out the Schuylkill to King of Prussia. He drove with two feet—right on the gas, left on the brake. First he'd floor the gas pedal and shoot up to ninety-five; then he'd weigh in on the brake and ease up at forty. He did this over and over in a regular rhythm like a sailor who was homesick for the crashing of sea waves against the hull of a ship. Landlubber Crusoe soon became seasick. The house-painter matched his two-footed driving with two-handed eating. He steered with his belly. That is, he held the car on a straight line by jamming his belly against the wheel and only using his hands to turn. Otherwise the hands were occupied by an orange and a can of beer. First a mouthful of beer, then a chomp at the orange. Three beers, three oranges by the time we lurched into King of Prussia. He offered me some, but I told him I hadn't found my sealegs yet. He looked at me strangely. I was too woozy to explain. When I got out, though, I did pocket two oranges and a beer. I had to take what I could get. I had nothing but the clothes on my back and a blue Navy jacket.

Two nuns gave me a lift to Downingtown in a black Chev-rolet with—of course—a plastic Jesus. The windows were rolled up tight. The car smelled of stale menstruation. Do nuns have periods? Do they bleed, or are their veins filled with freon? I asked for money. They said they'd say an *Ave* or something.

166

A fat man took me to Harrisburg. I sat in back. His wife filled the rest of the front seat. She was the classic fat lady: bleached hair, harlequin eyeglasses, lips a permanent pucker punctured by a cigarette, flaming red lipstick staining the filter tip, empty plastic cocktail glass on the dash, thumbing through a lurid magazine—'Buried Alive After Sex Session!' —while the fat man spoke over his shoulder to me. 'Just think. Wouldn't it be somepin if the price of clothes went up so high everybody had to walk around *nekkid*. Then we'd see what everybody *really* looks like. I hear in those nudy colonies, ninety per cent of the people are *ugly* when you see 'em with all their clothes off.' I asked for money. He gave me seven bucks. In a week they were flying to Vegas. I wished them luck.

A man in a gray suit. I asked him what he did.

'I'm in marketing.'

'What's that?'

He pointed at a black satchel. 'I go around. Show samples. Make sales.'

'Oh. You're a salesman.'

'No. I'm in marketing.'

'But you—'

'We don't call it that any more.'

I let it go. I couldn't complain. He bought me dinner in Carlisle.

A white Mustang. A beautiful dark girl sucking her fingertips. Long silver nails. Mysterious eyes. Could I? Would she?

'Where you from?' she said, removing fingers from lips.

'I dunno. Nowhere.'

She looked at me full face. The car swerved. 'You're from nowhere?'

'Seems like it.'

Her eyes returned to the road again. 'See that?'

'What?'

'There.'

'Where?' I was searching the road ahead.

'Not there. Here.' In the pocket of the door, next to her

167

thigh (thin, tan, slipping into a white miniskirt). A gun.

'What's that for?'

'Don't mess.'

'I won't. Don't worry. I promise.'

Prying a fingertip back into her mouth, the nail pressing into her upper lip. 'Coming from nowhere. Cripes.'

A men's room in Breezewood. At the urinal next to me a short jolly yellow-haired man was searching, fumbling in his fly. He seemed to be lost in the layers of shirttails and undershirt and shorts. 'I think it's here somewhere,' he muttered. 'Useta be. I know it was there last time I looked. Heh heh.' He winked at me. 'This is what you call fly fishing.'

I forget what kind, but it was a middle class car. Solid. Heavy. Quiet. And he was a middle class man. Educated. Friendly. He was talking about his wife: 'She's a Hungarian refugee. She's finishing a novel. She wants to make films. Not movies. Films. Very important. Films. She has moods. You've got to watch out for those moods.' He ticked his tongue. 'She used to be in women's lib but she couldn't figure out what she believed about it. It's like that.' He grinned wryly to himself. 'She hates materialism. She made me buy a washer and dryer and microwave oven. She's finishing a novel. Wants to make films.'

'Can I get personal?'

'You bet.'

'Do you love her?'

'Very much.'

A Detroit speedster. A necktie draped from the rear view mirror. The radio tuned to whatever was loudest. Weaving the lanes. Eighty. Eighty-five. Ninety. Eyes sucking up the road, estimating distances, speeds, openings. Fierce concentration. Fierce driving. No seatbelts. A weather report: 'It's snowing in Idaho. There's black ice in Nevada, rain in Oregon and Washington, snowy patches in Colorado. Berthoud Pass is closed. The Eisenhower Tunnel is open. Donner Pass is open; chains are required. Wyoming and Utah have six to twelve foot drifts. In Montana most of the state will have high temperatures below zero today. There's a cold front sweeping down across the Midwest. Heavy snows are predicted . . .'

'Where you going?' said my driver.

'West.'

A chatty man. We talked for an hour. I don't remember one word he said, nor one thought that I had. I don't even know what he looked like. It was successful socializing. Nothing — not a thing — communicated.

A small cafe. I had one quarter. A middle-aged woman was behind the counter. She was chatting with a woman on a stool who was blowing on a cup of coffee. 'I tell you,' she was saying, 'it's really something. I been on the wagon a week. Got drunk last night on three glasses of water.'

She strolled down the counter to where I sat with my quarter.

'Want a menu?'

'How much is coffee?'

'Fifteen.'

'And that doughnut. How much is that?'

'Twenty-five.'

'Just coffee.' I plunked the quarter onto the counter.

'Here.' She swept up the quarter and served me coffee and the doughnut. 'I'm ashamed to charge two bits for a doughnut.'

People are kind. I must remember. People are usually kind.

A pickup truck with KELLY'S PLUMBING & HEATING on the door. I climbed in back. There was already a couple in there. It was night. The wind whistled around the cab. The sky was clear and black and starry. We huddled under a blanket. A toilet bowl slid from side to side across the back of the truck as we swung around curves. The girl had blue lipstick. The guy had a mohawk hair cut. We were all shivering.

The girl lit a joint between her blue lips. We smoked it down. We hadn't said a word. The boy got out of the blanket and came around to my other side. Now I was between them. They pressed close. Still we shivered. The boy lay his head back. He looked like he was asleep. The girl slid her hand up my thigh. I looked in her eyes. She looked into mine. Stoned. Expressionless. She rubbed my thigh.

'He's broke,' said the boy.

The girl took her hand away.

I looked at the boy.

'We were gonna rip you off,' he said.

'Pickpocket?'

'Uh-huh. Bet you didn't notice.'

The girl produced another joint. We smoked all the way to Wheeling.

WHEELING

Wheeling again. Cloudy, gray Wheeling. Tired old Wheeling. The river. The mountains. The land. The land. There was always the land. The house up the hill.

Mrs. Patman: 'She won't come with yew? Well, *carry* her.'

'I can't force her.'

Mrs. Patman was heating a pan of milk on the old black stove. 'What's she weigh now? Ninety?'

'Looked better than that. A hundred ten. She's eating.'

'That child. I swear. You kids. Why do you do it?'

I shifted in my seat, a wobbly, straight-backed chair. I couldn't get comfortable. 'Why does anybody do anything?'

'People do what they want to do, Willy boy.'

'I don't think she does. I know I don't.'

'It ain't what you know, it's what you do. People do what they want to do.' She poured the milk into two beer mugs and spooned in the honey.

'I think she wants to be with me,' I said. 'And I know I want to be with her.'

'Mebbe. And this is the second time you've run out on her. She's there, and you're here. And here you set and tell me you all want to be together.'

'I love her.' Warming my hands on the mug. Still a little too hot for my lips.

'People do what they want to do.'

'You think we're crazy.'

'The whole world's crazy. Folks say they want to do one thing, then they go and do something else. Mr. P says he wishes he could be home with me, then he buys that truck and

171

goes away thirty days on a time. Because he wants to. He *cain't* admit it. *Nobody* admits it. But people do what they want to do. And if they're unhappy, they got no one to blame but themselves.'

'I'm unhappy.'

'Ha ha. Yore all right.'

'You think I love her?'

'Yep. Yore a *fine* pair.'

'Meaning we're both nuts.'

'Didn't say that.'

'Should I go back?'

'You figger it out.'

'I'll go back in a few months, if she's still there.'

'Ha ha!' When she laughed, her face was all crinkles.

I could sip it now. Oh my it was good. But I set it down so I could talk. 'Really. I'd like to know. What do *you* think I should do?'

'What you want to do.'

'Is that what you do? Do you want to be stuck at home raising a hundred kids 'til your hands are shaking and your knees won't hold you, while Mr. P's out there at some truck stop right now drinking coffee and winking at the waitress?'

She smiled. 'I could leave.'

'You can't! The kids—'

'Oh Willy.' She patted my hand. 'Drink your honey milk 'fore it gets cold.'

172

OUT WEST

Really moving now. I spent my days swept up in a gale of cars
and trucks, following the prevailing winds, sometimes swinging out in an eddy, always marvelling at the constant motion
over this land — Brownian motion it seemed — where are they
all going? Why? What pulls them? What is the mysterious
force that draws men and women? The salmon runs the
spawning stream; the bird follows the ancient flyways; the
wolf howls at the moon; the faith healer's touch, the mystic's
vision — forces of life, unseen and unmeasured but driving us,
drawing us — the flash of energy when eyes meet, gazes touch
— the magic of music, of dance — we are all acting in a vast
and wild energy field.

Flipside America. Warming my hands around a cup of
coffee at the lonely lunch counters of a thousand Formica
cafes from Texas to South Dakota. Sleeping at the Salvation
Army in Kansas City, the Holiday Inn at Memphis, the back
of a camper truck near Craig, Colorado. Bumming the cafes.
I'd nurse a cup of coffee and watch and wait until somebody
was getting up to go with leftovers on the plate, and I'd ask
for them. My luck depended on the mood of the clientele and
the charity of the waitress — at worst, shouting and threats
and hassles, at best a meal and a friend. Getting by. Usually
cold. Always dirty. Just getting by. Living not by the fat of the
land — the West in winter is not fat — but by the kindness of
people. I found the least kindness in the wealthy suburbs, the
trim houses. I found the most in the country. The city folk
were unpredictable — often cold and distant, occasionally
spectacular. I learned to search for the clear-eyed gaze of men

173

and women who live on and with the land, to avoid the fuzzy inward-turning eyes of the desk worker. I found jobs here and there. For four days I was a go-pher for a bunch of high-living oil drillers who would send me on one hundred fifty mile round trips driving their pickup to Wichita Falls for nuts and bolts and cases of Johnnie Walker Red. In a truck stop near Joplin, Missouri, I met a half-wild trucker who couldn't hold a cup of coffee without shaking it empty, who gave me a hundred dollars for driving his rig to Des Moines to meet a pay line while he slept like death through some of the worst gearjamming in the history of trucking. We arrived in Des Moines about the same time as a blizzard. The trucker set off to meet another pay line in Buffalo, New York, and I spent five days and nights in a skid row hotel waiting for the roads to clear and reading three novels by Ross Macdonald. There were other men on the road. They said they were looking for work, too. They were autoworkers, carpenters, bricklayers. Sometimes I'd get stuck somewhere. It took me three days to get a ride out of Grand Junction, Colorado. At such times I had to beg. When going house to house in search of a trade—work for a meal—a strange idea these days—people don't do chores any more—we have come to think of work as work, money as money, food as food; the relationship has blurred, and the idea that work could be traded directly for food is foreign, old-fashioned—anyway when going house to house I sought the cluttered yard, the old car, the toys in the driveway or the ragged lawn, the signs of a family too busy with the business of living to have time for Neatness, Preservation Of Order, Protection Of Investments and all the cold forces of death. I remember approaching a funky house in Kimball, Nebraska. The sun was setting and the wind was crisp. It was late winter or early spring, depending on your point of view. About a foot of crusty snow lay over the winter wheat. I had chosen a white Victorian house with three half-melted snow-men and one newer, ice-breasted snowwoman in the front yard. The sidewalk was trampled with footprints but hadn't been shoveled. One of the posts swung out from the front porch, leaving the roof to sag with the weight of giant icicles.

174

Through the steamy windows of the kitchen I could see a woman bending over an oven. A television glowed in a back room.

A brass door knocker.

A woman with yellow-dyed hair. I couldn't guess her age. Thirty-five or fifty-five, I just couldn't tell.

'Howdy, ma'am,' I went into my feet-shuffling act. 'I lost my bus ticket in Omaha so I'm working my way toward California and if there's any chores I could do that would be worth a meal to you I'd sure like to—'

'My meals!' She laughed. 'They aren't worth sic em. Tell you what, though. You shovel the walk, knock down those icicles and—and let Dirk help you, which means it'll take twice as long, but at least it'll get him out of my way for a while, and I'll give you three bucks so you can go somewhere and buy a *real* meal.'

Dirk was thirteen years old and full of questions. The farthest he'd been from home was Scottsbluff. What was Omaha like? Had I seen the Grand Canyon? Had I been to Dodge City, Kansas? It was a setup. I couldn't resist telling him about all my adventures, and I may have embellished a few details here and there (something about the West brings out the liar in people). I suppose I didn't *really* walk across the Great Salt Lake Desert to be rescued by Indians just as I was about to be eaten by a Gila Monster—but Dirk didn't seem to doubt me. He was sharp, though. He was leading me right into a trap. Before we'd shoveled half the sidewalk (that is, I shoveled and he trampled), he pushed his glasses up his nose and said, 'Golly, Mister, if you're going from Omaha to California you're taking a mighty funny *route*.'

I allowed to him then that I really wasn't heading any place in particular.

'You mean you're just *going* places?'

I nodded.

'Why?'

I shrugged.

'How long have you been *doing* this?'

It had been close to three months.

'Why?'

I shrugged again.

'Why?' Again he pushed the glasses snug against his nose. 'What's the point?'

What could I say? Well, you see, I'm married, I have this wife, she's only seventeen and kind of nutty, and she wants a baby but I'm temporarily indisposed, and I can't find work, and this thing happened in St. Louis where they think I did something that I really didn't, so I have to be sort of anonymous for a—

'What are you *talking* about?'

I rested on my shovel. 'It really doesn't make much sense, does it?'

'Nope.'

'What if I said I was doing it for fun?'

He shrugged. '*Is* it fun?'

'Well . . .' Standing all day in the cold and the wind at Grand Junction, Colorado—I stood there nine hours a day without getting a ride—that wasn't fun. Five days and nights snowbound in a hotel in Des Moines, Iowa—that wasn't fun. Panhandling, busted for it once, a night in jail in Green River, Utah; odd jobs, scrounging, giving out handbills in Phoenix, washing windows in Denver, shoveling snow, sitting for hours warming my hands on a cup of coffee in a truck stop near Tonopah, Nevada, because it's so bitter cold outside that I just can't face it and it doesn't matter anyway, one place is as good as another and what's the point anyway?

I recommenced shoveling. Dirk trudged along beside me in his bright red parka. He seemed to be set back by my lack of motivation. As he mulled it over, though, I think he shrugged it off—kids are used to inconsistency in adults, anyway—was I an adult?—creepy thought—and he reverted to thinking of me as some kind of adventurer. Soon he was asking for more details of my travels, and I tried to satisfy him as best I could. By the time I'd finished the shoveling and knocked down the icicles, Dirk was following me with bug-eyed admiration. I was a hero.

I went inside to collect my three dollars. Dirk's mother

was washing the dishes.

Dirk trotted in behind me. 'Golly, Mom, you should hear what he does. He *hitchhikes* all over the place. He's been to the Grand Canyon and Dodge City and all kinds of—'

'Oh yeah,' his mother said. She brushed a yellow-dyed strand of hair out of her face and tucked it behind an ear. Soapy drops fell to the floor. 'I hitched to California once.'

'Goll' Dirk gazed up at her in wonderment. 'When?'

'Long ways back. I was thirteen.'

'Thirteen! I thought you growed up in Oklahoma.'

'I did. I was an Okie.'

'Who'd you *go* with?'

'Nobody.'

'Goll'

'Went out to join my brother. Your granddaddy told me to. It was hard times.'

'You were a—what did you say?'

'I was an Okie.'

And I was a nothing.

Maybe that was when it all started to go bad. I remember leaving that house in Kimball, my fingers wrapped around the three dollar bills in my pocket, breathing puffs of steam out of my nose, kicking rocks, cracking the ice over puddles in the gutter. Who did I think I was? Huck Finn? Tom Joad? Neal Cassady? Crusoe, you asshole. Crusoe? *Middlebrook,* dammit. Couldn't even get my own name right.

I was walking by a Texaco station. I veered over to the office. A clear-eyed man in a greasy uniform was stacking credit card slips. When I opened the door, he clamped his hand over the slips before they could blow away.

'Excuse me.'

'Hmm?'

'You got a map?'

'Nope. Close the door.'

I closed it.

'Got no maps. They're too dangerous.' He looked up from the desk top, through the window and over the pumps to the fields beyond.

'Dangerous? *Maps?*'

'Yep. Whenever I got one, I go off following the little black lines.'

I laughed.

He sighed.

'You sound like a—an addict or something.'

He shrugged. 'Where you going? I can tell you how to get there good as any map.'

'Butte.' And as the name left my lips, I sort of stared at it in surprise.

'Montana?'

'Guess so.'

He looked wistful. 'Butte. Well. Stay on Eighty to Cheyenne, then hang a right on Twenty-five to Buffalo—that's Buffalo, Wyoming—then left on Ninety for a long long ways and it'll take you straight to Butte. Or if you prefer, stick with Eighty all the way to Salt Lake, then up Fifteen. That'll get you there, too. But if it was me, I'd cut right at Rawlins and go over the Green Mountains to the Sweetwater River and stop by Jody's ranch for a spell. Then you could head up through Cody and Yellowstone. Hayell, boy, get out of here before I take you there myself. Git. Go on, now.' He turned his back to me and resumed sorting credit slips.

I started walking toward my new-found destination. Butte. Elaine's uncle. Elaine. Maybe I'd known it all along.

I reached the entrance ramp just as the sun was setting. Magnificent purple shadows played over the folds of snow, but I hardly noticed. The wind was whipping into my Navy jacket. I was hungry, but I figured to wait. The three bucks was all I had, and I might need it toward a place to sleep.

Four hours later, I was still at the entrance ramp. I was clapping my hands and stamping my feet to fight off the spreading numbness.

A pickup stopped. I hopped into the cab. Sudden warmth. Like stepping into a steam bath. 'Thank God you stopped. I sure do appreciate—'

'Thank *who?*' He was a little man with a big beard.

'Thank the Lord! Praise God! Glory, glory, amen!' I was

suddenly high — high on warmth, on a chance to rest my tired legs — and woozy from semi-starvation.

'Where to?'

'Where you going?'

'Uh-uh. You tell me.' This guy sure wasn't high.

'Butte.'

'Montana?'

'Right.'

'I'm going to Salt Lake.'

'Great! That's fantastic. I can go all the way, and then I just have to —'

'You among the faithful?'

'Huh?'

'I took you for a Mormon. Looks like I made a mistake.'

I had a sinking feeling. This guy was as cold as the Nebraska wind. 'I'm not a Mormon.' I was flexing my fingertips. They were white, bloodless, painful.

'What are you?'

'Nothing.'

'Atheist?'

'No.'

'What church?'

'No church. I'm nothing.'

'Do you believe in God?'

'No.'

'Then what was that Praise the Lord stuff?'

'Just words.'

'You don't believe in God?'

'No.'

'Then you're an *atheist*.'

'No. Because I don't care. An atheist says there is no god. I say there may be a god and there may not, but either way I don't give a fuck.' If I hadn't been so tired, I would have chosen my words more carefully.

'You're an agnostic.'

'No. Because I don't *care*. An agnostic says I don't *know*. I say I don't *care*. You can't label me because I'm outside of the system. I'm in a whole different universe from all that. Not

179

agnostic because we don't care. Not atheist because we don't know. We're called the Whogivesashitters.'

He pursed his lips.

I rubbed my fingers.

He wiped his nose with the back of a finger.

I started unbuttoning my jacket.

He slowed down.

I looked around. We were nowhere. Absolutely nowhere.

He stopped.

'Get out.'

I argued. I pleaded. I had a sudden change of heart about the whole subject of religion. I wanted to learn all about it. Especially I wanted to hear all about those wonderful Mormons. Those wonderful, charitable, helpful, merciful, kind, open-hearted Mormons.

I watched his taillights disappear over a hill. The wind was so strong, I could hardly stand. Small white clouds were zipping across the black bowl of sky that seemed so much bigger than the sky back East. Grains of snow blew skittering over the crust to strike me like grains of sand. I couldn't stand up straight. With my back to the wind I leaned until I achieved some sort of balance. It was like leaning back on a sapling tree —springy, unreliable—but either I leaned or I'd be blown face first into the snow.

Not many cars. Spaced about a mile apart. Sometimes a truck. Nobody slowed down. They were doing seventy or more, and by the time I came into their headlight beams it was too late to stop, if they noticed me at all. I probably flashed by them like another lonely fence post.

I soon realized I wasn't going to get a ride. Already I was shivering. I figured I was about four miles out of Kimball. I started walking back. The wind pushed. All I had to do was steer.

About a mile later it didn't look like I was any closer to Kimball, but I felt a whole lot colder. It occurred to me that I might not make it. I might freeze to death, right here on the shoulder of the highway with cars and trucks rattling on by. They'd find me in the morning, write me up in the paper.

What an absurd way to die.

I started running. I jogged a while and suddenly—to my complete surprise—I fell. I hadn't tripped. I'd simply run out of energy. I hadn't eaten since breakfast, and that was only two doughnuts and a cup of coffee back in North Platte. I stood up again. My whole body was shaking. My toes and fingers were useless. My feet screamed with pain. The hairs in my nostrils froze with each intake of breath. My eyes felt funny. It felt like the water in my eyes was freezing. I had to do something. Not a car in sight. Nothing in sight. Empty plains. Rolling land. And a bump over there, something jutting up. Something round and black. Like a chimney. I walked toward it. I wondered if I was hallucinating; or maybe when you're cold, chimneys appear like mirages when you're thirsty. I could walk on top of the crusted snow. I walked a good ways and turned back to look at the highway. It had disappeared, as if it sank into the plains. I was alone, a human cow on a giant ranch. And not a blade of grass. The chimney didn't seem any closer. I walked on. I was really getting worried. I didn't trust my own mind any more. First the highway disappears, then the chimney seems to be walking away from me, teasing me. Had I already lost my mind? Was I wandering the snow like a madman, circling aimlessly until I collapsed and froze into the landscape?

No.

The chimney was closer. It *was* a chimney. Black, rusty stovepipe. But where was the house? The chimney was just sticking out of a lump of snow. Had the house collapsed? Closer. I trudged right up to it. Steps, going down. A door. No lock. No light. I couldn't open it. I jarred it with my shoulder. The door broke loose, opened. I was in an abandoned sod house.

When I closed the door, I was in absolute blackness. It was like a cave. And like a cave, it was a lot warmer than outside. I struck a match. About two dozen field mice dashed away from my feet. They disappeared through holes in the muslin sheets that covered the walls. The house was one big room. Bits of grain covered the floor. A harrow with a broken axle sat in one corner. And at the base of the chimney—oh beautiful sight—was a Franklin stove. A few wood chips were scattered about the base of the stove, and a stack of magazines —*The Saturday Evening Post*—were tied with twine and set like a stool exactly where a man would sit if he were warming his hands. Behind the stove, in a heap, lay a wooden chair with broken legs and a split back.

I built a fire. I tore up a *Post*, crumpled up the pages and lit it. I threw on all the wood chips I could find. Then I broke up the chair—good hard oak—and threw the pieces into the flames. I rolled up some more *Posts* and tied them with the twine. They made nice logs.

Soon it was cozy warm.

My shaking stopped. Suddenly I was sweating. I felt like I might have a fever, but I couldn't tell for sure because I was so tired and hungry. I sat on the floor by the stove. A mouse ran along the edge of the wall. I lay back. Immediately I fell asleep. I awoke once when a mouse ran inside the cuff of my pants and a ways up my leg, but no sooner had I thrown some more magazine logs into the fire than I was sleeping again.

The next time I awoke, daylight was bursting through cracks in the door. I stretched—stiff and sore. Still a little heat in the stove. I nursed the embers to flame, then stepped outside. The brightness hit me like a blast of wind. It was noon. It was a magnificent, clear Nebraska day. Not a tree in sight. I was alone with rolling plains of snow and a silent enormous sky and, way off, my only companion, a soaring hawk. Too much. Outtasight. I stood there marvelling while a plume of steam rose from the snow in front of my feet. I might've stood like that all day except I suddenly felt a nip of frostbite in a place where I couldn't afford any more problems. Quickly I zipped and returned to the warmth of the soddy.

I squatted by the stove and took stock. Definitely I had a fever. I was dizzy. I hadn't eaten for over a day. I had three bucks. I was hundreds of miles from Butte.

Nothing for it but to get moving.

Still I hesitated. It was warm and homey in this old soddy. I could live here, surrounded by earth, just like a potato. Erica would like it. Erica. What was that? There. At the base of the stove. A penny. Green, corroded. An Indian head penny. I fingered the copper, dropped it in my pocket. An omen of something. I felt uneasy. I studied the floor. There. Another. A nickel, this time. A buffalo nickel. It joined the penny in my pocket. When you are alone any friend will do.

We three, buffalo, Indian head, and I, had a hard day's hitching. We arrived in Cheyenne around nine at night. Some rancher's children had given me an apple and a candy bar. Otherwise I still hadn't eaten. I still had a fever. I bought a half gallon of milk and a dozen eggs, then found a hotel room for a dollar fifty a night over a honky tonk bar. I drank half the milk and ate half the eggs, sucking them raw from the shell, and then dropped on the bed and fell asleep to the sound of Merle Haggard on the juke box downstairs. In the morning I drank the rest of the milk and sucked out the other six eggs. All I needed was coffee. I had one dime left, plus the penny and nickel I'd found. For sixteen cents I knew I could get a cup of coffee, but for some reason I didn't want to part with the buffalo or the Indian head. I decided to see if I could find a place that still sold coffee for a dime.

Downstairs in front of the bar, leaning on the fender of a pickup truck, an old-timer was chewing tobacco and spitting in the gutter. I asked him if he knew where a dime would get a cup of coffee.

He eyed me closely. For about ten seconds he eyed me. Then he spat right between my feet.

I decided I didn't want a cup of coffee.

I walked to the highway and stood there for three and a half hours. Finally I got a ride to Laramie with a man wearing four hundred dollars on his body. It would have been cheaper to sew the suit out of dollar bills. He had a gold ring the size of a doughnut. I asked if he could help me out, as I'd lost my bus ticket and all that. He said he couldn't spare anything; he only carried small change. Later he bought some gas with a fifty dollar bill. Didn't even try to hide it from me.

I waited another two hours, then got a ride from one side of Laramie to the other. It was now four o'clock. No food since breakfast. Fever getting worse. Throbbing headache. Body shaking. Knees weak. My better judgment told me to head back in to Laramie, hustle up some money or find a Salvation Army or somehow find a way to eat and rest up for a few days, but I had a goal now and I was determined to make it to Butte as fast as possible, hitching night and day, forgoing sleep and food and rest if necessary, pushing my body to the limit because I'd catch up in Butte, everything would be all right in Butte, Butte was my purpose, my driving force.

A camper truck screeched to a halt in the gravel. An arm waved. I had a ride. I squeezed into the cab. A cowboy was driving. Another sat in the middle. They were in a hilarious mood.

'Which way you going, feller?' asked the driver. At the question the other cowboy started giggling helplessly. 'Don't mind Eddie,' said the driver. 'He's high.'

'I'm going to Butte.'

Eddie slapped his thigh and laughed out loud.

'What's so funny, Eddie?' said the driver.

Eddie stuffed back his laughter long enough to say, 'Where *we* going, Junior?'

Junior, the driver, considered the question. After some chewing of a toothpick he answered, 'Vernal.'

Eddie collapsed in mirth. 'Vernal?' he gasped. 'Where's Vernal?'

'Where's Vernal? Vernal, Utah? Why Eddie, ain't you ever pissed in a Vernal urinal?'

Eddie was helpless for the next three minutes. As soon as he composed himself, Junior started describing Vernal. 'They got a high school there. Vernal High. But we don't call it that. They got some nice gals there. Real nice.'

'What do you call it, Junior?'

'Venereal High.'

Eddie was gone again.

'No such thing as a Vernal Virgin,' Junior continued.

Eddie pounded the dash with his fists.

'Yes sir,' mused Junior, 'those gals suit my philosophy.'

'What's your philosophy?' said Eddie.

Junior removed the toothpick from his mouth. 'Find a need,' he said, 'and fill it.'

'Ooo, that's dirty.' Eddie turned to me. 'Hey, you falling asleep?'

I was. 'Sorry.' I said.

'That's all right. You just go on to sleep. We'll sing lullabies. Bye baby bunting, Daddy's gone a-hunting . . .'

Pretty soon I did fall asleep. I woke from time to time, picking up snatches of conversation. I remember Eddie saying, 'I don't want to fight, I'm as peaceable as the next guy, but when push comes to shove, you know . . . He lost nine teeth. *Nine* . . .' I was aware that day had turned to night, and that the Interstate had been exchanged for a bumpy country road, but I didn't think about it as long as we were moving.

We stopped. I awoke.

'Well here we are,' said Junior.

I peered into the darkness.

Eddie reached around and started unstrapping the rifle that was hung across the back of the cab.

All I could see out there was a gravel road, a mountain range, a three-quarter moon, and a lot of sagebrush. There were patches of snow, blue in the moonlight, but mostly the ground was clear.

'Where are we?' I said.

'Beats me,' said Junior. He opened his door and stepped out of the truck.

'Ain't this Vernal?' said Eddie, grinning. He had the rifle down now and was opening a box of bullets.

Junior rubbed his neck. 'I dunno, Eddie, I musta made a wrong turn somewhere.'

'See any jackerrabbits?' said Eddie.

'One.'

I stepped out into the cold. The sharp air had two effects. It jolted me awake, and it reminded me I had a fever. I asked Junior, 'Where's the Interstate?'

Junior spat and rubbed it into the dirt with the toe of his boot. 'Probably back where we left it. Less it's moved.'

I could hear Eddie giggling in the truck. He was dropping bullets into the rifle.

I was getting worried. Scenes from bad movies were flashing into my mind. There was an air of unreality about these two cowboys, a lack of cause and effect, a communication gap. Or maybe it was my fever. Maybe it was all me. It had to be me.

I approached Junior. Confidentially, in a low voice, I asked, 'Is this Utah?'

He looked me straight in the eye. 'Nope,' he said.

There. A simple answer. Encouraged, I asked, 'Is it far to Butte?'

'Butte? Where's Butte?'

'Butte, Montana.'

'Oh, *that* Butte. Heh. I reckon so.'

'Are you going any farther in that direction?'

'Nope.'

'Will you take me to the highway?'

'Nope.'

'Are you staying here?'

'Yep.'

'Would it be all right if I sleep in your truck?'

'Nope.'

'What are you doing here?'

'Hey Eddie!' Junior called. 'He wants to know what we're doing here.'

'Oh,' said Eddie. He was standing by the truck's front bumper, holding the rifle in one hand. 'Did you say you saw a jackerrabbit?'

'Uh-huh.'

'Ain't we here to shoot jackerrabbits?'

'Uh-huh.'

He shot. At my feet. A spurt of earth, by my right big toe.

'That's funny,' said Eddie. 'He don't hop. Can't you hop?'

I just stared at him.

He shot again. This time I felt a jerk in the heel of my shoe. I looked down, expecting blood, shattered bones, but he'd only grazed the shoe.

I started to run. Blindly. Anywhere. Away. Toward the mountains.

'Hee-yee-hah!' I heard from behind. Then another shot. I ran straight for the gravel road. I figured if they wanted to hit me they could. No use dodging.

'Hop, beatnik!'

Blam.

I reached the road and started running up it toward the top of the hill about a quarter mile away. Sucking for breath. Head pounding. Ears ringing. If you don't run . . .

Blam.

Had to stop. Can't breathe. Put one foot in front of the other. I looked over my shoulder. They were in the truck. Headlights on. They were coming after me.

I dodged off the road and ran sort of falling downhill to an arroyo. The truck was following my steps up the hill on the road. The arroyo had vertical banks about six feet high. I jumped in. The bottom was in a shadow from the moonlight. I worked my way along, tripping, walking fast. I heard the truck stop, back up, stop, go forward, stop. It was turning around. I saw the headlights sweep over the top of the arroyo above me. I kept on going. I heard one more shot. I had the feel of the bottom now. I could walk a steady pace. I couldn't hear the truck any more. The arroyo had gone around behind the hill so I couldn't see the truck either, but since I didn't hear it I figured they'd either given up or were following on foot. I kept going. I was climbing. Ahead were the mountains, a dark massive hulk in the night. Pebbles clinked under my shoes. Occasionally I kicked a dry branch.

I walked for an hour. I left the desert for the side of the mountain. The creekbed was still dry, but I came to a willow thicket and about a dozen startled cows. They bellowed and shuffled away. I couldn't go on. I found some soft grass between a willow and a cow pie, lay down, saw two shooting stars, closed my eyes, and fell into a restless, chilly sleep.

I awoke at dawn. A clear sky. The cows had returned. They paid no attention as I stood up. A magpie eyed me from the

187

branch of a willow. It flapped its wings once, but held its perch.

And there I was.

All alone in the West.

Fevered, half-starved, cold, tired. Lost. I could return down the creekbed to the desert and follow the arroyo back to the gravel road, but Junior and Eddie might still be there. Or I could strike out cross country and hope to hit a house or another road, but I could easily go fifty miles without hitting anything in this country. If there were cattle, there must be a ranch somewhere. I decided to scout around. I'd continue up the creekbed until I could get a view of the land.

A half mile up the creekbed I came to a dirt road. Just wheel tracks, really. Which way? I flipped the buffalo. Heads right, tails left. Buffalo up. Right.

I followed the tracks along the canyon to a fork. There was a handmade wooden sign with black lettering that had mostly peeled off. Back the way I'd been coming was an arrow and the words, STINKING SPRING 15 MI. Pointing up the left hand of the fork was STARVATION LAKE 5 MI. Neither sounded promising by the names. I chose the unmarked fork. The ruts led me around a hill, across a creek (with water, this time) to a dead end canyon and a ghost town.

The town consisted mostly of little puddles of wood where buildings had collapsed. There were two structures still standing: a roofless, false-front commercial building and a dilapidated log cabin with broken windowpanes and rusty venetian blinds. That seemed odd. Venetian blinds weren't something I expected to find in a ghost town. Behind the commercial building, on the side of a hill was a graveyard and a little shed. Leading out of town was a deep-rutted road that couldn't have been used for a long time because big bushes of sagebrush were growing in the ruts. A sign pointed up the road. I had to study hard to make out what the letters had said before all the paint fell away, leaving just a trace of a pattern on the wood. It said either SLEEPING LADY MINE or possibly STEPPING BABY MINE. I decided the sleeping lady made more sense.

I followed the ruts. They led to the narrow end of the canyon. Steep walls of rock rose on three sides. A mine shaft began in one of the walls, but it had collapsed after about ten feet. Judging from the pile of tailings, it had been quite a deep mine.

I walked back to the town. I checked out the little graveyard on the side of the hill. There were twenty-three identical wooden crosses laid in rows of five. On each cross was a man's name. I started hypothesizing. The fact that it was a ghost town, that it had been a mining town, that the mine had collapsed, that all the graves were of men and no women, that all the men had died at the same time (because otherwise there would have been dates on the crosses, and the cemetery wouldn't have had such a uniform pattern to it), all led me to conclude that there had been a mine disaster. The sleeping lady had stirred; twenty-three miners had died; the mine had probably played out anyway; and instead of reopening it, the mine had been abandoned, and the town along with it.

I looked in the shed. There was a pick head without a handle and two rusty old shovels, and resting against a corner there was another wooden cross. I brought it out into the light. When I picked it up, the bottom half broke right off. It was full of termite holes or dry rot or something. In the light I could see the name on the top half: JEDEDIAH KINGSMITH. It was as light as balsa wood from all the holes. Back in the shed I found the remains of three more crosses that had completely flaked apart. I wondered what had happened to Jedediah. Had they forgotten where they buried him? Unlikely. More likely they'd made crosses for all the men in the mine after giving up hope of rescuing anybody alive, and later when they recovered the bodies they'd found old Jedediah miraculously alive and in no need of a cross. Maybe he was injured and they kept the cross in storage, figuring they still might need it, and forgot about it when Jedediah recovered. In either case I valued this piece of wood. It was a testament to the stubborn tenacity of life. How does a rabbit survive the harsh and frigid winter? How can such delicate tissue surmount snow and starvation, predators, disease, cold? How does a miner survive his job? Jedediah Kingsmith survived. Perhaps he was living still. I carried his cross, what was left of it, back down the hill.

I glanced inside the commercial building, but it looked like souvenir hunters had picked it clean. I was looking for food. I then tried the house, and here I lucked out. There were signs of recent habitation. For one thing there was a Teflon frying pan on the table. There were three cans of Campbell's Pork 'n Beans on a shelf. And there was a bed with a mattress that still had most of its stuffing inside. Probably some hunters passed through here once or twice a year. I attacked a can of beans. I beat it against the corner of a shelf, which only dented it. Then my eyes spied a church key with a corkscrew, hanging on a nail on the wall. It wasn't the perfect instrument. I doubt if ever a tin can has been so abused. But I pried it open, and I gobbled the beans cold. Immediately I set to work on the other two cans, and soon I'd eaten three cold cans of beans. Then I headed straight for the mattress.

I slept all day. That night I got the heaves. Fortunately all the beans were digested by then and there wasn't much to come up. Then I made the mistake of drinking some water to clean out my mouth, and it came back with a vengeance. I spent the night sleeping fitfully, feeling the fever build, smelling stale vomit on the floor and tasting it in my mouth. When I slept, I dreamed of three faces. Dark glasses. A fist. A gold ring. Beckoning. Beckoning. An expressionless man. A man who was scared, who wore spectacles and had ears like little wings. A gambler? A loser. A man who is his own worst enemy. As are we all. When I wasn't sleeping I lay with my face toward the window, watching the parade of stars, wondering if I could possibly sink any lower, thinking that on the whole, I would rather be in Philadelphia. I clutched Jedediah Kingsmith in one hand.

In the morning I barely had the strength to obey a call of nature. I spent the whole day on the mattress, and then the night.

The following morning I felt stronger. My hunger returned but there was nothing to satisfy it with. I was trying to decide whether I had the strength to move on when I heard the sound of an engine. Clutching Jedediah, I stepped outside to see a jeep bumping into town, driven by a short-haired man with a neatly trimmed beard. We gaped at each other in surprise.

He was an archeologist. He had a dig about twenty miles away. He had taken the day off to do some exploring. He told me I looked like a ghost—fitting for a ghost town. I told him about hitchhiking, about Junior and Eddie, and getting sick and being hungry.

He didn't believe me. He said he could see I was sick and he could believe I was hungry, but as for the rest—well, he didn't know what I was hiding or how I came to be fifty miles from the nearest paved road, but he'd give me a ride back out again.

We almost didn't make it. The jeep ran out of gas. Seems it had a leaky fuel pump. Fortunately he was carrying a five gallon can for emergencies, and that got us back to the highway. He went straight for the nearest gas station. To pay for the gas, he peeled a five dollar bill from a wad in his jacket pocket. I couldn't help but think about that wad. I was feeling pretty desperate. For some reason, I had brought Jedediah with me.

'Want a beer?' he said when the tank was full. 'Come on. I'll buy you lunch.'

He was an all right guy, and I cringe to remember what I did to him. In that little cafe, in that little town in Wyoming, two events combined to inspire an instant decision that I will always regret. First a bus pulled up to the cafe. The driver stepped down, followed by a passenger. The driver opened up the side luggage compartment and pulled out a battered old suitcase. Then he closed it up and walked back toward the door of the bus. Meanwhile my archeologist had gone to the john. He'd left his coat on the chair, with the wad in the pocket. What can I say? In my favor I suppose I can point out that I only took half the wad, but still the fact is I grabbed that money and ran for the bus just as the driver was closing the door.

Ten hours later I was in Butte.

I had bought a clean undershirt. I was standing under a

191

streetlight in a swarm of flies. I still had Jedediah. I was staring into the window of a laundromat, staring at unattainable women. Their lives were aimed in directions I could not follow. There was a housewife folding towels while her harmless baggy-trousered husband played with their little boy. I knew she had a mortgage, a kid, and a husband who ate too much and couldn't hammer a nail straight; yet she had a soft, plain, unglamorous, healthy beauty in her freckles and soft downy face . . . Sitting in a plastic chair reading a magazine was a tall Montana woman with a magnetic presence, drawing my eyes to her again and again not by glamor or sexiness but the sheer strength of her, the energy about her, the aura of someone with whom you expect interesting things to happen—hilarity and parties and skiing and fast foreign cars and fingering a cocktail glass, wearing a stunning dress, her eyes merrily dancing while the men crowd around—her sharp features, with no apology in her walk but a sense of purpose and liveliness . . . Pulling bras from a washer was a compulsive toe-tapping girl, one of those eye-catching chicks who throws her head back in a certain way, who tosses her hand through her hair with a flair, who always knows who's watching, who chews gum, who will get pregnant, then engaged, then marry the son of the man who owns the hardware store . . .

I watched.

Me.

Willy Crusoe, petty thief.

Anonymous fugitive, naive suburbanite, tired-ass runaway, unlucky jobseeker, sexual suicide, husband on the lam.

Dangerous Romantic.

BUTTE

For two days I wandered the streets of Butte, streets named
Aluminum, Platinum, Silver and Iron. With every step I felt
more stupid for coming. I didn't even know Elaine's last
name. What had made me think I could find her? How did I
know she would be here? Why was I searching for her, anyway? Sometimes I feel like one of those miniature cars on
somebody's elaborate race track, guided over the roads by a
groove I cannot see, pushed by a force I do not understand.

On the night of the second day, late, one o'clock or so, I was
wandering along a street of wooden bungalows. All the
houses were dark. I was heading for a cozy little lean-to I'd
found down by Silver Bow Creek where I hoped for a good
night's rest before I left town early the next morning. Suddenly I felt a coin slip through my pocket and sliver down my
leg. I had only two coins: the buffalo nickel and the Indian
penny. I felt in my pocket. The nickel was there. The penny
was rolling across the concrete sidewalk—down an asphalt
driveway—into the street—teetering for a moment—almost
falling —now steady again, rolling back to the gutter and
under the wheel of a truck.

A yellow milk truck.

My Indian guide. I abandoned the penny and raced to the
door of the nearest bungalow. No light on, no sound. I
knocked. I tapped on the door with old Jedediah Kingsmith. I
tapped and tapped. At last, a light. The door. Elaine, in a
yellow nightgown. She looked sleepy and surprised.

'Well!' She smiled that big smile. Then she yawned, equally
big. 'Hello, Willy.' She rubbed her eyes. 'Come on in.'

I stepped in. She grabbed me and hugged me. I hugged back. I could feel her jaw against my chest, yawning.

An old man with white hair and white eyebrows and blinking white eyelashes and a white mustache came stumbling into the room. He might have been sketched by somebody who was trying to use up an oversupply of white chalk. He was wearing long johns and—by golly—a stocking cap. He squinted into the harsh light. 'Who's there?'

I let go, but Elaine clung on to me. 'Uncle Henry, this is Willy.'

'Friend of yourn?'

'Uh-huh.'

'Okay.' He waved a hand and turned his back. 'See you in the mornin'. Pleased to meet you, Will.' And he stumbled off to bed.

Elaine let go. She scratched her head sleepily. She pointed at Jedediah. 'What's that?'

'My teddy bear.'

'You sleep with it?' She yawned and scratched her stomach. The only sound was the ticking of a grandfather clock. She blinked, slowly. 'You tired? Come on.' She headed for her room.

'Where can I sleep?'

'I ain't makin' no bed this time of day.'

'I'll just sleep on the floor.'

'No.'

'Where else?'

'With me.'

By the time I had undressed and climbed into the bed, the warm sheets, she was fast asleep. She didn't even stir. I kept to my side of the bed. I held Jedediah on top of the covers. I heard a horse outside. It circled the house. What was a horse doing out there? It made about a dozen circuits around the house, then clopped slowly away.

In the morning we all had Cheerios. I asked about the horse.

'Hoss? What hoss? Elaine, you hear any hoss?'

'No, Uncle Henry.'
'Ain't no hoss hereabout.'

Elaine and I spent the day catching up on each other's lives. At one point she remarked, 'Either I slept through a rape or you've changed your ways.'

'I guess I've changed.'

'Funny.' She drew a circle on the table with her finger tip. 'So have I.'

I didn't tell her that when I woke up that morning I found my two arms wrapped tightly around her and my face pressed into her neck just below the ear, and that I jumped out of bed in a panic of confusion, and then I sat on the chair by the dresser and watched her for an hour and a half, watched her gentle breathing, her lovely soft neck where my face had pressed — watched and remembered Erica and wondered, If this is not why you came to Montana then what *are* you here for? Could we be friends? Is it possible for man and woman to be friends?

I asked about Al. She said they were through. She said he was a prick anyway.

'I'll buy that.'

'Drop dead.'

Her hand went to her lips. She reached across and held one of my hands between both of hers, jostling the coffee on Uncle Henry's table. 'I'm sorry,' she whispered.

'Bumpy said Al knows something.'

'He does. He knows the whole thang.'

'Ah.'

'What?'

'Thang.'

That slow smile: 'You silly.'

Elaine didn't want to talk about St. Louis: 'Don't mess with it Willy. There's nothing you can do.'

I coaxed. She said she didn't remember anything. Finally, bluffing, I told her that I was going back there to get the true story.

'Don't go to Saint Lou, Willy. *Please*. Don't *ever* go back.' As she spoke she was squeezing my hand. 'The police in Saint

Lou—you know how it is. There's this Mob. The old hoods. Useta boss the whole city. Now they got South Side and the suburbs. They lost North Side. It's gone Blob.'

'*Blob?*'

'That's what Al calls 'em. Black mob. Blob.'

'Are you pulling my—?'

'Listen. Some of the suburbs are going black. Places near Romey's. Blob wants to control it. The cops watch over the whole thang. Even in the suburbs, it goes through city cops. They sort of keep it orderly, you know. Course they favor the Mob every chance they get. This one cop—this is where I don't understand. They say he was working for Blob. There was trouble. Some stuff that was supposed to go to South Side disappeared. They say it ended up North Side. They thought this guy had something to do with it. I don't know what. Al could explain it better. Anyway, this guy hung out at Romey's. Course Romey's was Mob, but it's very near some Blob land and a lot more turf they think they oughta get. It was a hit. You just happened to be there. They hung it on you. If you go back, there's nothing you can do. 'Cept get killed. Cops would *arrest* you. Mob would *waste* you—you're dangerous to them. Blob would *get* you 'cause they think you got their man. *Everybody* wants-you. Stay the hell outa there, Willy. What do you want to do? Go in there with a couple of six shooters on your hip and clean up the place? Randolph Scott you ain't, Willy Crusoe.'

'Willy Crusoe I ain't, either.'

'Says you,' she pouted. And I wondered for the first time: Am I? Did Middlebrook die somewhere? Creepy, creepy. And this talk of gangs—how weird it all seemed out here in quiet Butte—how *unnecessary*—how unreal big city evil seems in the giant spaces of the West.

'Does Al—is he—I mean does he work with these guys?'

'He says he don't.'

'Do you believe him?'

She dropped my hand and slumped in her chair. 'Probably not.'

'Is he a junkie?'

196

'Sometimes. You know Al. He'd take rat poison if you told him it was good.'

'Are you?'

She shook her head. Emphatically.

'Ever take it?'

She nodded.

I hadn't. I've taken a lot of stuff—I once lived in the middle of the great chemical revolution. But never smack. 'What's it like?'

'Jeez, Willy!' She burst out of her chair and strode around the table. 'Don't even *think* about taking it.' Suddenly she went soft. Standing behind my chair, she lay her hands on my neck. One finger was drawing tiny circles under my ear. 'You know Willy,' she said gently, 'Uncle Henry won't be back 'til supper time.'

'Huh,' I said. 'You want to take a walk?'

Uncle Henry was a retired miner who now spent his days in barbershops and bars. He had once been the Manure King of the Midwest. He had founded a short-lived business empire on a foundation of shit. He cornered the market until he had a virtual monopoly. His manure was turning to gold. He had a whole trainload of the stuff—a hundred and seventy-five boxcars, to be exact—rolling through central Illinois when his empire collapsed through some shady wheeling and dealing that he refused to elaborate on with Elaine. All she knew about it was that he sneaked out of Chicago one step ahead of his creditors, bringing along enough cash to set up placer mining in Idaho, abandoning on a siding somewhere in central Illinois one hundred and seventy-five boxcars of high grade Texas manure which the bankers and lawyers are probably still haggling over to this very day. The placer mining failed. He came to Butte and worked as a salaried employee of the mines until retirement. It was the idea of being on a salary that he hated: 'No way to cheat the gummint on a salary. No room for the art of creative bookkeeping.' Elaine assumed that Uncle Henry's fondness for 'creative bookkeeping' probably had something to do with

197

the collapse of his manure empire.

He came striding up the street around dinner time. Elaine and I were sitting on the front steps, enjoying the spring air. He tipped his cowboy hat to me and spoke to Elaine. 'You already et?'

'No, Uncle Henry.'

'Hongry?'

We were.

'How 'bout some fry and some pone?'

'I cooked it all last night.'

'Well, greasewood and sagebrush! Any money left?'

'I'll get a job, Uncle Henry. You just don't get enough to feed me.'

'Don't you fret. No niece of mine's gonna wait on a pack of cowboys for a living. How 'bout a jam sandwich?'

Elaine explained to me: 'A jam sandwich is two slices of bread jammed together.'

It was Uncle Henry's favorite meal. He ate a loaf of bread without butter and washed it down with five bottles of Guinness Stout. Elaine and I split one bottle and ate a few slices of buttered toast. By the time we had finished eating, Uncle Henry had come up with a plan: 'This boyfriend of yours, Elaine, this—uh—'

'Willy.'

'Will. Yes. Right. Does he have a job?'

'No, Uncle Henry.'

I was sitting right there, but Uncle Henry spoke directly to Elaine as if I couldn't hear. Once again I had become invisible.

'He don't look to me like the type who *get* a job, either. You know the price of gold?'

'No, Uncle Henry.'

'Well it's high, darlin', it's mighty high. What say we go set up placer mining?'

Elaine thought it was a dumb idea. I thought it sounded interesting. Uncle Henry didn't really care what we thought, though. He had a hankering to see his old placer mine way back in the Idaho hills. Before dinner had ended, it was settled. We were going to Idaho. Tomorrow. What the hell.

That night I told Elaine I was sleeping on the floor. She was hurt, but she tried not to let on. I made a blanket roll and curled up on the bare planks of the living room floor. I lay Jedediah on an orange crate that was being used as a lamp table.

When the lights were out, the little bungalow was pitch black. I lay in the darkness and listened to the rustling sheets in Elaine's room. Elaine. Sheets. Her soft neck. Elaine. I counted the months. Four. Surely it was safe. But I was afraid. I wanted to be sure. I was scared of the pain. First I wanted to be checked out by a doctor. And I wanted to be ready for Erica. Above all, I wanted to be ready for Erica. I wanted Erica. My mountain child. My free spirit. My unlogical, nonbenevolent universe and our unlogical, non-benevolent love that made us so very happy when it wasn't driving us mad. I was determined. I will not blow it. I will not do anything stupid.

I heard the padding of bare feet on the floor.

'Lemme in.'

I let her in. She was wearing flannel pajamas. I couldn't see a thing. Far away, I heard the clopping of a horse.

Elaine's finger was drawing circles around my belly button.

'You wanna unbutton my pajamas?'

'No.'

'You wanna talk about it?'

'No.' I rolled over.

She kissed my back, wet lips between my shoulder blades. I heard the horse again. It was getting closer.

'Is it that operation you had?'

I didn't answer.

'Is there anythang I can do?'

'No.'

'Are you married?'

I didn't answer.

Now she was drawing circles on my back. She placed her mouth by my ear and barely breathed: 'There's something you can do for me.'

I rolled over. I started to do her the favor. The horse was right outside now. Elaine heard it, too. She stiffened. The horse was circling the house. She clutched my arm. The horse had stopped in front of the door. A hand was rattling the knob. Rattle bang bang. It was locked. *Bam! Bam! Bam!* Elaine and I were frozen. *Bam! Bam! Bam!* We didn't breathe.

The ticking of the clock.

Bam!

A muttered curse. The clink of stirrups. The horse, clopping away.

Elaine was shaking.

I held her to me.

The horse was gone. Elaine got up. 'I'm calling the sheriff.'

'I'm going.'

'Oh. I forgot.' Then her eyes got wide. 'You think that was the FBI?'

'No.'

She didn't call the sheriff. She made tea and sat up all night. I sat with her for a while, then sleep overcame me.

In the morning she told Uncle Henry. He stepped outside and walked around the house. He returned. He stroked his white mustache. He said, 'Go look at the mud.'

We looked. The soft spring mud showed not a single hoof print, only the path of Uncle Henry's shoes.

'Hoss. Hoomph. You kids.'

'I ain't a kid.'

'You're a kid,' said Uncle Henry.

IDAHO

Uncle Henry had a flatbed truck. He called it The Heap. He bought it in 1946, and it was a second hand truck at the time. He had no idea when it had been built. He knew that its present engine—its third—had been installed in 1958. It had no fenders. It had no hood. Just naked wheels and a naked engine. The boards in the flatbed were so rotten that you couldn't bolt them down, and Uncle Henry had tied them with twine. The gas tank had rusted out, and Uncle Henry had replaced it with an oil drum which lay on its side behind the driver's seat, connected by rubber hoses, rolling back and forth with a six inch margin, sloshing menacingly. There was no windshield. It was just as well that there wasn't, because the gas pedal was unreliable and the best way to start the motor was to stand in the cab with your right foot on the starter while you leaned out through the windshield gap and pulled the throttle in the engine with your fingers. Likewise, on a steep grade a passenger would be recruited to reach out and help feed the gas. The roof leaked. The seats were gone, replaced by wooden boxes. There were no doors. The clutch was so weak that the recommended method of shifting gears was to learn by trial and error what speeds caused matching RPMs in the gearbox and try to shift at those exact speeds, simply ramming the gears together by brute force. Every time I shifted, I imagined a trail of little gear teeth scattering in my wake across the highway.

I drove, Uncle Henry navigated, and Elaine cowered between us. I tried to reassure her by demonstrating that the brakes worked perfectly so that she could take comfort from the fact that there was no worry about being able to stop, although there was some question as to whether we would be able to go. Or that we would be able to control where we went: there was over a hundred and eighty degrees of play in the steering wheel.

Driving The Heap took a good deal of concentration, and I didn't notice too much about the country except that there were always pine trees and there were always mountains. I do remember passing through a little town called Wisdom, Montana. I am passing through Wisdom, I thought. My God. I am passing through Wisdom. And I remember Lost Trail Pass because we had a flat tire on the western slope. And Lost River, whose icy waters cooled our overheated engine. And I noticed the license plates. It struck me as remarkable that ministers and politicians and businessmen would be willing to carry a message like that around on their cars, but it made me feel welcome. I felt right at home with the potatoes, knobby and many-eyed, of the earth, like the people of the humble cafes and dusty bars, underground, where life is basic.

After the town of Chilly we hit the dirt roads. And I mean dirt. The Heap was truly admirable. It popped a hose and broke a fan belt and one of its tires split right in half, but otherwise we had no trouble over sixty miles of trail that I won't even dignify with the name road. I had the feel of it by that time, of course, which helped. During those last sixty miles I saw only one human being, a sheepherder looking cold and wet and miserable out in a thunderstorm trying to clear the road—I mean trail—of his sheep so we could pass through. We weren't exactly warm and dry ourselves. I drove the last thirty miles after dark with the aid of the one functional headlight. Twice I nearly hit deer. Once I just missed an owl who sat indignantly in the middle of the trail and peered down his beak at the front bumper three inches away, where I had screeched to a stop. Of course I couldn't honk at him—there was no horn—and shouting had no effect, so finally Elaine had to climb down and chase him away by stamping at his feet. In addition to the sheep and deer and owl, I thought I saw a wolf once. I ran over a snake.

I had to stop when the trail, which had been following a creek, dead ended at the head of a canyon where the creek came tumbling down a hundred foot waterfall. Uncle Henry said we could make camp here and hike the last eight miles tomorrow. We ripped dead branches from the pines for dry wood and built a giant fire. Dinner was a loaf of bread and a number ten can of creamed corn. Mountain bluebirds scolded us from the trees. We strung a tarp to some branches and rolled out our sleeping bags underneath.

The woods at night were full of little rustlings. We kept the fire high. Elaine told Uncle Henry she was too scared to sleep alone, and she zipped her sleeping bag together with mine. Uncle Henry shrugged and poured himself another tin cup of coffee.

I hid Jedediah under my sleeping bag so somebody wouldn't grab him in the middle of the night when groggy with sleep and toss him on the fire.

Elaine snuggled up close. She said I owed her a favor. I obliged. In the back of my mind I was listening for a horse. The fire burned brightly. Uncle Henry snored. Next to my head lay a clump of yellow flowers with an exquisite fragrance. They looked like yellow violets.

The fire burned low. Elaine slept with a deep peaceful smile. The woods were still. The mountains throbbed with a strong silent energy. I counted shooting stars. I thought of Erica. I wanted to call her. I was a hundred miles from the nearest telephone. I wanted her to hear the whistle of the wind in the mountains, the shaking of the white pine. Sometimes I thought that I had made up my love for Erica, that I loved not her but a fabrication of her filtered by my own delusions and deceptions. Sometimes I wanted to test my love for her against my attraction for another woman. And I just had. I was sharing a sleeping bag with Elaine, and my thoughts were all of Erica. Of her eyes like a meadow of black-eyed susans, the glimmer of dew. Of her breasts, her curves like the soft sloping tree-covered hills of her homeland. Of the rushing water of her mind, sometimes sparkling like a clear mountain stream, sometimes muddy and polluted by the work of man. My fingers were wet. I wondered if Erica was thinking of me. I knew she was ready. I was ready. Time had come. My thoughts reached for her over two thousand miles of wrinkle-faced land. I heard a horse.

I sprang out of the sleeping bag. I was naked. It was cold. I dove back inside. I clutched Jedediah.

Clop. Clop. Clop.

I reached for Uncle Henry. I could reach his toe. I shook his foot, his whole leg. He wouldn't wake up.

Clop. Clop.

I reached for my clothes and dressed inside the sleeping bag. Elaine rolled over, sighed, slept on. Clothed, I ran to The Heap. I wrenched open the toolbox and grabbed a tire iron. I crouched in the shadow of the cab.

Clop.

The horse had stopped in the shadows of the forest just beyond the reach of the firelight.

I called, 'Who—' My voice cracked. 'Who is it?'

No reply.

I heard the horse snort and shake its head.

'What do you want?'

How could Elaine and Uncle Henry be asleep? How could they not hear?

The horse was moving now, circling the campsite, staying just out of the light. Moving toward me. I checked my hands. I still held the tire iron in my right hand. In my left I held Jedediah. I hadn't even realized I was carrying him. I heard the clink of stirrups. Suddenly the horse was coming at me at a gallop. I dove into the cab of the truck. I raised the tire iron. The hooves beat. Closer. Still in shadow. I strained my eyes trying to see through the night. It was coming. It was—

Here.

I felt a cold wind like the breath of death. I saw nothing. I felt a wrenching, clutching hand—ice cold fingers—on my left arm. Cold and damp and heavy and irresistible. I flailed wildly with the tire iron. I could see nothing. The fingers pulled my arm. With all my might I swung the tire iron—missed—and smashed the rear window. A flashlight. Uncle

204

Henry. Shining the light on me. Nothing was holding me. There were no hoofbeats. I was wrestling dead air. I was alone in the cab of The Heap with the tire iron wedged between shards of the rear window.

'Damn, boy, that was the only glass left on the whole truck. You doin' whoopee?'

'No sir.'

'You chasin' a varmint?'

'No sir.'

The flashlight was shining in my eyes. I heard Elaine's voice: 'Willy? Did you have a bad dream?'

Yes.

The next day we hiked the eight miles—uphill—to the placer mine. There was scarcely a trace of it—just some piles of gravel and some rotten old four by fours with rusty bolts poking out of them. The stream was shallow and fairly level there. Uncle Henry said this was the first quiet spot after two miles of rapids. The gold, if any, would have settled here.

We couldn't carry all the supplies on one trip, so I went back to the truck while Elaine and Uncle Henry set up camp. At the end of the day I had walked twenty-four miles, sixteen uphill, carrying about a hundred pounds. I ached all over. I ached in places I hadn't even known were part of my body.

After dinner, Uncle Henry nibbled on a cup of coffee and explained the rules to us: 'No big fires. If John Law catches us here, he'll whup our ass. We got to get the gold and get out fast. Placer mining is rape. You can't do it without makin' a mess of the land. This here is my spot. I discovered it. I worked it once. I reckon I got a right to mess it up. But you can't explain nothin' to the gummint.'

Uncle Henry threw another branch on the fire. He poured another cup of coffee. Lacking Guinness Stout, he'd nibble on cups of coffee all evening long. He was telling us about an old hound he used to have when he was a prospector in New Mexico (which came after he was a stockbroker in Denver and before he was a farm machinery salesman in Iowa and, later, Manure King of the Midwest). The hound wandered into his campsite one day on Ceboleeta Mesa. It was half-starved and had a festering sore on a hind leg, full of pus and flies and smelling like a rotten egg. Uncle Henry got up to fetch it a piece of bacon when a rattlesnake stopped him short. Before he could go for his gun the dog jumped out like lightning and had the snake by the neck. He shook it dead. 'I took a shine to that old hound right then and there. Named him Mongoose. And he killed many a snake in his time. Saved my life moren once. You know how fast a rattler can move? You may not give credence to this, but I had a friend useta shoot rattlers with a bow and arrow. He'd always hit 'em in the head. Never missed. Couldn't figger it out. He knew he was good, but not *that* good. Finally he figgers it. "You know, Hank," he says to me. "I ain't hittin' those rattlers in the head. They seen the arrow comin' and they *strike* it. *They* hit the arrow. It don't hit *them*." ' But Mongoose hit them. Uncle Henry and Mongoose prospected all over the Southwest together. The dog met his end in Arizona, and it was rattlesnakes that did him in. Uncle Henry had stopped at a gas station. 'I had a case of the runs. I made straight for the privy. Ole Goose went sniffing around outside. Next thing you know I hear this awful racket. It's ole Goose barking and rattling and shaking something down. I hear shouting and wood tearing. I'm in the middle of my business and it takes me a few seconds to finish up. I'm pulling up my pants and running out the door as I hear a shot. The gas station man shot ole Goose. There was this snake cage he'd put up to attract business, filled with ten or eleven rattlers. Ole Goose had found it and done gone berserk. He tore it apart. The man had to shoot him. Had no choice. But here's the thing. The cage was already broken. And every one of the snakes came out in a line and headed straight for that man. They musta hated him somethin' fierce. I don't blame 'em. I wasn't too fond of him myself for shooting my dog. He looked like a mean ole cuss. Probably shook their cage and poked sticks at 'em. Anyways those rattlers are a-comin' in a line. Dartin' their tongues. He lifts his rifle and starts shooting. He hits three, four, but he misses on two shots and there ain't time anyway. Next thing you know, seven, eight rattlers on him. They strike his legs, his arms. One jumps up and sinks his fangs right in the old fart's neck. You think animals don't take revenge? They do! The son of a bitch never had a chance. I tried to get him to a hospital, but before a half hour had passed he swole up to twice his size. All the anti-venom in the world couldn't of saved him.' Uncle Henry nibbled the last drops from the tin cup. 'Can't say I wept for him either.'

I was sitting so close to the heat of the fire that some of the hairs on the back of one hand had singed, but I didn't even notice until later, I'd been so enraptured by Uncle Henry's tale. Not so Elaine. She was teasing the fire with a stick. She ruminated on the story for a few seconds. Then she threw down the stick and said, 'Aw bullshit, Uncle Henry.'

He cackled. 'Good night, darlin'.'

Elaine and I lay our sleeping bag by the low-burning fire. Two owls were hooting somewhere off in the forest, trying to locate each other in the darkness for fucking or fighting. I don't know which and probably they didn't either, simply swooping through the trees ready for whatever adventure life threw their way, be it love or war. Uncle Henry snored. Elaine rubbed my aching back. She wanted another favor.

'I'm too tired.'

'You're wide awake.'

'I'm listening for something.'

'That horse?'

'Uh-huh.'

'Would you get that god damn thang out of the sleeping bag?'

'What?'

'That sign. Jedediah.'

'No.'

'Can't believe you carried it up here.'

'Doesn't weigh anything.'

As long as I was awake anyway, I did her the favor. She was lost in a deep, satisfied sleep before I heard the breathing—a loud, rasping suck of air followed by a heavy sigh—tired, overworked lungs—old lungs—a miner's. *Hhh-hhh-uh-uhhh.*

And much too loud. It sounded like it was coming from the trees overhead. It wasn't branches in the wind—the sound was human. It wasn't Uncle Henry—his chest rose and fell in a different rhythm. The sound was everywhere. *Hhh-hhh-uh-uhhh.* I was freaking out. I shook Elaine. She was groggy. I got her to open her eyes.

'Listen!'

'What? The horse? Oh shit.' She sat bolt upright.

'No. Listen.'

Then she heard it too. The breathing, plus a new sound. A scratching, scraping noise that at first I couldn't identify. A sharp scratch, followed by a slower scrape, followed by a muffled thump.

'Somebody's digging,' I said.

'A bear?'

'With a shovel?'

Digging, and heavy breathing. But the sound wasn't coming from one point in the forest. It was everywhere. Elaine was terrified, clutching my arm. It occurred to me that I didn't have to be scared.

'It's like the horse,' I said. 'It isn't there.'

'Let's wake Uncle Henry.'

'He won't hear it. He'll just go out tomorrow and show us that there isn't a trace of digging nearby.'

'And then he'll call me a kid.'

'You are a kid.'

'Pig!'

She had shouted. The two words echoed back from the forest. And in the silence that followed, we realized that the digging, the breathing, everything had stopped. We'd beat it. Because it wasn't real.

'I didn't mean it,' I said as we both lay down.

'I'll show you I ain't a kid.' She reached for me.

'No. Please.' Her fingers brought swelling, thrust, strain. If she didn't stop I'd—

'Do me a favor.'

'I already—'

'Do it!'

I did, and I was worried. I didn't like the tone of her voice. She'd threatened me. She'd realized the power of her sexuality, and the helplessness of mine. I wondered if the way I was feeling was how it felt to be a woman.

Uncle Henry shook us awake a little after dawn. He was excited. 'Somebody's been diggin' in our creek!'

So they had. We went down and saw for ourselves. Uncle Henry said it was a claim-jumper.

'Aw, ain't no gold in there anyway,' said Elaine.

'Oh yeah?' Uncle Henry went back to the camp and returned with a pan. He waded into the creek. In ten minutes, he had two little kernels.

'There!' He brandished them in the palm of his hand. 'That's twenty, thirty dollars right there.'

Elaine's eyes were wide with wonder. 'Fantastic!' She bounced up and down. 'If only Al was here!' Then she caught me looking at her sort of strangely, and she blushed. She told Uncle Henry we'd heard digging last night.

'But it wasn't real,' I said.

'Well this here is real,' he said, and he kicked the pile of sand and gravel on the bank of the creek.

'No,' I said. 'It isn't.'

Uncle Henry shrugged. He dismissed me from his world. 'Elaine,' he said, 'go fix breakfast.'

'Willy,' said Elaine, 'go fix breakfast.'

I went.

We spent the day rigging up a make-shift sluice out of a bunch of old boards Uncle Henry found under the bushes. They were left over from the original placer operation, which must have been quite an ambitious one. What we ended up with was pretty rough and a bit too short, according to Uncle Henry, but it worked. Just before sunset we threw a few shovelfuls of gravelly dirt into the sluice, and from the bottom riffle we extracted one gold nugget.

'Can I have it?' said Elaine.

'It's yours, darlin'.'

Uncle Henry went to bed early that night. He was an old

209

man, after all. In the afternoon I'd noticed the sweat dripping from his white mustache, the shaking hands, the back that was too weak to lift a twenty pound board. Yet it was remarkable that he was alive at all. The trip had rejuvenated him. He had an inner strength that overcame the weakness of the flesh. He was another Jedediah. And he was happy here. He was a man of the mountains. In Butte he was an old man in a bungalow. Here he was a man by a campfire, a man driven by a dream, a man who could pull his wages right out of the earth. And the earth was waiting, waiting. Before Uncle Henry went to sleep he instructed us to wake him if we heard any imaginary digging.

Elaine and I sat by the low fire. I told her I wanted to separate our sleeping bags.

She reached into my pants. She is nothing if not direct. Instantly, I had an iron bar down there.

'Want me to stop?'

'Yes,' I said. 'No! I mean . . . Yes.'

She stopped. 'Let me know when you make up your mind. Now come to bed, and do me a favor.'

The little imp. The sweetest people can make you miserable. Elaine was coming all over the sleeping bag; I was surrounded by her smell, her touch, her liquid; I forgot Erica; I knew only a physical need that doesn't look at faces; I had a hardness and an urgency like the barrel of a gun—and I was scared of the pain. Simply scared. Such pain is never forgotten. That is, not the pain but the effect. You don't remember the actual *feeling* of the pain. Your mind mercifully refuses to remember. What it does remember is how you reacted to the sensation of pain. And the way I reacted was that I never wanted to fuck again. I would think of it, and I would wilt. I would smell the sleeping bag, and I would blossom. Up and down. I had to see a doctor. I had to know if I was ready. It was driving me crazy.

White fluffy clouds were scudding over the moon. There would be minutes of moonlight and minutes of darkness. I slept fitfully, and awoke to the sound of the horse. And the breathing. And the digging.

I shook Uncle Henry. He didn't stir. I poured the water from a canteen on his face. He woke up sputtering.

'Hear it?'

He heard. He pulled a shirt and pants over his long johns. The moon went behind a cloud. We sneaked through the darkness to the bank of the creek.

The digging sounded like it was coming from all up and down the creek. The horse sounded like it was behind every tree. The breathing was above us, below us, all around us. We could see nothing.

'Mountain echo,' whispered Uncle Henry. 'Can't locate nothin'.'

'It isn't there,' I said.

The moon came out. All the forest turned silver blue like a television picture. And all the sounds focussed into one point, behind us. The horse. Hooves pounding. The horse was coming right at us. We could see it. A dark shrouded rider leaned into the wind and spurred the horse's flanks. It looked as if he wanted to trample us. We had just a moment to move. Uncle Henry threw himself to the side. I stood. I clutched Jedediah in my left hand. With my right hand I found the buffalo nickel in my pocket. I brought it out and threw it directly at the oncoming horse. The moon went behind a cloud. The horse did not trample me. The hoofbeats stopped. The forest was silent. Horse and rider were gone. Vanished. The buffalo nickel did not hit the rocks. I would have heard it. It never touched ground.

'Damn, boy, what the *hell* is going on?' Uncle Henry picked himself up off the ground.

'It isn't real.'

'*Something's* real. What did you throw?'

'A buffalo nickel.'

'Was it just my imagination, or did that nickel disappear?'

'The moonlight. You know. The clouds—'

'Well howdy-do.' He stared at me, studying me. I think it was the first time he'd ever really noticed me as an individual, as anything except Elaine's companion. 'What's that?'

'Jedediah.'

211

'What?'

'A grave marker.'

Uncle Henry jerked back. He looked stunned. It was as if I had slapped him. 'Come to the fire, Will, and tell me about it.' His shoulders sagged. His head hung. Suddenly he seemed very old. I offered a hand. He leaned on my arm as we walked to the camp.

'Lemme get a nip of whiskey, Will. Then I want to know.'

I told him the whole story, starting with Eddie and Junior and the ghost town in Wyoming, the Sleeping Lady mine, explaining how Jedediah had come to be the life force to me. When I had finished, Uncle Henry drew himself another slug of whiskey. He was serious and sad and resigned.

'Don't tell Elaine,' he said. 'Tomorrow we'll start at sunup and work all day. Whatever gold we get goes to Elaine. *All* of it. Tomorrow night I will let Jedediah rest in peace. The next mornin', you and Elaine must go.'

'I don't understand.'

'Nemme you mind. Just do it. You were wrong about the Sleeping Lady. I knew her. I'm a miner. I know these things. Those extra crosses you found. They didn't live. Didn't make no miraculous recovery. They're just the ones they never dug up. Never found. They're still down there, deep in that mine. You stole a dead man's tombstone. And he wants it back.'

The next day we labored from sunup to sundown. We produced a handful of gold. Uncle Henry tied it up in a little sack and gave it to Elaine.

At dinner Uncle Henry was pensive. He didn't touch a bite. He drank a quarter of a bottle of whiskey, though—all that was left.

In the sleeping bag Elaine noticed: 'Where's that board?'

'Uncle Henry's got it.'

'Where's Uncle Henry?'

'He took a walk.'

I wanted her to sleep. I figured ecstasy was the best way to put her there. I sucked on her nipples and licked her belly button. I kneaded her back, brushed her eyelids, stroked her neck. I drank her lips. I poked a finger up her ass and two up her cunt. I tickled the clit with my thumb. Mechanical. But effective. An hour of squirming and thrashing and moaning. She slept like the dead.

I dressed and went to look for Uncle Henry. A half moon. A shooting star. Orion. I found Uncle Henry sitting on a rock by the creek. I watched from the bushes.

For a long time the only sound was the low gurgle of the creek. I saw two shooting stars. It always surprises me that they are silent. They should crackle and explode. Uncle Henry sat quietly. I could see Jedediah on his lap.

I dozed. I awoke to the sound of a horse. The moon was just above the mountains. Uncle Henry was walking upstream toward the sound of the horse, carrying Jedediah.

I followed.

The horse walked up the creek. I couldn't see it, but I could hear it splashing. We followed it into a narrow canyon. The slope got steeper. The water was cascading over rocks like stairsteps. I didn't see how a horse could negotiate such a trail, but still I could hear it up ahead. Uncle Henry was having trouble. I could see him slipping on moss, stumbling on rocks. His chest was heaving. Sometimes it was necessary to wade in the water. It was ice cold and running very fast. It burned the skin. Uncle Henry sat down to rest. I hid in a shadow. Up ahead, the unseen horse snorted and nickered. In the woods upstream I saw a soft glow. Foxfire? In Idaho? Or a reflection of the moon, perhaps. Way off in the distance I heard the howling of a wolf, so far that it might have been simply the wind. Uncle Henry was walking toward the glow. The low moon seemed brighter at this altitude, this thin air, reflecting from the rocks and the snowy peaks. I couldn't move any farther without stepping into the light. It would be like dancing into a spotlight. I crouched behind my rock. Uncle Henry tripped. I heard him curse as he picked himself up. The horse neighed. The sound came from the area of the glow, but still I couldn't see it.

'Jedediah!' Uncle Henry called.

The name echoed throughout the forest.

'Jedediah! You old rattlesnake!'

Uncle Henry was approaching the glow. The horse neighed and shuffled. There it was! I could see it in the dim light of the glow, and a dark-shrouded rider, in front of an outcropping of rock. I had to get closer. Uncle Henry was far enough away that I could dash across the open area. I ran into the moonlight. An odd thing happened. For a moment I could feel all the meandering forces of my life gathering at this instant, focussing on this anonymous man running madly across a clearing in the Idaho wilderness under the cold, unrelenting light of the moon. The moment passed. I reached the shade of tall pines. I circled Uncle Henry's path and sank in a bed of pine needles in a thicket of young trees. I could see the glow clearly now, coming from nowhere, and the dark horse with its faceless rider. Behind them I saw an opening in the rocks, a pocket of blackness, a cave perhaps or — and then I knew — it was the mouth of a mine. I watched Uncle Henry step up to the glow. I wasn't going to let anything happen to the old man. I could run to him in a few seconds if I had to.

Uncle Henry stood before the horse and rider. Not a word was spoken. Uncle Henry was trembling, wiping sweat from his face, Jedediah's sign in his hand at his side.

The rider dismounted. He took the horse by the bridle strap and led it into the mine. It disappeared in the blackness, but you could hear the slow clop-clop-clop echoing up the walls as the horse stumbled its way deeper into the earth. Uncle Henry stepped to the mine. He turned and looked back at the world and listened to its Mother Lode — the murmuring grass, the noble white pine whispering slightly to a gentle wind, the distant gurgling of the creek with its life-giving water and its paydirt full of riches, the ever-so-faint howling of a faraway wolf, the hoot of an owl, the chirp of a mountain bluebird, the strong silent presence of the mountains with their white peaks and green meadows, their skirts of dark forest, their glistening lakes and brutal rocks — he raised his eyes to the sky where the first hint of dawn was lightening the eastern ridges, the morning star shining, twinkling, and — dammit — the lights of a jet plane winking purposefully across the heavens. Then Uncle Henry turned his head in my direction, and though I knew I was hidden in my thicket of trees on my bed of pine, I could feel his eyes boring right into mine so that I felt utterly naked and exposed, as if all my secrets were his to know—and if he knew them, he didn't care; they were but the dreams of a child, the romantic musings of one who has yet to learn the mysteries of this life.

Uncle Henry turned back to the mine. He stepped into the blackness. I heard his footsteps, following the horse. I waited a minute while the sounds got fainter, the echoes deeper.

I came out of hiding. I walked to the opening. I hesitated at the edge of the light, one step from darkness. I felt a cold wind.

The earth shuddered.

Instinctively I stepped back.

The rumbling swelled up from deep in the belly of the earth. Dust and smoke and gas poured out of the mine. It was over in an instant. I was alone in the forest, standing by an outcropping of rock where once there had been a mine.

I ran for Elaine.

KETCHUM

In The Heap we roared banging and backfiring down the trail, totally lost, simply aiming downhill, Elaine and I not speaking but staring fiercely ahead while I battled to control the hulking monster of a rattletrap truck; I swerved around switchbacks and crashed through washouts; Elaine grimaced at every bump, tears on her cheeks, fingering Uncle Henry's nightcap in her lap (I had told her not to keep the nightcap, that it might haunt her as Jedediah had haunted me, but she said Uncle Henry wouldn't do that kind of thang and of course she was right); we plowed through giant puddles like lakes and nearly wiped out a herd of sheep, the sheepherder shaking his fist and cursing in Basque, wild with rage though we didn't hit anything but I think he rarely had a chance to get mad at another human being and he wanted to make the most of it, venting a year of pent-up rage; suddenly in the wilds we passed a pipeline and a giant pumping station full of painted valves and pipes curling and writhing like a basket of snakes and I knew we hadn't passed this monster on the way in, we were hopelessly lost, and then after another twenty miles of guesswork and logging roads we suddenly emerged from a thick grove of trees onto a smooth, black asphalt road. It was such a shock that I stopped the truck and sat there, stunned, idling the engine while camper trucks and station wagons went whizzing by.

I said, and it was the first word spoken since we had left camp, 'Where are we going?'

Elaine's fingers worried the nightcap. Tears had left tiny

216

cakes of salt on her cheeks. She wiped her nose. 'I'm going to Saint Lou.'

'Why?'

'Al's getting out.'

'*Al*?'

'We'll come back and work the mine.'

'You'll never *find* it.'

'*He* can.'

'But he's—He's such a—'

'You know what I used to do when I had to get out of bed in the morning? I'd say, "Al, kick me out of bed." And he'd *do* it. He'd *kick* me out. Nobody else would kick me out of bed in the morning.'

I then made the mistake of calling Al a creep. Elaine called me a creep. We had a big fight, while The Heap kept idling and the camper trucks kept whizzing by. The argument ended when there was a boom and a sheet of flame from The Heap's engine. We bailed out and watched it die. I tried to put my arm around Elaine's shoulder. She rolled away. She was still grim.

'So long, Willy.'

'So long, kid.'

'*I ain't a kid!*'

She stomped across the road. She was hitching east. In a minute, she had a ride in a Volkswagen bus.

But she *was* a kid. And that was what was so great about her. She'd never grow up. She'd always believe she could go back and find gold somewhere up in the Idaho hills.

I awoke shivering in my blue Navy jacket on a cold Idaho dawn. My head pounded. Where was I? I'd gone on a drunk, a two day drunk which hadn't been easy in the local redneck bars. I'd had a fight. I don't remember who or when or what for. I'd wandered. Passed out. My head ached. My tongue felt like a dry sponge. A sour taste in my throat. Ugh. Where was I? I'd slept on the ground without a blanket. No. Not on the ground. I sat up. My eyes swam. I'd slept on a flat marble slab

217

just an inch above the ground. Or maybe it was granite. I don't know. A flat slab between two small pine trees with grass all around and a little white wooden cross with plastic flowers intertwined . . .

A cemetery. A small grassy one, just like a thousand midwestern boneyards except this one was in a valley with the Sawtooth ridges soaring up on either side. And right above and overlooking the graveyard was a gleaming silver mobile home. And others, beyond. A sign: KETCHUM TRAILER PARK. From the near trailer I heard thumping, shouts, glass breaking, furniture scraping; I saw a woman pushed out the door and heard a man's voice: 'Tramp! Get away!' She walked slowly away, buttoning a dirty white coat, her hair hanging in long black tangles. Her stocking was torn.

Rest In Peace. It won't be easy. Cars rumbled on the highway. Down the road I saw a Holiday Inn.

I stood up and, gripping my temples, walked from grave to grave, reading the tombstones. It seemed like they were all babies. Many had died the same day they were born. Some were recent, some went back to 1895 or so. Bootie Hill? I was in a grim mood. I was getting a low opinion of local health care, particularly obstetrics. I was half expecting to find my own grave. I felt ready to crawl in and pull the dirt over me like a warm, heavy blanket. I paused before a picture of a lamb on a small white marble slab:

WILBUR BARNES
Drowned
June 12, 1881
AGED
3 yrs. & 12 ds.

Over the body a small white mushroom was growing.

I returned to see whose slab I had slept on, who it was who had kept me dry and off the ground for one more restless night. And then I saw. Well! Land sakes. You could have blown me over with a feather. *Ernie.* Ernie Miller. July 21, 1899. July 2, 1961. I'd never known his middle name was Miller. I'd slept on Ernie Miller's grave. I felt guilty, shabby,

218

hollow, disrespectful — and then suddenly I realized it didn't mean a damn thing. The old macho blunderbuss had supported me through the long night. I'd probably made better use of his grave than anyone ever had before. He'd probably be happy to see somebody benefit from it, even Willy Crusoe Middlebrook, suburban romantic, castrated fugitive, fellow potato. I could almost hear his ghost, Ernie Miller's ghost, chuckling at me at this very moment. Perhaps he knew, as I had been wondering, whether the violence we do unto others could possibly be worse than the violence we do unto ourselves.

I picked a yellow wildflower from along the fence below the trailer camp. I placed it on Ernie's slab and stood over him with my hands folded behind my back. I had the creepy feeling that a momentous change had come over my life. Some unseen hand had guided me to Ernie Miller's grave. It was an omen. It had to have meaning. The forces of my life were gathering strength for a grand push in a new direction. I walked purposefully toward the town. Enough of this fucking around. The sun was rising. I was going to do my daddy proud. I was going to step into my place in the world, my role in society. I could deal with the law face to face, man to man. I had a wife to take care of, children to raise, a job to find. I could be a productive citizen. I was ready to put my life in order.

Or at least, it was pretty to think so.

LEONARD AND CLYDE, *just out of jail*
Clyde *picked his nose with a ten penny nail*
Leonard *read a Bible, said, 'Hear me, oh Lord,*
Take me to Heaven in this Forty-nine Ford.'

  Mother America
  What have you done?
  All of your children
  Out on the run.

The Ford blew a rod, but Clyde didn't care
Tho Leonard he screamed and pulled at his hair
They set up house by the side of the road,
The world was their garden, and they were the toads.

  Mother America
  And Father, too
  Leonard and Clyde
  Me and you.

They lived in that Ford for years ninety and nine
Gurus of highway, at home in their shrine
If you think this is funny man you better be sure
Death's a disease only living can cure.

  Mother America
  Where's that, you say?
  Boston, Massachusetts
  To San Francisco Bay.

  Mother America
  It goes on and on
  The beginning of life
  Is the end of our song.

—Tony's Dance Band

TWIN FALLS

The new me. Purposeful. Organized. Businesslike. I set up office in a phone booth outside a Chinese restaurant in Twin Falls, Idaho. With a few collect calls I confirmed that, with or without my presence, the various streams of my life flowed on, and it sounded like some of the tributaries were about to converge. At St. Louis. The meeting of the waters. Mrs. Patman told me that she'd just heard from Erica, who was on her way to Wheeling at that moment. She also told me that Mr. Patman was on his way home from Tacoma, Washington, and that I could catch him in Twin Falls. He was going to call her tonight, and she'd warn him to watch for me at the truck stop. He was going to Denver, then St. Louis, then Cincinnati, then Wheeling. St. Louis. So I called Bumpy, who said Al was out, Elaine was coming— she'd called—they were talking about some crazy scheme about gold in Idaho which Bumpy didn't put much store by but at least it would get Al out of town so he'd quit hanging around the cafe, but before he left— Bumpy whispered over the long distance wires — Al had some scheme cooked up which he said would clear my name. Al had been meeting some guy in the cafe every day for a week — a guy named Double Arrow — weirdo hippy freak, this Double Arrow — and the two of them had left word with Bumpy that if he heard from me he was to tell me to call this Arrow feller. So I called John. It was the old John. I knew it instantly. 'Willy! Far fucking out! Hey buddy, it's getting mellow! What's this single arrow bullshit? Double all the way! Thought you might be *dead*, it's been so long since anybody heard—Erica went home. Did you know? How come you

221

didn't tell me about her? You ran out on her, schmuck. Of course I know. The Shadow knows . . . Oh, I made a few phone calls. I'm Philip Marlow's illegitimate son. Well anyway. Listen, come to Saint Louee and we'll tie up the pieces, man. Me and Al did all the legwork already. We made a deal with some people. That Al. Kee-rap, man, he'd sell his mother into white slavery. How'd you ever get mixed up with a dude like that? Don't worry, he isn't helping you out of charity. There's an angle. It's pretty complicated. There's this thing here—you won't believe—called The Blob. They—Oh, you're hip to all that. Good. Cause I can't explain it on the phone anyway. Meet me in Saint Louee, Louee—I mean Willy—meet me in Saint Willy, Louee—I mean—Christ I'm stoned. Good to hear your voice, man. Me and Lucy split. I'm gay. Can you deal with that?' And suddenly he sounded unsure.

'Yeah man. I can deal with that.'

'I *knew* I could count on you, Willy boy! Lucy blames you. If she seemed hostile—Yeah. Right. So I dropped out of med school. What a zoo. In a class of a hundred, two committed suicide, three got shipped to the nutty farm—and they're the *sane* ones, I mean you should see what they left *behind*—twenty-two flunked out, nine transferred, and fourteen dropped out. It's like war, man. They expect a few casualties. This one guy—I'll tell you when you get here. You *are* coming, aren't you?'

Sure. I was coming. Hadn't I resolved to put my life in order? First I'd straighten out this messy little legal situation in St. Louis, then move on to Wheeling and settle things with Erica. I'd get a job. She could have a kid. Or even two kids. We'd buy a house—*near* the river, this time, right smack dab *on* the river if she wanted it—and stop this business of running away from each other. Running away from our problems. Our responsibilities. Our commitments and duties and obligations. Our . . . places in society.

TRUCKIN'

Love. A man in love. With a truck. Erica's father loved his truck. He loved trucking. He loved the hundred mile coffee. He loved screaming downslope in Georgia overdrive between purring stacks and whining tires, and he loved the low growl of the diesel as he double-clutched through twelve gears trying to bring twenty ton of payload uphill against the wind. He was no longer a man. He was a piece of a monster machine with eighteen wheels on five axles carrying forty feet of Consumer America, and yet it wasn't a monster to him; it all fit in the space between his eyes. He looked like a giant perched on that air suspension saddle where you can see road like you've never seen it before — when a car passes, all you see inside is legs — he had a penthouse on wheels and he grew ten inches taller as soon as he stepped into it, then shrank back to a little stogie-chewing fiddler as soon as his boots hit the pavement of the parking lot. And he was in love. Driving truck. I had to admit, it sure looked better than chugging Coca-Cola over the pot-holed streets of Wheeling. He owned a ten-year-old Kenworth cabover that had already seen over a million miles of concrete and asphalt. Definitely it was past its prime, but even an old Kenworth is still a Kenworth — like an old Jaguar is still a Jaguar — and Erica's father carried a full set of tools so if he needed he could do a complete overhaul at the side of the road, which in fact he had already done. Twice. A man in love. In baby blue letters he'd painted NO NO NANOOKIE on the door — a vow he'd made to Mrs. P — a vow he broke the way a politician breaks promises — casually, constantly, at every massage parlor, with every pavement

223

cess at every truckers bar but with the understanding that
dn't matter because it was only nanookie, his love was
lready taken by a rig with a dash like an airplane with speed-
writer, tachometer, air pressure gauge, temperature
gauges, electric gauges, heater switches, light switches, red
lights, orange lights, headlights, spotlights, cab lights—a
whole lighthouse. But Lord, he loved that truck. He loved it
with a passion equalled only by his hatred for I Can Catch
him (ICC), Death on Truckers (Department of Transporta-
tion, state police, the whole state of Ohio, the whole popula-
tion of New York. He could laugh at the big rig men, he could
live with a kidney buster. He knew that GMC and FORD
stood for General Mess of Crap and Fix Or Repair Daily. He
respected the Bulldog, the Emeryville, the Pete, the Freight-
liner, the Cat, the other Katydids. He didn't mind hauling
reefer, he could watch for the bubble gum machines, his belly
could deal with a heartburn palace. No cackle crates for him,
no pork chop express, no garbage, he wasn't a relocation con-
sultant, a bedbug hauler. He was a sailor on a concrete sea.
He had a three speed hat and a chain drive wallet. He knew
that music meant KLAC in Los Angeles and WWL in New
Oleans, KNEW in Frisco and KXWL in Iowa, WBAP in
Texas and WWVA back home and KOB all over the West
from midnight to dawn. He'd followed the taillights of
Phantom 309; he'd hauled alongside Giddy-Up Go. He could
keep the rubber side down, keep her between the ditches,
keep the lipstick offa his dipstick.

Half the time I hardly knew what he was talking about.
The other half, when he wasn't talking truck, I could still
recognize the same old half-crazy hillbilly, or crazy half-hilly-
billy—whichever—that he always had been.

'So you're gone back, hey? Gone face the music. Cain't hide
forever, huh Willy boy? Cain't run away from all the problems in the world. Police in Saint Looey, wife in Wheeling. I
was you, I'd ruther face a cop than that kid of yourn. Yep,
she's a kid—ain't no woman yet. Shouldn't never a let her get
married in the first place, ceptin we thought it was a godsend
—a chance to get that wild critter outa the house fore she

killed us both or drove us to the poorhouse with all her bills for
being a loony.'

'Hey. She's not a—'

'We thought you was the number one sucker wantin to
shack up with a bobcat like that. Marriage like that cain't
last. You're way too old for her, anyways.'

'We're both young,' I said with a sigh and a shrug.

It was late evening. We were grinding through the
Wyoming desert somewhere between Rock Springs and
Rawlins. Earlier in the twilight I'd seen antelope skittering
over the sagebrush. Now I saw nothing but blackness beyond
the edges of highway. There were no people out there, no
lights, no houses or human warmth.

Mr. P relit a stogie. The smoke made my eyes burn. He
poked it into the gap in his teeth and nibbled with his lips,
ruminating, staring at the road ahead, leaning his weight on
the big steering wheel. Clipped to the sun visor was a picture
of John F. Kennedy. Shepherd of the Interstates. Mr. P saw
me eyeing it. He asked, ' How old were you when young
Kennedy was shot?'

'Sixteen.'

'You reckymember what you were doing when you heard
the news?'

'Sure. I was in school.' I paused. The memories flashed.
Wyoming disappeared. 'They announced it over the P.A.
Then they cancelled all the classes. I had a dentist appointment. Everybody on the bus was listening to this old black
lady's transistor radio. She was sitting in the front seat with
tears running down her face. Everybody was quiet. I remember I didn't even feel any pain at the dentist's. I bought a
newspaper on the way home—they ran an extra, the first one
I'd ever seen—and I read the front page over and over again.
The radio station I always listened to—a rock and roll
station—was playing nothing but this real subdued music,
muted trumpets and crap like that. My older brother came
home that night—he'd moved out and was living with a girlfriend downtown, and my parents had disowned him—he
came home for the weekend because we had a TV set and he

wanted to watch it. He sat in front of that set for four days
We all did. We didn't even fight. We just couldn't believe it
Christ. I remember little John-John saluting, and that rider-
less horse that they couldn't control. And DeGaulle marching
in a plain uniform. Wow. I haven't thought about that in
years. I remember *everything*.'

Mr. P was rubbing his eye. 'Erica don't.' He sniffled. 'She
didn't even know it happened. She's eight years old. Didn't
even know who the President *was*.' He seemed to recover
now—I think he'd been moved by my memories. 'And that's
the point. You reckymember every little thing that happened
that day, and she don't know jack shit about it cause she was
just a little twerp back then. Don't tell me you're both young.
You're a whole different genee-ration from her. You was disappointed. You had eye-deals. Does she have eye-deals?'

I reflected a moment. 'Sure,' I answered. 'Sure she does.'

'Like what?'

'*Life*.'

'*Life?* That ain't no eye-deal. That's a *thing*.'

'It's also an ideal.'

Mr. P rubbed his chin. 'Talkin' to you is like talkin' to a
woman. Now I'm askin' you, does Erica care one lousy half
damn about politics?'

'No.'

'Do you?'

'No.'

'You don't care who's President?'

'Nope. One of these days, one of them will push the button,
and we'll all be charbroiled. Doesn't matter which one does
it.'

'But you *used* to care?'

'I guess so.'

'You *guess* so? You just told me every little bitty thing that
happened on the day Kennedy got shot. You even told me
what music was on the *radio*.'

He paused to relight the stogie.

'I don't think that's our problem,' I said. 'I mean I guess it's
true and everything, but it doesn't affect our relationship.'

'Well then what is it? You shore as hell got a problem some-wheres. You keep runnin' out on one t'other.'

'I guess . . . I think we didn't want to . . . face up . . .'—for some reason I had to pull the words out—'. . . face up to . . . our . . . responsibilities.' There. I'd said it. What was so hard? Responsibilities. We had to pay our dues. Love is more than fucking and feeling tender and having fun. We had to support each other, help each other. And to do that, we had to understand each other. Which we didn't. As a matter of fact, we hardly even related to each other in a rational way. We related through a current of feeling that flew between us like a million volts. Sometimes touching Erica was like touching a spark. A look—that first look after we had been separated for a time, or maybe just for the day, or even that first look when we woke up together at the beginning of a new day with the sun pouring in the window when we'd both turn our heads on the pillow in that grimy apartment in Wheeling and suddenly our eyes would meet—and rivers of feeling would run between our pupils to that space in the mind where unknown forces are propelling us through our lives, and in those precious moments I understood her perfectly, impli-citly, absolutely, I understood her wants and fears and her every need, and then she would look away or I would scratch my belly or a car would honk, and suddenly with the contact broken we became two strangers together in a bed thinking our own thoughts, following our separate dreams. Rationally, analytically (focussing my perception from the old logical and benevolent world of the suburbs where I was raised), what could I say about Erica? She had freckles. That was my first requirement in a woman. She was left-handed. That was my second. Freckles to me are simply beautiful, but as to why a woman must be left-handed I am hard put to explain. It sets her apart, I guess. It shows that her brain is organized in a different mode. It shows independence, perhaps alienation. But mainly, it grabs me in the gut. Which isn't rational. Which I'm trying to be. Rationality: There is a definite physical attraction. So what? Physical attraction is the easiest thing to talk about, easy to describe, a cop-out. I am physically attracted to thousands of women—intensely attracted—but I don't pursue them. Or of the few I did pursue, the relationship didn't last long because physical attraction wears thin fast after you have seen somebody groggy with sleep on a work day morning or crabby after a hard day—after you have seen her drunk and silly—after you have seen her on the toilet. There's got to be more. And there is. But what? What else about Erica? She talks to birds. She sings. She's a good fuck and a bad cook. She's clean. She's pretty. She likes to smoke dope. She wears dresses from the 5 & 10. She doesn't shave her legs. She likes to play Monopoly. When she goes for a walk, she has to stop and make friends with every dog she meets. She wants to have a baby. She flips out from time to time. I am older than her by a period equalling half of her lifetime.

Which explains nothing. What draws her to me? She says she thinks I'm handsome (most women don't). She thinks I'm smart. She thinks I'm strong and calm at times when she gets too excited. She likes the fact that I like her parents. It's important to her even though she doesn't like them much herself. She likes the fact that I've been to a lot of places, especially San Francisco. She wants me to take her there. She likes the way I fuck. She likes me because when she's living with me she doesn't have to live with her parents. She used to like me because I could give her a baby. She thinks I'm wise and worldly, and she looks up to that because she thinks of herself as a country hick. A hillbilly woman. A wild child. A nature girl. A blossoming flower. A woman. Wo. Man.

Mr. P was talking. I hadn't been listening. I had to ask him to repeat.

'I say, it ain't responsibilities. It ain't relationships. Don't gimme them ten dollar words. Here it is for two bits: you got to run away, cause it's so nice to come back. You don't know how nice it is to breathe unless you stop. You ever been sick, laid up for a week, and then when it's over you walk around feelin' how nice it is just to *walk*? And then a day later you forget, it's just walkin', just like you always done. So you 'n her forget. You stop feelin' that old nice feeling. So you run. And

228

then when you come back, there's that old nice feeling again. The worser the pain, the better the relief. The longer you're apart, the nicer when you get back. It's like pounding your head against the wall because it feels so good when you stop. You keep workin' at it, you'll figger out that the best way to separate, to make your love never die, is to kill yourself. And that's crazy.'

'You think we're crazy?'

He removed the stogie from his mouth and tapped the end on an ashtray. 'Didn't say that.'

'Mrs. P does.'

'Then so do I. Ah me . . . Mrs. P. Lawd, lawd.' He poked the stogie back into the gap in his teeth. 'Two more days and I'll see her again.'

'How long has it been?'

'Thirty days.' He sucked, then gave loose with a giant cloud of smoke. 'Thirty long days. Lawd, lawd. Got to cut out this life.'

'You don't mean that.'

'Shore do.'

'You love trucking.'

'Never see Mrs. P any mores.'

'But when you see her, is it nice?'

'Why, boy! Never been better!'

'You'll never quit this life.'

'Thirty days. Lawd, lawd. Can't *wait* to see her again.'

I 70

At a truck stop near Colby, Kansas, a spaced-out dude in
tattered pants asked Mr. P for a ride. He was just a kid,
maybe seventeen. From the hairline to the eyebrow, a scab
was oozing pus. Every minute or so, the kid wiped it away with
the cuff of his shirt. Mr. P would have refused the ride, but I
asked him as a favor and he consented. We took the kid to
Topeka where he directed us to a shopping center parking
lot. He had spent the whole ride shivering and refusing to
talk. Now he pointed to a Goodwill pickup box and asked Mr.
P to drive up to it.

'You gonna make a donation?'

The kid shook his head.

'You gonna steal some of that trash?'

The kid shook his head. He shivered — you could see it
move up and down his spine. A drop of pus ran into the
corner of his eye.

'Can't you walk that far?'

'There's people I shouldn't . . . see . . .'

He would say no more. He simply sat there, shivering.

Mr. P gunned the engine and pulled the giant semi
through the parking lot and stopped right beside the Goodwill box.

The kid looked around. He checked every corner of the
parking lot. He was scared to death. He crouched low.
Cautiously he opened the cab door and without setting foot
on the pavement climbed directly from the truck to the Goodwill package door. He slid in. I heard a thump.

For a full minute Mr. P and I sat watching the box. There was no movement, no sound.

Mr. P shook his head, tooted the air horn, and headed back for the highway.

ST. LOUEE, LOUEE

No doubt about it. Spring had arrived. The air was warm and moist and brimming with life. Everywhere I looked, it seemed like every patch of grass was covered with a flock of robins; every tree was full of cardinals. The sky was swirling with birds. Leaves were budding. The land was green, that special light fresh green of beginning life, of new photosynthesis, of countless burgeoning cells bursting one upon the other, of egg meeting sperm, the dance of the chromosomes, pollen and spore, cubs and nestlings and mothers and the wetness of birth and all the exploding forces of life. And I was in a phone booth at a truck stop in St. Louis, choking on diesel exhaust, straining to hear over the rumble and roar. Right outside the booth, a forklift was darting about, unloading pallets, dropping them with a clank and a crash. I could barely hear the dial tone, the ringing, John's voice: 'What's happening, man?'

'Arrow Comma One calling Arrow Comma Two. Do you read me, Arrow Comma Two?'

'Ah.' He was always quick. 'Arrow Comma Two reads you loud and clear. You idiot. And Arrow Comma Two would like to say for the record that he is very very pleased to hear from Arrow Comma One. Where are you?'

'I'm at the—'

'Whoops! Shh!'

'What?'

'You at a public phone?'

'Yeah.'

'Give me the number. I'll call you back from a pay phone.

That way they can't listen in.'

'Who can't?'

'The Commies.'

'Yeah. Well. I'm at the—'

'DON'T SAY IT!'

'You mean it?'

'Al said we oughta take precautions.'

So I gave him the phone number. We'd play Al's game. I waited ten minutes in the diesel-soaked air. I watched a caterpillar crawl up the side of the booth.

The phone rang.

'Okay,' said John. 'Now we can talk.'

'I don't like this game.'

'It's Al's game. The whole deal is his game. I think you oughta play along. He's doing you a big favor.'

'Al? Al doesn't do favors.'

'True. But if in the process of doing what he happens to be doing, you get the charges dropped, that's a favor.'

'You really think it can work?'

'Dunno. But it sounds promising. He's here. You want to talk?'

'All right.' I didn't, really. I was watching the caterpillar hump along the side of the phone booth.

Al's voice: 'Hey. You there?'

'Yeah,' I said. 'What's these games?'

'*Games?* Willy boy, your *life* is on the line in this town. You should *see* these guys. If *anybody* finds out you're here—and I mean *anybody*—except me and John and Elaine and Bumpy—'

'Bumpy. He's cool.'

'Yeah—if *anybody* else finds out you're in town, your ass is grass and I don't mean Acapulco Gold, man. You savvy? You connote?'

'Yeah.' Crap. Games. 'I connote.'

'You hip?'

'I'm hip. And you're . . .' Crazy, I was going to say, but why bother? I'd scooped the caterpillar off the side of the booth and was letting him cruise up and down my fingers. It was a

233

jolly little furry thing, green with red dots.

'Hey!' Al was shouting. 'Do you understand?'

'Yeah. Sure.'

I noticed a ladybug had landed on the coin slot. I cradled the phone on my shoulder, kept the caterpillar occupied with my left hand and tried to nudge the ladybug onto a right hand finger. Nothing doing. Every time I nudged, the ladybug skittered a few inches away. I tried placing a finger on both sides, but my lady took to the air. Meanwhile, the caterpillar was crawling up my sleeve. And John was back on the phone explaining how I should meet him at the corner of Skinker and Delmar—he would be there already, and I was to approach cautiously and double back to make sure nobody was following me, and when I saw him I wasn't to reveal myself if he was standing with his legs crossed, which meant it wasn't cool and I was to split.

I consented to play it Al's way. I'm an easy-going guy. But I knew I couldn't take it seriously, not just because it was unpleasant to live that way but because taking it easy was necessary for my survival. You can stay away from The Man as long as you don't fear him. He'll see your fear. He knows how to handle fear. What he doesn't know, what he can't handle, is being ignored. If you just live your life, have fun, enjoy yourself—and don't let your name, your *real* name, get on any documents—you're invisible. You're just another potato. And potatoes are invisible—under the ground. Out of the light.

So I had Mr. P drive me to the corner of Skinker and Delmar, and I even had him double back to see if we were being followed, which of course we weren't, and I saw John standing with his legs set apart, so I arranged to call Mr. P at his motel room and jumped down from the truck.

John hustled me away to a cafe around the corner. He was all grins. He no longer looked like a med student. He had a beard like a wild man and hair to his shoulders. He looked great. This was the man I would expect from the boy I had known. The med student had been an aberration, a wrong turn. Now he was back on the highway of his life. I was glad.

But I wanted to talk about this cops and robbers routine.

'John,' I said when we were settled in a booth in a dark corner at the rear of the cafe, 'it's a beautiful spring evening, and the air smells pretty as perfume, and it's great to see you, but god damn it I have never *ever* seen such paranoia.'

'Willy.' He lost the grin. 'We're not hiding you from the cops. The guys who want you here, they aren't gonna read you your Mir*anda* rights. They don't *need* a search warrant. They don't *care* about your social security number.'

We ordered barbecue beef sandwiches, which came with salad and potato chips and coffee, and John told me he was annoyed by my attitude and that I had to be extremely cautious or the whole complicated deal — which he couldn't explain here — would fall apart and I'd probably get dumped in the river. I promised not to make a spectacle of myself. I was cocky. Looking back on it, I can see just how cocky I was.

Since John refused to talk about what I'd come all the way to St. Louis for, we talked about ourselves, and John started grinning again. I told him some of my adventures, and he his. His medical school sounded more like a loony bin to me — a highly competitive loony bin. He reeled off story after story, casualty after casualty. I got the distinct impression that med school is like jail. It breaks people. I was worried that it might have broken John — this intense, hairy man who was once like a brother to me — and I tried to probe.

'How's Lucy?' I began with my usual finesse.

He grimaced through his wild hair. 'I told you we split.'

'So how is she?'

'What do you care about that cunt? She hates you, too, I know. She blames you.'

'*Should* she?'

'No.' He scratched his ear. 'Well. I don't know. I mean you and I never —' He stopped talking and stared rigidly, fixedly at my face for a few seconds. I met his gaze. Our eyes burned. Something passed between us then — a moment of absolute wordless truth. Some mechanism within the mind released its gate behind the eyes and opened a direct line to the soul. John sipped some coffee. Then he spoke into his cup, 'I'm

235

homosexual, but sometimes . . . I don't exactly . . . feel *gay*.

'How — uh — John — how long — has. . .'

'Always.'

'You mean even when we were — like —'

Softly: 'Always.'

It boggled my mind. 'Remember the night — you and Gai
in the front seat while Emmalee — and me — in the back? Eve
then?'

'Of course.' He was no longer speaking to his cup. He spoke
to my eyes. '*Especially* then. What do you think it means
both of us in the same car like that?'

I'd never thought about that before. But how could he hav
carried such a secret when we were so close; how could thi
friend who I had loved and trusted and shared my adole
scence with, how could he turn out to have been a stranger a
that time? I felt like a teacher had just graded the paper of m
youth, and I had flunked.

'Does it matter?' John was studying my face, reading m
response.

'No! It's — I mean —' I struggled for thoughts, and th
thoughts struggled for words. 'It's just . . . that I thought . .
I *knew* you.'

'You did.'

'Were you ever with . . . boys . . . back then?'

'No.' He was still studying me. Judging me. I squirme
under his probing gaze.

'Did you ever . . .' Could I really say this? 'Did you ever . .
want . . . you know . . .'

'What?'

'Me?'

He looked pained. 'That ain't the meaning of Doubl
Arrow.'

'But did you?'

'I don't know.'

'Do you?'

'You mean now?'

'Yeah.'

'No.'

I think a straight person's greatest fear of gays—mine, anyway—is that one will make a pass at him. And he'll say yes. Maybe I will some day. I sort of hope I do. Then I can get over this fear.

Whew. I felt better. We had weathered this maudlin scene, and we could still sit together in this booth at the rear of the cafe ordering refills of coffee.

I asked when it had started.

'Like I said, it was always there.'

'But when did it . . . happen?'

'At Yale.'

'Without me.'

'Yes.'

I took comfort at this news. Like, he *needed* me. 'I was a steadying influence, huh? Me, and Putt-Putt, and old Emit Godwin.'

'Who?'

'The probation officer?'

'Oh. You mean the'—holding up his fingers like little quotation marks—' "Youth Counselor"?'

We both tested a chuckle, sort of chewing on it to see how it felt.

John said, 'We should've taken his sign.'

'It would've meant taking the whole door.'

'That's right. We should've.'

'But the door was in the *police* station!'

'We should've. Dressed up like carpenters and carried it right out.'

'You're right. We should've.'

We shared a laugh. Things were okay. John lit his pipe.

'When did you start smoking a pipe?'

'At Yale.' Squeaking against the old leather of the booth, fingering a spot that had torn and been patched with adhesive tape, John settled back in his seat. He sucked peacefully on the pipe. A grin crept into the corners of his mouth. 'You see, our House had a dog. His name was Botts. Botts had a brick. Everywhere he went, he carried this brick around in his mouth. Wore his teeth down to stumps. Wouldn't chase

237

sticks. Just wanted his brick, and no substitute bricks either. Slept curled up around it. Once somebody hid it from him, put it in his car and drove off. Parked the car across campus and went to class. When he came back, half the paint had been scratched off the car door and Botts was sitting on the hood. If Botts really liked you, he'd drop the brick on your lap if you were sitting or on your feet, which kinda hurt, if you were standing. You were supposed to pick it up, admire it, and give it back.'

'I guess I lost the thread of this somewhere.'

'So if Botts could have a *brick*, I could have a *pipe*. We all need *some*thing.'

'Are you stoned?'

'No.'

'Did you really decide to smoke a pipe because some dog was carrying a brick around in his mouth?'

'No.'

It was the same old John. I had no doubt of it now.

'When are you going to tell me about this great scheme of yours?'

He wouldn't. Not there. In fact he didn't want to tell me at all. It was all set up. My role was minor. I could perform it without understanding all the mechanics behind it. I just had to make a certain delivery to a certain person at a certain time. I'd probably do it better if I didn't understand it. Which is when I realized that what John was implying was that if I knew just what it was that I was supposed to deliver, and to whom, and why, I'd be scared out of my wits. I remembered The Black Spot, McDonald's, Philadelphia. Games. I didn't ask any more. But I began to be scared.

'Hey John.'

'Hmm.'

'Let's get drunk.'

John was amenable to the idea. We walked down the street to a bar called the Cameo Lounge. We sat in a booth way in back and got quietly, pleasantly loaded. We relived some old times, and then we realized that to celebrate our reunion we should go steal a sign. Nothing fancy—couldn't risk getting

238

arrested in this town—but something simple and symbolic. We hit the streets. I was overwhelmed with possibilities. I wanted the giant interstate sign that said

DANIEL BOONE EXPRESSWAY ↑
MARK TWAIN EXPRESSWAY →

The idea of an expressway named for Mr. Boone particularly appealed to me, but the sign was simply beyond our means. Poor Daniel would have to remain, a concrete monument to the free spirit of the green Virginia mountains and soft Kentucky rivers, the flintlock rifle, the man who felt crowded. There were more signs. There were billboards of all shapes and sizes touting beer, cars, waterbeds, candidates for mayor. All too big. Everything is too big. Poor Daniel. We walked down streets named Westminster, Rosedale, Kingsbury, Nina. The air was a curious mixture of moist spring rising life and some horrible chemical odor that John said came all the way from a Monsanto factory across the river. The evening vibrated with an excitement—a sense of possibilities and opportunities and the end of the cold forces of winter, the victory of life, the coming of summer's pleasure, of sun and fishing and growth on the land—folks were sitting on front stoops, smoking and drinking and laughing; music blew out from screen windows; I smelled a steak frying in garlic—or maybe the magic was just the reunion with an old friend, firming a relationship that had decayed, rediscovering old fine feelings of trust and comradeship and adventure, plus the chance to relieve a burden that had been hanging over my freedom so long now that I'd forgotten that I had once lived without any fear of the law. I was wandering in such a haze of good feeling that it was a shock to suddenly focus my eyes and not know where I was. I looked at John. He saw my surprise. He didn't understand. I couldn't explain. I was totally lost. What city was this? What movie theater of the mind? There was a vacant lot, a burned building, a broken shopping cart. A drunk in a doorway. Headlights. A car burning rubber. A couple dudes in fancy hats, jiving. 'John! Where—?' I was freaking out. The wasted landscape. An acid flash. It looked like Philadelphia. It looked like Oakland. It looked like Chicago and Boston and Wheeling, like every crummy run-down city I'd ever seen. What movie had I been watching? When I stepped out of the lobby, what streets would I encounter? I ran. I passed a laundromat, a palm reader, a pornie theater, a boarded-up window. I came to a corner, a street sign. I was on De Baliviere Avenue. John ran up behind me. 'John!' I clutched his arm. 'John. Where am I?'

'De Baliviere. Willy. What's the—'

'What city? Dammit. *What city?*'

'St. Louis. Hey Willy—'

I wanted that sign. It denoted the intersection of De Baliviere and De Giverville. It was the intersection of every street in my life. No matter where I travelled there would always be a De Baliviere. John didn't understand, but he helped me with the sign and in five minutes it was mine. We walked home silently. I was shaken. I carried the sign. I couldn't explain. John didn't ask. Good old John. He knew when to shut up. And Daniel—he understood. A slow smile came over his face as he lay in his tomb, his body crowded for eternity, his soul free at last, free of the lawyers who stole his land, free of the De Baliviere Avenues that had chased him across the continent. John and I walked to his one bedroom apartment on Waterman Street where I met Ron, his shadowy roommate. Ron said hello and retreated to the kitchen. I scarcely saw him again—ever.

'Ron's a bit shy,' John explained.

I called Mr. P to tell him I was spending the night with John. A woman answered. I asked for the fiddler. She said, in an easy-going sort of sexy voice, 'He's a-fiddlin' in the john. Who's calling?'

'Tell him it's Willy.'

'Willy who?'

'He knows who.'

'Well *I* don't.'

'Who are you?'

'Laureen.'

240

'Have I got the right room?'

'Dunno. It seems all right to me.'

'Is Mr. Patman there?'

'Hey Tiger! Is your name Patman?'

I heard him call back, 'Yeah. What's yours?'

She giggled. 'It's the right room.'

'Well, Laureen, tell Mr. P I'll see him in Wheeling in just a few days. And thanks for the ride.'

'Oh, you're welcome any time,' said Laureen. 'Bye-bye, Willy.'

John asked, 'Who was that?'

'Laureen,' I said.

'A friend?'

'Nope.'

'You told her your *name?*'

'Yep.'

He scowled.

I made a bed on the floor.

I couldn't sleep.

After an hour I got up and sat in an overstuffed chair in the dark apartment. John and Ron were asleep behind closed doors. I was tense. I searched through the kitchen but couldn't find any booze. I needed something to knock myself out. I dressed and walked a few blocks to the neon sign that said CAMEO LOUNGE. I ordered a beer and watched the big color television over the bar. Johnny Carson was introducing Johnny Mathis.

'He's fruit,' said the man to my left.

'Yeah,' said the bartender, wiping a glass. 'He's fruit.'

Two men in blue business suits and a young pretty-looking woman walked in. The two men sat at a table and ordered beer and drank without expression. The woman sat at the bar next to me.

'Bud,' she ordered, and then she looked at me. I looked back. She met my eyes. I was the one who looked away. I looked at the two men at the table. They were smoking and drinking and avoiding all expression. I looked at her again. She met my eyes again. She had clear eyes.

241

'Aw, he's *really* fruit,' said the man to my left.

'Yeah,' said the bartender. 'They're all fruit.'

The woman pulled a Winston out of her purse and turned to me. 'You got a light?'

'No. Sorry.' I really *was* sorry.

'That's okay.' She smiled. The bartender threw her a book of matches. She was sitting with her legs crossed, one leg swinging rhythmically. She was looking at me. She was about to say something when a man in a green parka burst into the lounge and ran up to the man at my left, spun him around on the stool and socked him in the jaw.

'Hey, you fruit!' He raised his hands in front of his face.

The man in the green parka hit him again.

I stepped away. I looked around. Nobody was doing anything. Everybody was watching the fight. Nobody was going to stop it. The man in the green parka was landing all the punches. Slap. Crack. Thud. The victim's nose was bleeding and his lip was cut.

'All right,' announced the bartender.

The fight stopped. The man in the green parka stood with his fists clenched at his side. His chest heaved.

'You made your point,' said the bartender.

The man in the green parka walked out. He never did say one word. The bartender handed some napkins to the victim to catch the blood from his nose. The other customers resumed drinking and watching television.

I noticed that the woman, and the two expressionless men in blue business suits, were gone.

The next morning John drove me to Bumpy's cafe to meet Al and Elaine. He insisted on driving down alleys and doubling back, signaling for turns but not taking them, and generally acting totally paranoid.

'Stop it, John, you're making me nervous.'

'We're being followed.' He studied the rear view mirror.

'Bull.'

'That blue Chrysler.'

I turned around to look. Two men in business suits.

'The one that's turning?'

'Uh-huh.'

'It turned.'

'It'll be back. You'll see.'

It didn't come back.

I walked into the cafe and Al said, 'Hello, sucker.'

'Hello, creep.'

Al scowled.

Elaine told us to cut it out. John and I sat down. Bumpy brought us water. He winked. I nodded. He glanced at the door. Nobody talked. Tension was high. It was ridiculous. I said, 'Where's the violin case?'

'The what?' said Al.

'We should all be in zoot suits. With tommy guns in violin cases.'

Elaine laughed. She could always laugh. Forgive and forget. She was too warm a person to hold a grudge. Al was somber. John was serious.

Al looked ten years older. His hair was cut short. His eyes were hollow, haunted. His skin was pale and dry. His fingers were stained brown where he clenched his Gauloise. He smoked with a fury. The cigarette crackled when he sucked. Smoke poured from his lungs. One side of his mouth was twitching uncontrollably. He'd spent less than half a year in jail.

Elaine was still Elaine. She sat with her legs crossed, completely relaxed, one hand on Al's shaking knee, the other holding a glass of orange juice. She met my eyes and smiled pleasantly. You'd never know we shared a sleeping bag in Idaho. It seemed like another world. It was.

'What are we doing?' I said.

John looked to Al. Al glared at me. 'You gonna do it?'

'Do what? Would somebody please—'

'Hey.' Al spoke to John. 'Shut him up.'

John tapped my arm.

I got mad. 'What are you—his enforcer?'

John looked annoyed. 'We can't talk about it here.'

'So when is the little creep gonna tell me what's happening?'

Al bounced up and stomped to the rear of the cafe. Elaine made a tut-tutting noise. I shouldn't have said creep. It was a trigger word with Al. John pushed his chair back. 'Come on, Willy. Let's go.'

I walked out fuming. I sat in John's car with my arms folded across my chest. John—his eyes regularly flicking up at the rear view mirror—said, 'You've gotta understand, Willy. This is for real.'

'It's a game.'

'Right, Willy. It's a game, and it's for real. Reality *is* a game.'

'Don't you think I should know something? I'm for real, too, you know.'

'It's tonight. Unless Al hears anything different. And it's very touchy.'

'*Al's* touchy.'

'He oughta be. You aren't the only one in trouble around here.'

'How's it going to get me off the hook?'

'You're going to set somebody up. Somebody the cops want to use.'

'They're in on this?'

'Sure.'

'They know I'm in town?'

'Probably. Anyway they expect you.'

'Great jumping jehosephat.' I sank deeper in the seat. 'Then who are we hiding from? This Blob bunch?'

'Blob's helping us. It was their man who got killed at Romey's, you know.'

'And they think *I* did it.'

'No. At least they won't hold it against you. As long as you help them with this thing.'

'Does the Blob know that the cops are in on it?'

'Yes. But the cops don't know about the Blob.'

'And just who are we after?'

'The guy who sent the two guys who killed the cop that

244

you got blamed for.'

By now I had sunk so deep in the seat that I couldn't see over the dashboard.

'What's in it for Al?'

'Freedom. Right now he's on a screwy sort of probation.'

'What's in it for *you*?'

'Nothing.'

'*Really*?'

He nodded. A true Double Arrow.

'You're full of shit.'

'Really. There's nothing in it for—'

'Not that. You. And Al. Al's full of shit. He's just a two bit punk. He couldn't swing this. He doesn't have the connections. You're talking about a big city. The cops. These guys —Al couldn't pull all that together.'

'It's not all that big a city.'

'It's bigger than Al.'

'It doesn't take much. This town—the key to St. Louis is —it doesn't *care*. They don't *care* about politics. They don't *care* about glamor—city stuff—art—nightclubs—excitement. All they care about is their paycheck and their baseball team. Football team. Hockey. Basketball. Go to a bar and try to strike up a conversation. What can you talk about? Sports. Cars. Beer. Look at the selections on a juke box. It's all *old* songs. They don't *care* what's on the hit parade. Listen to the radio. The top ten songs here are already dead and buried on the coasts. They don't *care*. Look what surrounds them. *Dirt*. Farms. You're maybe seven hundred miles from New Orleans, maybe nine hundred from the east coast, probably more from Denver. What is there? Just *land* out there. It never changes. Nothing changes. Why should they care? A few people with energy can take over this town. Nobody cares what happens across town. Nobody cares what happens in the next block. You want it? You can have it. Who *cares*? Al cares. He's an operator. He makes connections. In jail he met one of the guys who killed your cop. He connected. Now he knows who the other guy is. He's got information. Information is as good as money if you know how to trade. He traded.

He knows a cop. Another *connection*. The cop wants more information. The way to get information is to make a guy rat. The way to make a guy rat is to have a lever. A bust is a lever. The deal is, we set him up. Then they bust.'

'You mean *we* do the dirty work?'

'Yep. Because *we*—namely you and Al—want the results. Cops won't stick their neck out just because some jerk like Al fingers a guy.'

'So let Al set him up.'

'He knows Al.'

'So it has to be me.'

'Or me.'

'Me.' I couldn't let John get messed up in this. 'But how do we know he'll rat about Romey's?'

'Because *you* will identify him.'

'You mean I'll have to *talk* to the cops?'

'You were the only witness at Romey's. Who else could—'

'But you mean, I'll actually have to . . . meet . . . cops?'

'You'll probably have to appear in court.'

'You mean we're actually working *with* the system?'

'Sort of. But the system has two levels: above and below. Most of our work is below.'

'Like, underground?'

'Uh-huh.'

'Like me?'

'Uh-huh.'

'You're saying they're just like me? I'm just like them?'

'Nope. You're saying it.'

Touché. But . . . 'You sure this isn't some bullshit fantasy of Al's? And yours?'

'Can't be sure. You know Al.'

I knew Al. 'But you—if it isn't a fantasy, I mean—you really think it can work?'

He pursed his lips. He stroked his wild man beard. 'I sure hope so.'

'What if it doesn't?'

'Well, Al's probably betting his life on it.'

'What about me? What if it doesn't work?'

'Like I said, Willy, this is for real.'

Real . . . Meaning life. And death. Reality. What a drag. Suddenly I didn't want any part of it. Look at us. What a pair, John and I. The hippie and the half-ass romantic. We just didn't belong here.

'So,' I asked John, 'how could it go wrong?'

'They could find out about it.'

And they could find out from the cops, from Blob, from one of us—or they could simply find out I was in town and start working from there. But nobody knew I was here—except Mr. P, who was safe, and some broad named Laureen, who wasn't.

'There it is,' said John.

'What?'

'That blue Chrysler.'

'Turn!'

He turned.

The Chrysler went straight.

That night was a fiasco. John drove me to a loading dock behind an abandoned warehouse on the riverfront. He dropped me off. I was alone. I could hear the lapping of the river. A train creaked over Eads Bridge. Trucks growled. The loading dock was dark as a cave. Every window—every last shred of glass—had been broken from the warehouse. The walls were brick, black with age.

I hadn't expected to be scared, but this place was creepy. The longer I waited, the creepier it got. A little fog blew off the river, shrouding the lights. A perfect spot for a murder. I was exposed and alone. And scared. I was so scared that I had diarrhea. In the black shadow of the warehouse I had to squat and take a dump, hoping that whoever was meeting me wouldn't pull in while my pants were down. I waited an hour. Every shadow seemed to move. Every rustle was an assassin. I am a coward. I died a thousand deaths.

Headlights.

It was only Al. 'Come on. We're late.'

I got in. He zoomed out of the lot and down Broadway.

'Can't depend on *any*body,' he muttered.

'What's the matter?'

'Guy didn't show.'

'Is it off?'

'Hope not.'

Suddenly Al swung off Broadway and plunged into a neighborhood of rowhouses. He ran stop signs. He ran red lights. My fear took a new direction. I was afraid I'd die in a car accident. Al ran one last stop sign and swerved into a park. There were swings, jungle gyms. He screeched to a stop. 'Get out,' he said. 'Wait here.'

'For what?'

'They'll tell you.'

'Who?'

'You'll see.'

I got out. Al roared away. I sat on a swing. I could see a sign telling me I was in River Des Peres Park. I was a few feet from the River Des Peres. I could see it. Worse, I could smell it. It was an open sewer. I swang, gently. The swing chain creaked. I was alone. I waited. After a half hour, a car pulled into the parking lot, shut off its engine and turned off its lights. I waited. Nothing happened. A frog was croaking. I was listening for a horse. I walked over to the car. I couldn't see any silhouettes in the windows. I knew nobody had gotten out. Somebody had to be in there. Was this a trap? Cautiously, I approached. I made no noise. My bowels screamed. I clenched them back. My heart was pounding. My hands were shaking. I was in a cold sweat. I held my hands up to the glass and peered into the window on the driver's side. I expected to see death itself.

Instead, I saw one naked back.

Four naked legs.

One furious face.

I backed off. The car door opened. The man stepped out in his shorts.

'Sorry,' I said. 'There was—I was supposed to meet somebody.'

'You wanna die young?'

248

'Sorry. Hey. Listen. I'm supposed to meet somebody. I thought you—'

'Aw shit.' He got back in the car. Slammed the door. Started the engine. Backed out. Roared away. I'm sure he was still in his shorts.

I walked back to the swings.

I waited.

I swang.

I waited.

A frog croaked. A whippoorwill sang.

I waited.

At dawn, I walked out of the park and called John.

While I was waiting for John to pick me up, I called Wheeling. The phone rang and rang. Finally Erica's mother answered.

'Who's that?'

'Willy.'

'Willy. You know whut *time* it is, boy?'

I got Erica on the line. She said, 'Where *are* you?'

'St. Louis.'

'Pop's comin' home tomorrow.'

'I know. He brought me here.'

'When *you* comin'?'

'Very soon. I was hoping to clear up this thing, you know, but it looks like—'

'Why?'

'Why what?'

'Why bother?'

'So I don't have to worry about it. So I can be free.'

'You *are* free.'

'The Law—'

'I never *seed* anybody so free.'

'Yeah. Well. I'd like to be able to—'

'Willy. Come on home. You ready? I mean, can you—'

'Yeah. I can.'

'Come *on*, then. Ma's drivin' me *crazy*. I gotta get *out* of here.'

'Don't go crazy.' What a dumb thing to say. 'I'll get you out.'

'Hurry *up*, then.'

'I love you.'

'Don't gimme *words*.'

'I'll be there.'

Suddenly softly, she whispered: 'I miss you.'

She hung up.

Why, indeed?

John met me and I told him Al was full of shit. What a bunch of clowns we were. John said, 'Yeah. Maybe.' Smoking that damn pipe. We drove to Bumpy's cafe. Al was there with Elaine. In front of him, the ashtray was overflowing with butts. He drank coffee like a man dying of thirst. His eyes were wild. *Now* I was seeing death itself. He shoved the front page of the *Globe-Democrat* under my gaze. 'There's the guy you were supposed to meet.' He pointed to a little box in the corner of the page: BODY IN CANAL.

I read the article. Just one paragraph. Just an unidentified body.

'It doesn't even give his name.'

'I know his name.'

'How?'

'I hear.'

'You're full of shit.' I looked at John. 'Isn't he full of shit?'

John sucked his pipe. He scratched his wild man beard. He rocked back in his seat. He said nothing.

'You still game?' said Al.

'You still got a game?'

'I got one. You gonna play?'

'I've *been* playing. That's all I do is play. When are you going to deliver?'

'Tonight. Just wait.'

'You're full of shit.'

'You'll see. You're gonna meet a gambler tonight. And watch it. Be very, very careful today.'

'I'll be careful.'

As we drove away, I asked John again: 'Don't you think he's full of shit?'

'No,' said John.

And I wasn't so sure myself.

I couldn't help it. Despite all my best efforts, I was getting paranoid. When we parked in front of John's apartment, I could've sworn I saw a blue Chrysler pull away about a half block down the street. I didn't say anything about it to John.

I had the rest of the day to kill. I went to a coffee shop. I sat at the counter and ordered coffee and pie. I bought a *Post-Dispatch* and lounged on my stool, reading the paper and drinking endless refills of coffee until suddenly I smelled her hair. She was sitting on my left. She was the woman from the Cameo Lounge. She had a plate of french fries and a cup of tea. Her shiny bright hair flowed like a river of silk all the way down her back, and she couldn't have washed it more than an hour ago because it smelled like I was still standing in the bathroom with her as she towelled that massive bundle of color amidst the steam and lavender soap which she still carried here in the coffee shop on a stool next to mine. I remembered it was spring. She had freckles. I held my breath, my lungs full of lavender. She was reaching for her cup of tea. She held it in her left hand. That did it. Her left hand. I was out of control. Erica, forgive me. I said something stupid, anything, I had to start somewhere so I said, 'The trouble with tea is they don't give you refills like they do with coffee.'

She looked at me calmly. 'Yes they do,' she said.

'They do?' I said.

'Yes,' she said.

She returned to her french fries.

Fiercely I chugged my whole cup of coffee.

'But they don't give you a new tea bag,' I said. 'Just hot water.'

She looked at me again. 'That's right,' she said. She kept looking at me. She expected me to say more. I had to say more. What? What do you say in a lavender cloud with your

251

eyes swimming at a face full of freckles while a left hand deli‐
cately balances a cup of hot tea?

'I could never get into tea,' I said.

'Hmm,' she said, and she returned to her french fries.

Shit.

I mean, *shit*. If there was ever a time when I felt justified in
using that word, it was at that moment. I felt like a fresh
steaming turd.

I sat in desolation while she picked up the french fries one
by one with the fingers of her left hand and dabbed them in a
blob of ketchup and raised them to her unpainted lips. She
drained her tea. She moved to pick up her check.

My hand had a will of its own. It shot out from my body and
clomped on that check and snatched it from under her palm.

She looked at me and laughed. Neither of us spoke. We
walked together to the cashier. She'd known all along. I felt
like a fool, but I didn't care. It was spring. My blood surged.
A flock of sparrows swooped to the pavement outside the glass
door.

I paid the two checks. The woman stood at my side, carry‐
ing a cloud of lavender wherever she walked. My lungs
couldn't suck deeply enough. I was spinning plans, where
would we walk, what would we do, how could I—

The cashier counted the change into my palm and winked
at my lavender companion and said, 'Hiya, Laureen.'

I dropped the change and ran like hell.

From a phone booth I called John. I was afraid to go to his
apartment, afraid I'd see a blue Chrysler. When he answered
the phone I told him to go to a phone booth and call me. He
did. I told him they were hip to me. He said he'd get in touch
with Al and call me back in an hour. I hung up and waited.
Sixty minutes. The phone booth was on Hamilton Avenue.
There was a grocery store on the corner. I was hungry. I
walked directly away from the grocery store for a block and a
half, then suddenly spun around and walked back. No blue
Chryslers. No green warts. Nobody. I bought two apples and
an ice cream sandwich. I sat down next to the phone booth

Across the street, two teenagers were throwing knives into a billboard on the side of a building. The billboard showed a woman sipping a Bloody Mary made with a certain kind of vodka: 'For a bloodier Mary.' The teenagers were throwing knives at her eye. I noticed I was blinking every time they hit the billboard. I met the eyes of every pedestrian, every person in every car. People who didn't care about my social security number. And what was I doing in this city? I was going to sink into the festering pit of evil known as law and crime, where one cannot exist without the other, where the one cooperates with the other to shoot their evil into the veins of the children, where dollars and death are part of the same thought, where money is a force of death, where law is a force of death, where law *needs* crime for without crime there could be no law, where law and crime play secret underground games with each other, underground just like me, every man has a secret underground soul, some for good and some not. Elaine said it: Randolph Scott you ain't, Willy Crusoe. Willy Crusoe I ain't, either.

Finally the phone rang. John said Al thought we could still pull it off. He said anyway that it might've been the Blob or even the cops checking on me. Not to worry. Be at the corner of Euclid and Washington at 8:30. Look for a black man driving a Dodge van.

'Will you be there, John?'

'No.'

'Will Al?'

'No.'

'How will I know what to—?'

'Listen to the guy in the van.'

'Can I trust him?'

'You got no choice.'

'Good-bye, John.'

'Good luck, Willy. Good-bye.'

'Okay. Good-bye, John. And thanks.'

'Uh-huh.'

'Yeah. Well. Bye, John. Take care.'

'Bye.'

'Hey John—'

'Huh?'

'It's been good.'

'Uh-huh.'

A long pause. I could hear his breath blowing gently into the mouthpiece.

'John, I hate long good-byes.'

'Oh.' He hung up.

And I stood with the dead receiver to my ear and read the Instructions for Dialing over and over again.

Listen to the guy in the van. One's bigger. He's got an orange and a red headband. What'll he do when I give it? Take it. What'll he do to *me*? Nothing. You chickenshit? No. Yes. Clarkie's dead. Who? Clarkie. They got Clarkie. We got two of them. Shot one in the spine. Huh, muhfuck? It isn't real. Well, *something's* real. Jedediah. You old rattlesnake. Wilbur Barnes. Drowned. June 12, 1881. Aged 3 yrs. & 12 ds. Under ground. Another potato. Guess you ain't gonna marry me. Marry! Thought so. You stupid idiot. Why? I never *seed* anybody so free. I guess . . . I think we didn't want to . . . face up . . . face up to . . . our . . . responsibilities. This is for real. Reality. Meaning life. And death. You're saying they're just like me? I'm just like them? Nope. You're saying it. Analyze, Willy. Put your life in order. *C* is *a. B* is *a. B* is *c. A* is *b* is *c*. Consider the contrapositive. If *c* is not *a*, then . . . I will not consider the contrapositive.

What Willy?

I said I will not consider the contrapositive.

And so it has come to this: after all the clowning, all the running, all the games, all the bullshit fantasies of my life I am a passenger in a Dodge van driven by a silent black man wearing a digital watch on his wrist that counts out the minutes, the seconds of our passage through the endless American suburb of lights, of signs, of a neon STIX BAER AND FULLER followed by a FAMOUS—BARR separated by a MOBIL, a KENTUCKY FRIED, a CENTRAL HARDWARE and a JACK IN THE

BOX as we are swept by the flow of lights and the hum of rubber over the asphalt pathways of the Daniel Boone Expressway following the footsteps of the Indian, the buffalo, the horse and the wagon guiding us past the mighty SHOPPING PLAZA — 101 STORES — COVERED MALL and the humble JIFFY LAUNDERETTE — EDIE'S BAR-B-Q — QUIK GROCERY & CIGS while I wonder whether I am actually going to set up some guy for the copblobmob bunch to grind up in their mill although the more I think about it the more it seems that the copblobmob is the fantasy and Al is the reality, clowning and cunning and bullshit are for real, are all you really have in this life, this game, this amusement called living.

The van stopped. The driver turned off his lights. In the sudden darkness I felt the onrush of silence, of the smell of a spring night on a quiet street of brick apartments, grassy lawns, gas lamps flickering warmly. The man handed me a paper bag. Inside the paper was a plastic bag. Inside the plastic was genuine pure cocaine. I was to deliver the bag, collect x amount of money and walk to y corner where I was to light a match. That's all. Just light a match.

The van departed. I stood and listened to the murmur of the night. I knelt and touched the grass — a full, lush lawn — all rye, no crabgrass. I studied the brick apartment building. Each unit had a little balcony. One balcony held a barbecue and a bag of charcoal, another had a ten speed bicycle, another was covered with flower boxes.

The building's double door burst open. Out walked a girl. She was wearing white shorts and a white jersey. Her legs and face were tan. Her hair was gold. Her cheeks glowed. Her teeth sparkled. Her eyes were full of life. She was so . . . clean. So *healthy*. So innocent. What was I doing here? She was waving. A boy ran by me. He was waving. He bounced over the sidewalk. He too was clean, tan, healthy. Innocent. Benevolent. Logical. He took her hand.

'Where you going?'
'Baskin-Robbins.'
'Can I go?'
'Sure.'

I felt like a potato in a garden of truffles. I felt totally out of sync. I didn't belong here. This was suburbia. This was fantasyland. How dare I intrude with my grubby little business?

The boy and girl walked hand in hand down the sidewalk. As they neared me, the girl looked directly into my eyes. She smiled. *Smiled*. At *me*. They passed.

I walked into the building and up the stairs—good lighting, fresh paint, soft carpets—and knocked on apartment 3A.

Footsteps. A shadow over the peephole. A voice through the door: 'Who is it?'

'Delivery.'

'I didn't order anything.'

'Al sent me.'

Click. Rattle. The door opened a crack, held by a chain. A hand appeared. 'Give it to me.'

I looked at that hand. The fingers were pale white, long and skinny. Deep creases under the knuckles and across the palm. A short lifeline. A faint health line. No rings. The hand started shaking. In five seconds, it was fluttering so badly that I couldn't have placed the bag in it even if I'd wanted to.

'All right,' said the voice. The door shut. The chain rattled. The door swung wide open.

'Come in.'

He was a plain man in a white shirt and baggy trousers. He wore spectacles. He had a receding hairline. He had ears like little wings.

So. I knew him. His hairline had receded another inch. Otherwise, he hadn't changed. He didn't seem to recognize me. He looked scared. He might have been half-drunk. He just stood there with his hands at his side. Again, the hands were shaking. He'd looked scared the other time we met, too. A gambler? A loser.

'Where is it?' he said.

'Here.' I held up the paper bag.

'I'll take it.'

'Wait.'

'What?'

'I want a glass of water.'

He walked to the kitchen. I followed. He removed a glass from the dishwasher. It sparkled under the bright fluorescent light.

'How about a beer?' he said. 'The water stinks.'

'Just water.'

'It comes from the river.'

'I've had worse.'

He had one of those single-handle washerless faucets. He set the full glass on the Formica counter. On the wall, in a frame, was a paper print of an embroidery:

Bless this food to our use
And us to thy service
And make us ever mindful
Of the needs of others
    Amen.

'Thanks.'

He eyed me while I sipped the water.

'You don't look like you belong here,' he said.

That was exactly the way I felt. 'How should I look?'

'I don't know. Tough.'

I lied, 'My friends are tough.'

'Don't I know it.'

I finished the water.

'Now,' he said, 'are you ready for business?'

'No.'

'What, then?'

'Let's sit down. Get yourself a drink.' He looked like he needed one.

He didn't have to be asked twice. He poured a glass of brandy. 'You?'

'No thanks.'

I sat on a naugahyde armchair. He sat on a sofa.

I said nothing. He drank.

Outside, a car engine started, drove away.

He finished the drink. His hand was shaking less. He said, 'This isn't the way they do it on television.'

'You ever done this before?'

'Hell no. I'm just—' He stopped, sat back, retreated from his words.

'You live alone?'

'Yes.'

'Who's that?' I was pointing to a framed photograph on the coffee table. It was a picture of a slightly plump woman in a blue wedding dress.

'My daughter.'

'Are you—uh—divorced?'

'Yes.'

'Where does your daughter live?'

'Belleville. She's a dental technician. Husband's unemployed.'

I felt like Billie. I felt the same compulsion. 'What do you do?'

'I'm a State Farm agent.'

'What else do you do?'

'What is this, a loan application?'

I wasn't quite as good as Billie.

'Your daughter's husband—what does he do when he's—uh—not unemployed?'

'Why do you ask?'

'I might know him,' I lied. I didn't even know where Belleville was.

'I hope you don't.'

'Why?'

'But then you might. Considering your line of work.'

'I don't usually do this kind of thing.'

'Neither do I.'

'You don't look it.' He looked to me like—well—like a State Farm agent. I asked him, 'Does this guy—your son-in-law—is he involved in this—uh—transaction?'

'No. His friends are. I gotta admit, he tried to help me.' He was running a finger around the rim of the brandy glass. 'He couldn't—you know—*stop* them, but at least now I've got a way to . . . work it out.'

'Do you trust them?'

'Of course not. But I did . . . something . . . once before for these guys.'

'I know.'

He looked at me sharply. Did he recognize me? No. But I could see him resist the temptation to find out what I knew. He returned to running his finger around the glass, but now the finger was trembly. He said, 'I don't trust them. But I have no choice.'

'You could leave. Run away.'

'Where?'

'Anywhere.'

'Sure. Just leave. Just disappear. Leave my job, my friends, my family, my home, my team—'

'Team?'

'Little League.' A quick smile. 'I've sponsored a team for six years now.'

'Jesus Christ! You sponsor Little League, and here you are mixed up with these—'

'Don't rub it in.' He rested his forehead on his knuckles. 'I've got my . . . weakness, I reckon you've got yours.'

I reckon I do. I returned to the idea of leaving. 'Maybe you could come back sometime.'

'A *long* time.'

'Change your name. Start over.'

'It's impossible.' He sat up. 'I couldn't.'

'Why not?'

'What do you know? You're too young. The world's too complicated. People have roots. You can't change everything just by running away.'

'Can I have some more water?'

'How can you drink that stuff?'

'Tastes okay to me.'

Reluctantly: 'Help yourself.'

I came back with a full glass of water. As I sat down I asked, 'Your team any good?'

'Fair.' He was cleaning the lenses of his spectacles with

259

a white handkerchief.

'It's hard to find a good pitcher at that age.'

'All right.' He pushed the spectacles emphatically back onto his nose. 'Let's do it. There's no way around it. You gotta do what you gotta do.'

'No you don't.'

'I say you gotta do what you gotta do.'

'I say you don't gotta do what you gotta do.' I set down the empty water glass.

'Quit stalling.'

'I've stalled all my life.'

'I never stall.'

'You should try it.'

'Why?'

'You could save your life.'

Suddenly he looked at me with fear. 'Are you—?' He stood up, backed away. His ears fluttered. I think he was trying to fly away. 'Is this—?'

'No.' I stood up. 'I'm not. And this isn't.'

I walked to the door, still carrying my paper bag. 'Good luck,' I said.

WHEELING

I went to no corner. I lit no match. I deposited the paper bag and its contents in a mailbox that had a 5:30 pickup.

I signalled a taxi. Earlier John had 'loaned' me a hundred dollars. I took the taxi to the airport and caught a jet to Cincinnati. I sat in a window seat and watched the lights of St. Louis pass below me. A strangely lovable town. I set down in Cincinnati and transferred to a prop to Wheeling. Late that night I was climbing the steep hill amid a chorus of spring peepers to the house over the river. Mr. P was right. You have to run away because it's so nice to come back. If you don't run, you don't live.

We walked the dark streets. The touch of her hand was magic. The head on my shoulder, or picking flowers with her left hand, or looking up to me under a streetlight with a face full of freckles, delight in her eyes, magic in her lips. After midnight we sat in the hanging chair on the porch over the river. Enough of this mushy stuff. She cuddled up and whispered, 'Kin you flush?' I was somewhat curious myself.

We tried.

It flushed.

UNDER THE GROUND

Maybe I blew it. I guess I'll never know. Maybe if I'd stayed in St. Louis for just a few more hours, I would now be Willy Middlebrook again, nice guy from the suburbs. Instead I'm Willy Crusoe and I'll always be Willy Crusoe, and when somebody follows me down the street I'll cross to the other side to see if he crosses behind me. I made the choice. They opened the door and I chose not to enter. I have no regrets. Maybe other people would have done it differently. Maybe they are disappointed in me. If they are, then I am disappointed in them. They don't understand. They watch too much television.

I spent a magic week in Wheeling. I slipped off for two days and made a quick trip to Doc Bates, who informed me that I would never have children. I did not tell Erica Crusoe. In fact, Mrs. Crusoe and I devoted a good deal of time and effort alone together in an attempt to conceive a child. We found the work not at all boring, but not at all fruitful.

We live in California now, Erica and I. Her pa took us on a run to Oakland, and then we sort of wandered. For a while we lived on the Stanford Golf Course — that is, we slept in blanket rolls under a tree near the eleventh hole. The accommodations weren't much, but you couldn't beat the rent. Nobody bothered us. We came by night and left at dawn, and soon a couple dozen coons and possums and even a skunk or two had learned to expect our arrival and Erica's offerings of bread and affection. When the rainy season began I lied my way into a job as a computer operator, and we rented a shack in the Santa Cruz mountains. We lived up a foggy holler that

262

took Erica right back to Harlan County, except it was full of down and out hippies instead of down and out hillbillies. I made a sign and set it in front of our shack. It said WELCOME TO HARLAN COUNTY. Some son of a bitch stole it. I can't say it was a perfect life. We had our moments. When a year of steady effort still hadn't produced a baby, Erica started getting distractable and nervous and finally stopped eating; and after two days of sitting in a corner without food, screaming at me whenever I set foot in the cabin, she ran away. I searched. I lost my job because I spent all my time searching. One month later, she returned. She was pregnant. I ran away. I hitched down to San Diego and got involved in this weird sort of relationship—weird things *always* happen when I get too far from the fortieth parallel, mainline America. She was a right-handed, fair-skinned woman who was divorced and lived in this gigantic ranch house with two kids and three cats. Her refrigerator was bigger than some houses I've seen. She didn't love me. I didn't love her. She wasn't my type. I wasn't hers. I think we were both in transitionary phases where we wanted to touch a side of the world that had always seemed out of reach. Her phase had been going on for seven years, ever since her husband had left her to marry his uncle in San Bernardino. My phase lasted about a month. I walked into her house one day to find a woodie parked in her driveway, a surfboard parked in her living room and a surfer parked emphatically in her bed. I can't say I was broken-hearted. I went back to the cabin in the mountains and—as I've said—it was nice coming back. It's always nice coming back.

Right now I'm working at the Alpha-Beta Supermarket. I won't be here much longer, though. A neighbor of mine is doing carpentry, and I've been helping him out on weekends. He wants me to join him in a full time partnership. Erica stays home a lot with the baby. I would never have thought that such little breasts could make so much milk. She's a natural mother. She was made to give life. She's pretty calm now. I suppose she'll want more kids, and then we'll have to deal with some things or start this running business again. I think

263

we can deal with it. The kid is beautiful. She named him Dale—I think that's the name of the father. We get along. We all get along. I love the kid. I love her. I don't resent what she did. Why should I? She had the right. She still makes me happy. I think she tames me. She tames the wildness in people as well as animals, though none can tame her. I try.

I had a scare once. This man pounded on our door in the middle of the night and showed me a badge that said FBI. Turned out he was looking for somebody else, though. Occasionally I read in the newspaper of another potato, a more famous one, being unearthed by the government or simply tiring of the underground games, the anonymous life, and turning him or herself in. That's their choice. I made mine.

I got a postcard from Elaine in Idaho. She and Al were driving around the mountains in the yellow milk truck looking for Uncle Henry's camp. I hear from John every once in a while. He went to India for a time and then started wandering all over the place 'searching for energy,' he says. Right now he's living in Nigeria. I think he's teaching English there. There are lots of people I don't hear from who I think about from time to time, like the duck lady, and Billie, and Claire in Champaign-Urbana, and a hundred more whose names I can't even remember, whose faces I will never forget, whose lives touched mine and bounced away. I imagine their stories are about what you'd expect. They pursue their dreams and make do with what they can get, and I wish the best to all of them. Their lives are buried where newspapers and television will never dig them up, their roots are the roots of this land, their dreams are the dreams of us all, their failures are our own, their weakness is our weakness, their strength is the backbone of every man and every woman, their story is our story. They have rough brown skin and soft wrinkled eyes. They are round and they are usually dirty. They are hard because they have to be, but if you warm them they get soft and you can make them sweet. They come by the thousands, by the millions. We depend on them, and we take them for granted. They lived the only way they knew how. And if they have not died, they are living still.